"How much time have you spent in the U.S.?" Hannah asked as she swept.

"Almost none," Jake admitted. "I have a small work studio in Costa Rica, but I'm hardly ever there, either."

Lord. Hannah couldn't imagine living like that, with no real home, just a suitcase.

"Traveling can be fun, but I'm mostly a homebody," she said, raising her chin and practically daring him to comment.

"Yeah, I figured. The domestic stuff is okay, but home, marriage, kids—those things would end my career."

Hannah stared. "That isn't the first time you've mentioned that, and it's starting to sound like a warning. I don't need to be told to keep my distance. If I get married again, it's going to be to someone stable and caring who can put me and my son first. It certainly won't be to a man with one foot out the door and a habit of risking his neck. So save your warnings. I'm not interested."

Hannah began putting cups in the dishwasher, thinking about the mixed emotions on Jake's face... emotions too complicated to fathom. One thing was quite clear, however—Jake Hollister didn't understand people

Dear Reader,

Please note that the heroine's home town, and the nearby lake and mountain in *Jake's Biggest Risk* are fictional, set around very real locations in the State of Washington.

When I was growing up, my father usually had two or three cameras hanging around his neck. One of our family jokes is "Just a little closer to the edge." Why? Dad would frequently pose us on places like giant logs or an ocean bluff to get the desired photo. We were never in danger, but I'm certain my mother had a few nervous moments.

Some people will do anything for a great picture, and my hero in *Jake's Biggest Risk* is that kind of photographer. Jake Hollister has no intention of giving up his roving, adventure-filled life, even after being injured in a plane crash. Enter Hannah Nolan, a divorced mother, determined not to fall in love with a footloose risk-taker with commitment issues. Jake and Hannah have one problem...hearts don't always listen to what the brain is telling them.

Instead of a classic movie alert, I recommend *The National Parks, America's Best Idea,* a 2009 documentary by Ken Burns. The six-part series uses new and historical footage to provide terrific views of U.S. national parks. Three cheers for public television!

I hope you enjoy this third book in my Those Hollister Boys series. I love to hear from readers and can be contacted c/o Harlequin Books, 225 Duncan Mill Road, Don Mills, ON M3B 3K9, Canada.

Wishing you all the best,

Julianna Morris

JULIANNA MORRIS

—

Jake's Biggest Risk

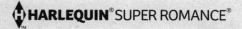

HARLEQUIN® SUPER ROMANCE®

Recycling programs
for this product may
not exist in your area.

ISBN-13: 978-0-373-60875-1

Jake's Biggest Risk

Printed in U.S.A.

www.Harlequin.com

ABOUT THE AUTHOR

Julianna Morris has an offbeat sense of humor that frequently gets her in trouble. Her interests range from oceanography and photography to traveling, painting, walking and reading. Julianna also loves cats of all shapes and sizes. Her family's feline companion is named Merlin, and he's currently a little grumpy from being on a diet. The family is discussing adding another dog to their menagerie just to make him happy (Merlin is a feline anomaly—he enjoys canine companions).

Books by Julianna Morris

HARLEQUIN SUPERROMANCE

*Those Hollister Boys

Other titles by this author availabe in ebook format.

For my father, who took thousands of pictures over the years, visually preserving our childhood with love and talent. I miss you so much.

PROLOGUE

JAKE HOLLISTER PEERED above a crest of snow, spotted his quarry and began taking pictures of the polar bear and her cubs. He was barely aware of the numbing cold.

"You're out of your frigging mind," whispered his assistant, using the sotto voce they'd perfected over the years they had worked together.

"That is entirely a matter of opinion."

"Fine. It's my *opinion*. We're miles from nowhere. It's the time of year when nobody is crazy enough be out here except Inupiat and scientists. And that money-grubbing bastard pilot is probably drunk. Oh, and did I mention? We're thirty feet from the largest bear on the planet, hiding behind a chunk of ice the size of my girlfriend's ass."

"Vera has a very nice ass. I'm sure she'd be pissed that you're comparing it to a piece of ice," Jake murmured, focusing on the mother bear's face. She was wary, possibly venturing out for the first time with her cubs since their birth. He'd never come to the Arctic so early in the season, when the polar bears were leaving their winter birthing caves. It was risky, but what was life without a few risks?

This was their twenty-first day of shooting. They had at least another two months planned, though they might be able to wrap up earlier if he got the shots he needed. *Maybe.* Editors sometimes failed to recognize that wild animals didn't show up on cue. Jake wouldn't compromise, so if he wasn't satisfied, he didn't turn in a single photo.

Toby handed him another camera, taking the one Jake had been using and tucking it into a case. They'd worked together so long that Toby seemed to instinctively know what equipment Jake would need next.

"These days Vera is pissed whenever I leave," Toby grumbled. "She's starting to talk marriage."

Jake refocused with the second camera, most of his attention on the bear and her cubs. "That is why it's never a good idea to get into a serious relationship when you're in this line of work."

Toby mopped his face, somehow sweaty despite the cold. "Hell, it isn't a good idea to *be* in this line of work. Why do you always have to get so goddamned close? You've got telephoto lenses that could photograph Cindy Crawford's mole from the moon."

Jake didn't bother explaining.

The camera whirred as he continued taking pictures. He'd never wanted to have an assistant, but when he'd taken an assignment to Indonesia eight years earlier, the magazine had insisted he take

Tobias Mahoney with him. Short, wiry and endlessly complaining, the guy had risked his life to save Jake when an uprooted tree had knocked him into a rain-swollen river. They'd been a team ever since. Complaints included.

"I'm running if she starts this way," Toby announced, settling the camera bag straps around his neck for a quick getaway. "I'll save the cameras, but she gets the rest of your equipment."

"She's too fast—you'd never get away from her on foot. But unless the wind changes, she'll never know we're here. Provided you pipe down, of course."

With a faint smile, Jake continued working. There was an amazing quality to the silence around them. It was both an absence of noise and an extraordinary clarity of the few sounds they *could* hear. Ice cracking. Wind across the snow. The faint snuffling cries from the bears. None of it could be captured in a photograph, yet he kept trying, because most of the world would never experience the Arctic. He was lucky to have been this far north several times in his career, though usually in the middle of the summer when there was a relative abundance of insect and animal life. Now it was mostly ice and the three bears they'd spotted from the plane.

The cubs were playful; one even lay on its back, grabbing at the mother's tail. Then suddenly the adult bear whirled their direction, standing on her hind legs and sniffing the air, some instinct telling her that danger might be afoot.

Toby choked and Jake nudged him with an elbow, still shooting. If he could just catch that look in her eyes…the wildness of an animal protecting her young.

When the bear dropped to all fours and took several steps in their direction, even Jake was considering a strategic retreat. Then the bear stopped and bawled to her babies. They headed west with amazing speed and were soon hidden behind a ridge in the landscape.

"Gawd," Toby gasped, clasping his hand to his forehead. "This is the last time, Jake. The last *frigging* time I'm doing this for you."

"You say that every trip."

"This time I mean it."

"You always say that, too."

They hiked back to the plane with Toby still issuing a long stream of grievances. Their pilot was watching for them. Gordon was a seasoned bush pilot—Toby's comments on his ancestry and drinking notwithstanding—and couldn't be blamed for charging a fortune to fly a photographer around northern Alaska to look for an animal powerful enough to destroy his plane.

"Ready?" Gordon asked.

"What do you think?" Toby stomped snow from his boots and climbed into the back of the plane. "Let's get the hell out of here. I want a hot meal, or whatever passes for one in that village."

"Does he ever shut up?" Gordon muttered to Jake in a low voice.

"Not so you'd notice."

Takeoff went as smoothly as it could for a plane on skis, and Jake spent the first few minutes of the flight methodically putting the SD cards from his digital cameras into pouches, which he then tucked into a zippered pocket inside his parka. When he finally looked out, they'd climbed high enough that the land below them was mostly a featureless field of white.

"I hate the cold," Toby griped. He was drinking a cup of coffee from the thermos they had filled that morning.

"You hate everything."

"Huh. You want some coffee?"

"Not right now."

Just then a low grunt from the pilot caught Jake's attention. Gordon's face was gray and beads of sweat had broken out on his forehead.

"What's wrong?"

"Chest…tight…hurts like one of your bears is sitting on me."

Jake leaned over and loosened the other man's collar. He took the pilot's pulse; it was fast and thready and his fingernails had a bluish tinge. Jake had a fair amount of experience with first aid from working in remote areas, but this was more than a cut or busted leg.

"Do you have any health conditions—asthma or

something?" he asked casually, figuring the mention of a possible heart attack could cause panic.

Gordon groaned. "N-no."

"Okay. Maybe we should radio ahead to the village."

"Yeah. And I'll have to...to bring us down. Won't have time to find...a good spot."

"Just get us down. Try to relax and breathe deeply." Jake shot a glance into the backseat and saw Toby's alarmed expression, but there was little he could do to reassure him.

The pilot called for help on the radio, giving their position as he angled the plane downward. Jake murmured encouragement, at the same time taking quick looks outside; the featureless field of snow looked more and more irregular the closer they got.

At the last moment the pilot groaned and lurched forward. There wasn't any time to react. Jake's side of the plane took the hardest impact and his last thought before losing consciousness was that all that soft-looking snow was damned hard on contact.

CHAPTER ONE

HANNAH NOLAN RACED into the real estate office. She was running late, but she wanted to touch base with the leasing agent for the house she'd inherited from her great-aunt. She would have loved to live in Huckleberry Lodge, but the upkeep and utilities were too expensive. It was more practical to live with her son in Silver Cottage—the guesthouse located over the detached garage—and rent out the main building.

"Hey, Lillian," she called.

"Hannah, I was just going to phone you. I have a fabulous offer you're going to flip over."

"I'm *not* selling my great-aunt's property," Hannah returned.

Lillian routinely tried to convince her to sell rather than rent, and she wasn't interested. Great-Aunt Elkie had been devoted to the lodge; it was the home her husband had built when they were first married and hoping for a large family. And despite Hannah's attempts to be practical, deep in her heart, she was desperately sentimental. If she'd had her druthers, she would be living in the lodge with a man she loved as much as Great-Aunt Elkie had loved Great-Uncle Larry.

The real estate agent waved her hand dismissively. "I'm not talking about selling. You have an offer to lease Huckleberry Lodge on a monthly basis, with utilities paid on top of the rent. It will mean ten times the income you've been getting with those short-term winter rentals. The first three months are guaranteed, but it'll probably be for a full year or longer."

A full year...?

Hannah's knees wobbled as she mentally added up the amount she'd receive. She grabbed a chair and sat down. It was a fabulous offer, but it also meant the lodge would "belong" to someone else the whole time. There wouldn't be any going over and using the hot tub when the house was vacant, and she'd have to collect her favorite movies from the large DVD collection in the library, along with other favorite items.

Still, what a break. Her renters were primarily wealthy skiers who came up over the winter from either Portland or Seattle. Summer was beautiful in the Washington Cascade Mountains, and the town was located on a picturesque lake, but the town's biggest tourist draw remained skiing, both downhill and cross-country.

"What's the catch?" she asked.

"No catch. It's a photographer—that guy whose plane crashed in Alaska when the pilot had a heart attack. It was big news because he won a Pulitzer for his war photos a few years ago. Imagine having that kind of recognition at his age. He can't even be thirty-five."

Hannah frowned thoughtfully. "Why does he need the lodge for so long? We aren't in a combat zone, and the nearest polar bear is in a zoo."

"I've only spoken to Mr. Hollister's agent, Andy Bedard. You know Andy—he rents the lodge two or three times every winter. Tall, lanky and a whiz on skis?"

Hannah nodded, picturing the nerdy guy in her mind. Andy could be socially awkward, but when he strapped on his skis, he was unrivaled. She'd had so many people in and out of Huckleberry Lodge it was hard to recall them all, but he was one of her best tenants. Although he always brought a large group of clients with him, they never caused problems.

"Anyhow," Lillian continued, "apparently Mr. Hollister's injuries were more severe than the news reports made it sound. It will take at least a year for him to recover and get back to the kind of photography he's known for, so he's doing a book on the Cascade Mountains while he recuperates. Andy calls it *The Cascades Across Four Seasons*. Kind of dull, but it's just a working title. Anyhow, I can fax the lease over tonight if you agree. I already told his business manager there's a large damage and cleaning deposit."

"Go ahead. It's too good to turn down."

"That's what I thought. There's just one other

thing…Mr. Hollister wants someone to do a bit of light housekeeping twice a week, for a couple of hours. But only when he isn't off working, and he'll pay extra for the service. You could hire somebody else, but I'd hate to see you lose the income. He shouldn't be around that often with the book to photograph."

Hannah hesitated. She was accustomed to cleaning the lodge after weekend skiers, but the prospect of having a regular tenant had given her a brief, appealing vision of spending more time with her son over the winter.

"Do it," Lillian urged. "He's offering an obscene amount of money per hour. If nothing else, you can put it toward Danny's college fund."

It was an argument that could convince Hannah to do a lot of things. Her ex-husband never sent child support—she wasn't even sure where he was most of the time—and her salary as an elementary schoolteacher didn't allow her to save much.

"All right." At least this way she could keep an eye on the house and make sure Mr. Hollister wasn't doing any damage. Not that being a daredevil photographer meant he'd be a bad tenant, but he took chances with his life that no sane person would consider.

"Excellent. When the lease comes back, I'll call and you can sign, as well. Mr. Hollister wants to move in next week, so I'm sure he'll return the paperwork quickly. It's going to be fun having someone famous staying in Mahalaton Lake, even if he has a reputation for being a loner. You'll have to convince him to come to some of the town events so we can all get to know him."

Hannah wasn't sure about fun, but it would be a relief not having people constantly in and out of the lodge. Just cleaning up after each group had taken two or three evenings following a long day of teaching, so it wouldn't be bad getting paid for light housekeeping on top of the rent. She'd probably still have more time with Danny.

"It's great news, Lillian. Just let me know when the lease is ready. Talk to you later."

Hannah headed to her mother's house to pick up her son. The school year had ended earlier in June than usual, and she'd needed to clear out her classroom. Normally they had more snow days to make up for missed classroom hours, but the weather had cooperated this winter, so they'd had fewer than usual. Unfortunately Mahalaton Lake wasn't offering a summer session because the budget was too tight; having Huckleberry Lodge leased full-time was an unexpected boon to her finances.

"Mommy, Mommy!" Daniel yelled, running down the porch steps when he saw her.

She returned his hug. "Have a good time with Grandma?"

"Yup. Can we eat our pizza at Luigi's instead of at home? Grandma gave me quarters to play the games."

"Okay. Say goodbye and get in the car."

Danny dashed up the porch steps to give his grandmother a kiss, and just as precipitously, ran to their car and climbed inside.

"Thanks for watching him, Mom."

"I enjoy it, though I admit he tires me out," Carrie Nolan said with a laugh. "He hardly ever stops moving, and I'm not as young as I used to be."

"None of us are," Hannah replied drily. "What's this business about giving him money for video games?" When she was a kid her mother had claimed the same games would rot her brain.

"I'm a grandmother now. I don't have to be sensible."

"Ha." Yet Hannah smiled. "By the way, I have good news from Lillian. A photographer is doing a book on the area and wants to rent Huckleberry Lodge. It's month to month, but he'll probably stay for a year or longer."

"That's wonderful, dear, though if you ever need help...well, you know we're here, and..." Carrie's voice trailed off.

"I'm fine," Hannah said firmly. She was determined *not* to ask her parents for anything more than babysitting. She'd married the wrong man and it was up to her to deal with the fallout; the hardest part was knowing that Danny didn't have the father he deserved. But at least his grandfather was his male role model instead of a chronically unemployed dad with restless feet and a wandering eye.

On the other hand, her parents were all the family she had left, and it bothered her that Danny didn't have a larger support structure. Maybe if she knew her ex-husband's parents… Hannah shook her head as soon as the thought formed. Steven had refused to talk about his family whenever she'd asked. Apparently the relationship was so bad, he hadn't even wanted them at the wedding. As far as she knew, they were unaware their son had even *gotten* married. Just because Steven had turned out to be a jerk it didn't mean his folks were the same, but she'd rather not open *that* can of worms.

She said goodbye and they headed to Luigi's. Aside from the supermarket freezer case, it was the only place to get pizza in Mahalaton Lake, since large restaurant chains hadn't discovered their small corner of Washington. Aside from Luigi's, they had Elizabeth's Tea Parlor, the Lakeside Bar and Grill, McKenzie's BBQ, Pat's Burger Hut, three cafés, a bakery, a deli and the Full Moon Bistro for natural-food fans. If you were looking for anything exotic, you were out of luck. Of course, in winter there was both a coffee cart and restaurant at the ski resort, but few people in town went up there to eat.

"Hello, Danny," called Barbi Paulson, Luigi's delivery driver, as they came through the restaurant's double doors. It was before five and the place was still empty. "Didn't you want me coming out to the house with your Friday-night pizza?"

"I was at Grandma's," he explained, "so we're having pizza on the way home."

"Glad to hear it." Barbi gave him a wink. "I don't want to lose my best boyfriend."

"Nuh-uh."

Danny skipped to the arcade tucked into a side room of the restaurant. It was a bright, cheerful place that was scrupulously clean and maintained. Hannah had played those same games as a girl, her mother's objections notwithstanding. Luigi hadn't bought anything new for the arcade in years, saying a classic was a classic.

"You sure got a great kid," Barbi said.

"I'm pretty fond of him."

"And he's real smart." The other woman grinned, but her smile faded and she leaned on the counter, the bangles on her arms clattering on the polished wood. "I've been thinking about you being a teacher and all. You know I never finished high school."

Hannah nodded, recalling that Barbi had dropped out of school to get a job. Though only thirty-two, she'd already had a rough life between a hard-drinking father and a mother who'd died when she was nine. People in Mahalaton Lake weren't always comfortable with the way Barbi dressed, but they admired her honesty and how diligently she worked.

"Anyhow, Luigi keeps bugging me," Barbi continued. "He says I got to get a high school diploma because you can't get anywhere without one. Luigi treats me great, but it sure would be nice to have one job, instead of these part-time gigs all over town."

"You might earn more with a general equivalency diploma," Hannah agreed diplomatically. It was hard to say what would make a difference in Mahalaton Lake, but statistically, graduates did better financially than dropouts. "I can check when the next exam will be."

"I already got the schedule." Barbi fidgeted with the bangles on her arms, looking embarrassed. "But right now there aren't any night classes to help study for the damned thing—that is, the test. And I wondered...I know you do tutoring and stuff. I'd pay, of course," she added hastily.

"I'd be happy to help you study," Hannah assured her. "But as a friend. I wouldn't want to be paid."

"That isn't right," Barbi protested. "You got a kid to support."

"What isn't right is the school board failing to offer enough adult courses." It was something that deeply irritated Hannah. "But I have access to the study materials and we can go from there."

Barbi chewed her lower lip so hard that most of her bright red lipstick disappeared. "I don't know."

"I do," Hannah said. She'd been lucky to have parents who'd encouraged her to get an education and were there to help if she needed it. Offering the same support to a friend was the least she could do. "I'll call when I have everything together. We'll have fun."

"Barbara," Luigi hollered as he came out of the kitchen. "That pizza is ready for delivery."

"Gotcha."

Barbi left with the insulated pizza bag and Luigi came to the counter with a broad smile. "*Ciao.* I'll take care of you, Hannah. Your usual pizza?"

"You bet." Hannah thought about the lucrative lease she'd been offered and decided to splurge. "But add a garden salad and an order of garlic chicken wings."

"Excellent. I heard Barbara speak to you about tutoring," Luigi said as he took the money. "I'm glad she's finally doing this."

"She mentioned you've been urging her to get a GED."

"I was sixteen when we came to America from Sicily. My mama told me to study hard, not just to get ahead, but because learning is how to stay young." He thumped his chest. "My heart is *not* sixty-eight years old—it is strong like I'm still a boy."

Hannah's lips curved into a smile. "How *is* your mother, Luigi?"

"Ah, she goes to the church every day. She tells the priest when he makes a mistake in Mass and then works in the kitchen, making gnocchi to raise money for another stained glass window. She will not be happy until every window in the sanctuary is done. And she is reading *War and Peace*. So far, she likes Tolstoy better than Hemingway."

"*War and Peace* is a good book. Say hello to her for me."

She paid the bill and went into the arcade to watch Danny play as she waited for the food. He was an exceptionally bright kid, a year ahead of children his own age and curious about everything, including his deadbeat dad.

But whenever she started to feel bad for Danny or got upset with her poor judgment, she should remember Barbi Paulson. An absentee father was surely better than one who was drunk all the time. God knew what Barbi's childhood had been like, and Hannah suspected Vic Paulson still came around now and then to make life difficult for her.

DRIVING HIS NEW Jeep Wrangler, Jake followed his agent's car to Mahalaton Lake, Washington, grateful to be away from doctors and the hospital.

Andy Bedard, his agent, had offered to stay and help for a few days, but Jake would have none of it. That was why he'd insisted they bring two vehicles; if Andy had his own transportation, he'd have less excuse to become an unwanted houseguest.

It would have been worse if Jake had let his half brother drive him. Matt had been the one who'd arranged for Jake's transfer to a hospital in Seattle and gotten top specialists to treat him…including Matt's own father-in-law, Walter McGraw. Matt wasn't a bad sort, and he'd chartered a flight and flown to Alaska as soon as news had come of the accident.

Still, Matt had become depressingly domestic since giving up his carefree party days and getting married. At least he'd traveled extensively before; now he wore a suit every day and handed out money for a charitable organization.

His wife was nice, though, full of energy. And while Layne worked as a researcher for a weekly regional news magazine, she hadn't asked him to do an interview.

Jake shifted his aching leg as they drove through the little town and out onto a road lined with tall evergreens, before turning right onto an even smaller road. It opened to a clearing where a two-story structure sat overlooking the lake.

Not bad.

It was a large mountain lodge, built solidly of natural beams, with a hint of the Arts and Crafts architectural style. In fact, it was reminiscent of some of the work done by Julia Morgan, an early twentieth-century California architect. Andy was right—if he had to be trapped in one place, Huckleberry Lodge was more palatable than most locations.

Small-town America made Jake shudder, and the cities were worse. Not that he'd spent much time in either, but even that was enough to know he preferred the solitude of locations like Nepal or the Australian outback. There were too many cars and people in most places.

Andy honked his horn and a young woman came out of the lodge, followed by a small boy. The dog lying on the doorstep got to its feet, tail wagging furiously. Jake frowned; he knew the landlady lived in a guesthouse over the garage, but neither Andy nor his business manager had mentioned her having a kid.

He opened the SUV door, stepping out in time to hear the woman call, "Hi, Andy."

"Hey, Hannah. Sorry we're early—we made better time on the road than I thought we would. Jake, this is Hannah Nolan," Andrew said. "She owns Huckleberry Lodge and teaches at the elementary school in town."

"Good afternoon," Jake muttered.

He couldn't tell much about Ms. Nolan from her appearance. She was dressed in faded jeans and an oversize man's shirt. She had a long, rumpled braid of chestnut-colored hair and her face was pretty in a wholesome way. Apparently she'd been cleaning, because the faint odor of bleach permeated the air.

"You aren't ready for me to move in?" he asked coolly, gesturing to the bucket she carried.

"I spoke to Hannah late last night and asked her to do extra sanitizing as a precaution," Andy explained hastily. "It seemed a good idea because you just got out of the hospital."

Jake's jaw tightened. He was damned tired of hospitals and disinfectants and people trying to protect him without understanding the first thing about what he wanted. His body was damaged, not his brain. His mother had actually trekked out of the Andes to urge him to take it slow. Josie wasn't a sentimental mom—he'd rarely seen her since becoming an adult—but she had her moments.

Hell, his *father* had even breezed through shortly after the accident. Since Sullivan Spencer "S. S." Hollister was a true hedonist and had been in the middle of yet another romance at the time, he must have been really worried. Nevertheless, Jake was done with doctors and everything associated with them. His only concession would be physical therapy—anything to get him back to his peak.

"Sanitizing won't be necessary in the future," he growled. "I only asked for light cleaning. And you won't need to come until Tuesday. I'll be fine until then."

"I always do extra polishing before someone arrives, Mr. Hollister, and you *are* earlier than expected," the landlady said, the chill in her voice equaling his own. She put a hand on the youngster's shoulder. "By the way, this is my son, Danny. Danny, this is our new tenant, Mr. Hollister."

"Hi, mister."

"Uh…yeah. Hi." Jake didn't know anything about kids and didn't want to.

"Let me give you a tour of the lodge," Hannah offered after an awkward silence.

"I'll show myself around." He turned and limped to the Wrangler to begin unloading his luggage and equipment. "I don't need that thing—take it with you," he snapped as Andy took out the cane recommended by the doctor.

"The doctor said—"

"I don't care what he said."

Over Andy's protests, Jake carried one load after another into the lodge, despite the pain that was becoming intense. Danny Nolan wanted to help, but Jake sharply told him not to touch anything. The last thing he needed was to have his equipment damaged by a snot-nosed kid.

Hannah Nolan promptly sent her son to their home over the garage, her expression turning less friendly by the minute.

Andy began to look alarmed. Much to Jake's displeasure, he pulled Hannah aside and started whispering in her ear. Jake ignored them both and carried two of his tripods up the lodge steps. He didn't need his agent being a diplomat and making excuses.

Perhaps he *had* been rude, but the sooner everyone left him alone, the better.

HANNAH WAS SEETHING.

She'd seen the excitement on Danny's face disappear at a single sharp word from Jake Hollister and she wanted to strangle the man. For some reason her son had been drawn to the tall photographer, only to be rebuffed. She didn't expect her tenant to be buddies with a seven-year-old boy, but was common courtesy too much to expect?

"Honestly, he's a nice person," Andy repeated urgently. "Don't be misled by first impressions."

Hannah fixed her gaze on Andy. How could he be associated with such a bad-mannered, pompous ass as Jake Hollister?

"You mean he's rich and talented, so he gets away with murder."

Andy made a helpless gesture. "*No.* I'm the first to admit that Jake is focused and intense when working on a project, but that's the perfectionist in him. He has his faults, but you have to understand how much pain he's in right now—it's a miracle he survived that plane crash and being hauled by dogsled for fourteen miles. Then there was the delay in flying him out for medical care. He'll recover, but it's hard for him to accept limitations, however temporary."

Hannah shifted her feet.

In the five days since she'd first talked to Lillian about leasing Huckleberry Lodge to Jake Hollister, she'd learned plenty about him. Some had come from a telephone conversation with Andy and the rest from Lillian, who was dazzled at the thought of meeting someone famous. Yet Hannah wondered if she would stay impressed with Mr. Hollister once she got a dose of his bad manners.

"It's all right, isn't it, Hannah?" Andy asked anxiously. No doubt he was accustomed to working with temperamental artists who flew off the handle at the slightest thing. Hannah had a healthy temper as well, but she couldn't afford to try breaking the lease agreement.

"Don't worry, I'll deal with it," she assured him, though she already regretted agreeing to clean house for her new tenant.

Andy smiled his awkward smile. "Good. I'd hate it if I wasn't welcome in Mahalaton Lake."

"No chance of that. But since I'm not needed here, I'm going to check on Danny."

"I… Oh, sure. I'll probably leave as soon as Jake is unpacked, so take care."

"You, too."

She hurried away with her bucket of cleaning supplies. Silver Cottage—the living area over the four-car garage—was a very nice home, with a third-floor family room, two bedrooms, lots of closets and a splendid kitchen. Best of all, it had a spacious living room and a deck with a view of the lake. When Great-Aunt Elkie was alive, she'd rented out Silver Cottage to skiers instead of Huckleberry Lodge. It wasn't that she'd needed the income; she had just liked having people around.

Danny was lying on his stomach on the living room floor, drawing a picture, their golden retriever next to him.

"That's a great dragon," Hannah said.

He shrugged, a small pout on his mouth.

"Don't be upset about Mr. Hollister," she murmured. "He got hurt awfully bad a while ago. You saw him limping, didn't you?"

Danny didn't look up. "Uh-huh."

"Well, sometimes people in pain don't feel very friendly."

"But if he doesn't feel good, why couldn't I help?"

She sighed. How did you explain adult pride to a child? "Maybe he wants to prove he can do it himself. Remember when you were mad at Grandpa because he wouldn't take the training wheels off your bike as soon as you wanted? It's kind of like that."

Understanding dawned in his eyes. "Oh, I get it."

"Good. We should both be understanding of Mr. Hollister and remember he doesn't want people bugging him. Deal?"

"Deal."

Her son stuck out his hand and they solemnly shook.

Danny returned to his drawing and Hannah was relieved that he seemed happier. Badger got up and followed her around as she took care of various chores. She'd gotten the retriever as a puppy when they moved from town to live on Great-Aunt Elkie's property, and he'd grown into a magnificent dog with reddish-gold fur and a calm, protective nature.

She was fixing dinner when a knock sounded on the door. Badger let out a sharp yip, his ears perked forward; it was his someone-I-don't-know bark.

"I'll get it," she called.

But Badger and Danny both beat her to the door and she heard her son give a friendly greeting to their visitor.

"Uh...yeah. I need to talk to your mother," said a deep male voice.

Hannah wrinkled her nose. *Jake Hollister.*

"Is there a problem?" she asked as she turned the corner into the entry area.

"Not at all. I just wanted to ask if there are any restaurants that deliver out here from town."

She thought about the sacks of groceries she'd seen in the trunk of Andy's car. On top of which, she had put one of Luigi's menus by the kitchen phone.

"Luigi's delivers pizza on the weekends, but when things are slow he's willing to send someone out on other days. If nothing else, he'll usually come himself at closing time. I'll get their number for you." She brought another copy of the menu to the door and gave it to him. If Hollister had let her show him around Huckleberry Lodge, she would have pointed out both the phone book *and* the menu, along with other things he might need. Still, the guy was in pain, she could see it in his face.

Jake left with a low, almost grudging "Thanks."

When they were alone, Danny looked up at her. "Maybe he's just hungry, Mommy. It makes me grumpy, too."

Hannah ruffled her son's hair. "I know, but don't forget we aren't going to bother Mr. Hollister. We're going to let him have peace and quiet so he can rest and get better."

Danny crossed a finger over his heart. "I'll be good."

YOU'RE A DAMNED fool, Jake thought as he walked back to Huckleberry Lodge with the menu Hannah Nolan had given him. The doctor had warned him not to overexert himself, so naturally he'd insisted on driving alone to Mahalaton Lake from Seattle and had sent Andy packing.

And now he'd offended his landlady to the point she probably wanted to drown him in the lake.

He collapsed on the couch and glanced at the menu without much interest. Ironically, the doctors had urged him to eat nutritious, high-protein meals, but the crap he'd been served at the hospital was barely edible—even the limited diet he'd shared with the Inupiat had been better.

Or maybe it was just the environment. He'd grown up in the far corners of the world with his mother and they'd always eaten native when feasible; Josie believed you couldn't learn about a culture if you didn't eat their food and sleep in their beds.

With pain throbbing in every inch of his body, Jake let the menu drift to the ground.

Maybe he'd try ordering something later.

Much later.

CHAPTER TWO

THE NEXT MORNING, Jake woke as the sun was rising and realized he had fallen asleep on the couch.

He was stiff, but some of the pain had subsided and a fine view greeted him through the windows overlooking the lake. The snowcapped peaks beyond were reflected on the water's surface and he stared out for a while. Where was his impulse to capture the view in a unique way? Taking pictures had been his driving force since childhood, yet he had zero desire to start working.

God.

Maybe it was too pretty. That must be the problem. Why he'd ever agreed to doing a damned book on the northern Cascade Mountains was beyond him. The Cascades had been photographed to death; there was nothing new or unusual about them. He was going to be bored out of his skull.

But even more important...how was he going to put his trademark adventurous stamp on the book? The thought of people rolling their eyes and saying he'd lost his touch because of the accident was unacceptable. And he'd already faced that scenario once before.

Jake gritted his teeth.

He had never intended to be a traditional photo-journalist. He'd gone to the Middle East to help out an acquaintance whose wife was having a difficult pregnancy, but after receiving the Pulitzer, at least a dozen interviewers had asked, "How will you top this?" Hell, "topping" pictures of people killing each other was the last thing he was interested in doing.

His stomach rumbled and he got up.

Andy had insisted they stop and buy groceries in Mahalaton Lake, so Jake made his standby in all climates and altitudes—a peanut-butter-and-jelly sandwich. It wasn't inspiring, but cooking was *not* one of his skills. He always kept peanut butter in his backpack while traveling, and it wasn't bad on most local breads.

Munching on the sandwich, he wandered around the lodge. The spacious sunroom off the kitchen had tall windows on three sides, providing a view of the lake, the guesthouse and the wooded drive leading in from the road. A huge master bedroom suite was on the opposite side of the house. Other main floor rooms included a well-equipped utility room, two powder rooms, a library and formal dining area. Upstairs there were additional bedrooms and baths, with a family room in the center, and beneath the house was a half basement that provided storage.

It was far more space than Jake needed, but had the benefit of being outside a town, and the natural wood beams and high ceilings gave it a relaxed, faintly rustic feel. And there were artifacts scattered here and there from around the world, such as jade carvings, masks from various tribes and pottery. In a curious way it was soothing to be surrounded by some of the things he'd seen in his travels. Perhaps that was why Andy had urged him to lease the lodge.

Slowly he began sorting out his equipment and other supplies. The cameras he'd taken to Alaska had been destroyed in the crash, but Toby had personally brought Jake's backup gear from the studio he kept in Costa Rica.

Toby...

A reluctant grin creased Jake's mouth. Toby had bitched his usual stream of complaints, saying the magazine was willing to wait for its photos since they didn't have any "goddamned choice," and if Jake planned to go back to that frigging place, he was going alone.

This time it actually sounded as if he meant it.

Even so, Jake had expected he'd come along to Mahalaton Lake until Toby had sheepishly confessed that he and Vera were getting married in a few weeks and he was starting another job. Marriage was a career ender as far as Jake was concerned, at least for any career that involved extensive travel. Vera was a terrific woman, but she'd made it clear often enough that she wanted Toby at home.

Jake rubbed his face, rough with beard stubble, and stepped to the bank of windows. The day was lighter now, though the sky was still pink from the sunrise. The dog he'd seen the previous day was racing along the shore below, his fur flying in silky waves. It stopped, grabbed a stick in its mouth and ran back to its human companion—presumably Hannah Nolan.

He grimaced. An apology was in order; he'd behaved with the grace of an ill-tempered water buffalo. He let himself out a side door and walked down the grassy slope toward his landlady. The dog noticed him first, dropping his stick and hurrying to his mistress's side.

"Did you have a good night, Mr. Hollister?" Hannah asked politely when he got within earshot.

"Good enough."

He'd slept for eleven straight hours on the wide leather couch—much longer than he would have in the hospital with their constant health checks. Getting chilled and stiff from his position on the sofa was his own fault.

Jake gestured to the golden retriever who was regarding him suspiciously. "Who is this?"

Hannah put her hand on the animal's head and stroked it. "His name is Badger. But don't worry—I won't let him come into Huckleberry Lodge."

"He's welcome. I like dogs. Where is your son?"

"Still in bed. Danny isn't a morning person."

"Neither am I," Jake said absently.

Her lips pressed together in a flat line and he wondered what she wanted to say—it was amusing the way she was obviously trying to guard her tongue.

"Anyway," he continued, "let me apologize for yesterday. I didn't behave well."

"Okay. You've apologized."

"Uh…how far do you have to go from here to see any wildlife?" Jake asked, despite her flat response. It wouldn't hurt to be on decent terms with his landlady.

Hannah's face became less guarded. "Actually, you can sit on the deck and see a whole range of birds and mammals. I've spotted almost everything except bears and mountain lions."

"That's promising. I also noticed a couple of trails leading away from the lodge. Where do they go?"

The retriever yipped and she patted him again. "The one to the south leads into town, winding back and forth between the water and woods. The north trail is similar, but it's rougher, with far more ups and downs. It extends around the lake to Mount Mahala."

Jake looked at the snowcapped peak behind the water. "I'm guessing it would take a while to reach the mountain."

A grin tugged at her mouth and he suddenly became aware of her as a woman. He still didn't have any hint of Hannah's figure, but if it matched her smile, he could be in trouble. Making a move on a woman with a child was a bad idea—in his experience, they were usually looking for commitment, and that wasn't something he would ever be willing to offer.

"You're right—it's much farther than it appears.

You can't see it from here, but there's a spur of the lake that goes way north beyond that point." Hannah gestured to an outcropping of land covered by tall evergreens.

"What made you smile just now?" he asked curiously.

"A memory. When I was a kid I decided I could hike to the mountain all on my own. My parents didn't argue, but Dad followed a few hundred feet behind me. We spent the night out there, not even a quarter of the way, with my feet hurting like mad. Not that I admitted it."

And Jake would bet she was just as stubborn now. That kind of obstinacy wasn't something people typically outgrew.

"I take it you grew up in the area," he commented.

"Except for four years at college, I've always lived here."

"Hell, I could never stay in one place for so long." It wasn't until Jake saw the look on Hannah's face that he realized how rude he must have sounded... *again*. "Sorry. I'm a born wanderer."

She raised an eyebrow. "Then you must be dreading the next twelve months."

"That's an understatement. I just want to get past this damned accident and have my life back."

Nobody understood how he felt except Josie, and she was back in the Andes—or maybe she'd gone somewhere else by now. The doctors had preached patience, Matt's attitude was that it was only a year and Andy was just pleased that his client had finally agreed to do a book based in the United States.

But Jake didn't want a conventional existence; he wanted what he'd had before the plane crash—international travel, seeing new places, his photography…and as few complications as possible.

"It isn't because of your house," Jake added hastily. "The lodge is great. Why aren't you living there, instead of in the guesthouse?"

"It's too expensive on a teacher's salary. It makes more sense to rent it out and live in Silver Cottage."

"But surely you get child support," he said. Before leaving the day before, Andy had explained she was divorced. Jake had gotten the impression that his friend was attracted to Hannah. Not that it would go anywhere. Andy was an excellent agent, skilled at professional negotiations, but he was notoriously inept in his personal life.

Hannah's green eyes narrowed. "My son's father and his financial contributions are a private matter."

"Well, yeah. That is, I didn't mean to pry."

"Whatever." She turned and hurried away. Badger followed with a glance over his shoulder, clearly warning Jake to watch his step.

Jake groaned.

He hadn't meant to be inquisitive, but even *his* father had never skipped out on financial responsibility for his kids. And S. S. Hollister was generally considered one of the most irresponsible men on the planet, with children and ex-wives all around the world.

Of course, Jake's mother wasn't one of S. S. Hollister's ex-wives. Josie had refused to marry "Sully" as she called him...probably the only woman to turn down one of his marriage proposals, though she'd agreed to give their son the Hollister name and let Sully set up a trust fund. The trust fund had been a huge concession for Josie, who considered money a necessary evil.

Evil or not, Jake found his trust fund useful. From the very start of his career he'd been able to choose his assignments based on interest rather than just the need to pay bills. The money had also meant he could purchase the finest photographic gear that money could buy.

Unfortunately, no amount of money could repair his injuries. Only time would do that. The doctors were optimistic, yet nobody could guarantee he *would* recover enough to go back to the life he loved, and it scared the hell out of him.

As HANNAH MARCHED back to Silver Cottage, she realized she'd overreacted. Admittedly, she was still annoyed by Jake's behavior toward Danny, but she didn't have to be so sensitive. She needed to remember the monthly rent check she was getting. The amount Jake was paying should make his abrasive qualities easier to handle.

She went inside and checked on Danny; he was

still asleep, sprawled across his bed with childish abandon.

A faint whine came from Badger, and she rubbed him behind the ears. "Patience, boy. He'll be awake later."

The golden retriever was a tireless, protective playmate for Danny. Hannah kept a close watch on her son, but it was reassuring to have the golden retriever as a second pair of eyes; he wouldn't even let Danny get near the water except when an adult was nearby.

Badger padded into the room and jumped on the bed. Danny rolled over in his sleep, flung his arm across the retriever's neck and buried his face in his pillow.

Hannah drifted into the living room, annoyed with herself for mentioning her finances to Jake Hollister. It was none of his concern how she met her expenses, and neither was the question of child support from her ex. Steven wasn't a pleasant subject at the best of times—they'd gotten married during her senior year of college and were already divorced by the following Christmas.

The part that continued to puzzle her was how she hadn't recognized what kind of a person he was earlier. Somehow she'd convinced herself they were the next great love story only to discover how quickly it fell apart in the face of infidelity and other problems. Thinking she'd been blinded by romance wasn't any comfort; lots of people fell in love but didn't marry someone utterly wrong for them.

The phone rang and Hannah hurried to answer. The caller ID showed it was Brendan Townsend, and she smiled as she picked up. "Hi, Brendan."

"Good morning, Hannah. I hope I didn't wake you."

"I just got back from walking Badger. You know me—I'm up with the sun, same as you."

It was one of the ways they were alike—she'd finally agreed to go out with Brendan because of what they had in common. She didn't have a list of dating requirements, but it was important not to start caring for someone who didn't share her belief in commitment.

She still hoped to find the passionate love she'd wanted her entire life but couldn't afford to break her heart over the wrong man again. She wasn't sure how many more times it could heal.

Brendan chuckled. "I drove my college roommate crazy getting up so early. He was the party-hearty type and never went to bed before 3:00 a.m."

"Did he flunk out?"

"Amazingly, no. He's the multimillionaire owner of a computer software company. They create fantasy games."

"Impressive. Maybe you shouldn't have settled for law school," she said with a laugh.

"Not at all. I wouldn't have met you if I wasn't a lawyer." The tone in Brendan's voice was warm and she squirmed. He wanted their relationship to move much faster than she did. But even if her marriage hadn't taught her caution, she needed to be careful because of Danny.

"That's a nice thing to say. What's up?" she asked briskly.

"It's short notice, but would you like to go out tonight? We haven't been able to see much of each other lately."

"Oh, I'm sorry, I have plans," Hannah said regretfully. It had been several weeks since they'd gotten together and she would have enjoyed talking to a sane adult male. "Barbi Paulson is coming over."

"Barbi Paulson?" Brendan repeated with obvious surprise. "The pizza-delivery woman?"

"She's a friend. We're going to…uh, watch a movie or something." Hannah couldn't explain that she was tutoring Barbi for her GED exam—Barbi might prefer to keep that information private.

"Maybe we can go another day. What's on tonight's menu? You're such a wonderful cook, I'm envious."

"No call for envy. I'll probably do macaroni and cheese. It's easy, Danny likes it and Barbi isn't coming until after dinner."

After they said goodbye, Hannah sat at the breakfast table with a cup of coffee. The sun was fully up now and she gazed out, loving the changing view. Honestly, she didn't think there was anything more beautiful than the Cascade Mountains.

Finally she opened one of the adult-study manuals she'd gotten from the school district office. She taught elementary-age children, and it had been years since she'd looked at the high school curriculum. It wouldn't bolster Barbi's confidence about taking the GED test if her tutor wasn't familiar with the material.

BRENDAN WENT BACK to work at his desk, disappointed that his great plan to sweep Hannah off for the evening had failed. He would have thought that in a quiet place like Mahalaton Lake, with only a few thousand people and her parents available for babysitting, they wouldn't have trouble getting together, but she was so busy it was a challenge.

Yet as he dealt with his email, he formulated a plan—if Hannah didn't have enough time to go to dinner, he would take dinner to her. He'd surprise her by bringing something from Luigi's, and leave when Barbi arrived.

Hmm.

He frowned thoughtfully.

Barbi Paulson and Hannah?

The two women couldn't be more different. Luigi's was the only restaurant in town that delivered, and he ordered regularly from them on weekends. While Barbi didn't mouth off when she brought his pizza, she wore garish, low-cut outfits that were always a little too tight and a little too short. She even managed to be eye-popping in the winter when she wore things like hot pink ski pants and equally colorful parkas.

With a shake of his head, Brendan reviewed his appointment schedule. It was far less full than when he'd practiced law in Seattle. Relocating to Mahalaton Lake the previous year might be the only impulsive decision he'd made in his entire life, but it had seemed right at the time.

Yet even as he thought about it, he felt a pang of sorrow, remembering the woman he'd once hoped to marry.

Maria had been an associate in his high-pressure Seattle law firm, but she'd died suddenly of a brain aneurism. The other partners hadn't appeared troubled by the loss; they'd simply divvied up Maria's client list between them. Yet Brendan had been devastated. For the first time he'd questioned the sanity of working more than a hundred hours a week. Maria had been having headaches and dizzy spells, but she wouldn't even take time off to see a doctor—success came before marriage, before kids, before *everything*.

What sort of life was that? Hell, it *wasn't* a life. She was gone at thirty-one.

At first he'd tried to cut back his hours—much to the displeasure of the head of the firm, who'd "suggested" resuming his original schedule or finding other options for practicing law. About the same time Maria's father had told him he was trying to sell his law firm in Mahalaton Lake. Brendan had visited the town a couple of times with Maria, and the idea of completely changing his scenery had caught his imagination. He'd quickly purchased David Walther's shabby practice and moved.

Of course, in Seattle, he'd also dreamed about Maria every night, hearing her voice urging him over and over to go to Mahalaton Lake. Moving to a small town might seem unusual, but moving because of dreams? He'd never dared tell *anyone* about that.

Brendan glanced around the office, no longer shabby now that he'd had it redone. The only thing left from David Walther's days was a carved wood plaque saying, "Work to live, don't live to work." He'd kept it as a reminder of the reasons he'd made such a huge change in his life. Maria hadn't learned the lesson from her father, but maybe he could.

A career here wasn't going to make Brendan rich, but it wasn't a bad life, at least for a while. No matter what the reasons, moving to Mahalaton Lake *had* been a good decision. It was in his professional capacity that he'd met Hannah—she'd asked him to review her rental paperwork for the lodge.

All at once Brendan straightened his tie and checked his cuff links. Life was more casual in Mahalaton Lake than in the city, but he came from a long line of attorneys and had been raised to do things in a certain way. He'd rebelled to a certain extent, but there were some things he couldn't abandon.

THE DAY PASSED slowly for Jake. Part of the time he slept, and part of the time he did the exercises the physical therapist in Seattle had taught him. He was starting to understand why the specialists had recommended a couple of weeks in a rehab center, but inactivity wasn't something he handled well. Freedom had beckoned, even the freedom of a small American town.

Anyway, he had arranged for a therapist from a nearby community to come to Huckleberry Lodge twice a week. It was well worth the expense of having them come to him rather than dragging himself to the clinic.

Jake finally loaded up his computer and began looking through the shots from northern Alaska. It was time to confront his memories of the crash. The photos taken on days before the accident didn't bother him...a lone male polar bear hunting for seals, one climbing from the frigid sea with water streaming from its fur, another moving with long, purposeful strides. And still more of daily life in the Inupiat village where they'd stayed part of the time.

Then a shot of Gordon popped up and took Jake off guard.

The pilot's weathered features were creased in a smile and he was lifting a cup of coffee to his mouth. Jake stared for several minutes before clicking on the next image. Several dozen photos later there were more of Gordon, playing with Inupiat children, and others of him talking with the elder members of the community.

Jake had almost forgotten that he'd taken these pictures. He didn't often take photos of people, but the magazine had suggested it would be nice if his Arctic photographic study could include some of the tools used by the Inupiat for hunting. As a kind of lazy exercise, he'd wandered around, interested by the juxtaposition of modern and age-old technology in use. Pictures of people had inevitably crept in.

His nerves tightened further as he pulled up the images from the day of the crash. The doctors had asked about the accident and he'd refused to answer. Assuming it was because he couldn't remember, they'd said not to worry, that it was common to block everything out after a trauma. Yet it wasn't that at all.

Jake's memories of that day were crystal clear—he sometimes wished he *couldn't* remember. He still could feel the purity of the air and hear the sound of ice cracking, along with the noises from the bears and the crunch of their boots as they returned to the plane. And he could see Gordon's gray face, his bluish fingernails, the snow getting closer, the painful impact…and the realization that the old bush pilot hadn't survived.

It wasn't the first time Jake had seen death. When he was a boy, half of his mother's climbing party had died when they'd tried to climb Sagarmatha—Mount Everest to most people outside Nepal, except the Tibetans, who called it Chomolungma. At eight, he'd been too young to do anything except stay in base camp, but he would never forget the blanket-draped stretchers waiting for transport and Josie's silence as she sat with a cup of coffee and gazed into the distance.

Two of the bodies hadn't been recovered. The climbers had died on the upper slopes where the air was so thin that anyone making the attempt would be risking their own lives.

Pushing darker thoughts away, Jake mentally evaluated the collection of photos. Since the magazine still wanted him to complete his assignment, returning to Alaska would be his first real effort once he was back to full strength. He didn't count the picture book on the northern Cascades as genuine work—it was mostly to keep himself from going crazy until things were normal again.

Late in the afternoon Jake was working in the bright, airy room off the kitchen when a car pulling into the driveway caught his attention. The expensive, late-model sedan was out of place in the natural setting, and the same was also true of the man who climbed out with a bouquet of red roses in one hand and two white sacks in the other.

Uptight, Jake decided. Obviously conventional, wearing a suit and tie and sporting a short, conservative haircut.

Hannah Nolan came down the stairs, her long

chestnut hair shining with red glints in the afternoon sun, and Jake leaned forward to get a better look.

Nice.

While he hadn't been able to distinguish much about her figure in their previous encounters, right now she was wearing snug jeans and a T-shirt that nicely displayed her feminine curves.

The sight reminded him that he hadn't died in the airplane crash. Sex was fundamental to the survival instinct, and Hannah Nolan was a *very* sexy woman.

Jake grinned. His apology and attempt at small talk had gone badly that morning, but he'd enjoyed his landlady's response. She hadn't humored him the way everyone else had been doing since the accident, saying what they thought he wanted to hear. She'd gotten mad and let him know she was pissed.

Was she as frankly honest with her visitor? She appeared surprised to see the newcomer, but it obviously wasn't her ex-husband, who Jake suspected fell into the deadbeat-father category.

The stuffed shirt handed Hannah the flowers and bent down for a kiss that landed awkwardly when she turned her head at the last moment. Courting customs varied around the world, but it was a good guess they hadn't arrived at the lover stage. After another few words, they went up the steps into the guesthouse.

Though he was getting hungry again, Jake decided to stay in the sunroom to see if anything else happened. Aside from Hannah's undeniable visual appeal, the whole exchange hadn't been particularly interesting, but after spending so much time confined to a hospital, his standards for entertainment weren't high these days.

CHAPTER THREE

IN THE GUESTHOUSE kitchen Hannah tried not to react as she took out the three entrées Brendan had brought with him. Eggplant parmigiana. Her favorite dish, but not the sort of thing Danny liked. Okay, so Brendan didn't understand kids; that wasn't the end of the world. He could learn. The baby greens in the salad were even worse for a little boy than the eggplant, but the cheesy breadsticks would be popular—when Luigi called something "cheesy" it was an understatement.

"This place is really nice," Brendan said with approval as he gazed around the kitchen. "I never asked, did you do a remodel when you moved in here?"

"Uh, no," Hannah murmured, thinking of the fortune it would have taken for her to update the property. Her father was both an architect and contractor and had insisted on doing the work for Great-Aunt Elkie at cost when she'd renovated a few years before, but the materials alone had been hideously expensive. "My great-aunt kept things fixed up. She was quite particular."

"I'm impressed. A lot of older people seem to want their homes to stay the same, out of sentiment I suppose."

"Not Elkie, at least not about Huckleberry Lodge. Before he died, Great-Uncle Larry made her promise she wouldn't be maudlin and leave everything the same."

"You must have been very close."

"I was crazy about them both." Hannah smiled at the memories. "I used to spend weekends here. We'd make banana splits and watch old films like *Key Largo* and *The Big Sleep*. My great-aunt was a big Humphrey Bogart and Lauren Bacall fan. There was a line she loved from an old pop song...'we had it all, just like Bogie and Bacall.' I think that's how she saw her marriage to Great-Uncle Larry, but instead of Key Largo, they had Mahalaton Lake."

"Oh...right."

It was just a guess, but Hannah had the feeling he wasn't entirely sure who Humphrey Bogart and Lauren Bacall actually were.

She checked the clock as she arranged the flowers he'd given her in a vase. Barbi wasn't due for a couple of hours, so there was time to eat and visit. Nevertheless, it was exasperating that Brendan had come, even though she'd told him that she had plans. Between taking care of Danny and work and community activities, she didn't have as much time to socialize as he wanted. Of course, maybe he'd never dated a single mother before and didn't realize how much a child changed things.

Still, if she ever wanted to fall in love and get married again, she needed to remember how it felt to be a woman, not just a mother.

She set the table and called Danny from his room. He greeted their guest politely, only to scrunch up his face when he saw his plate; he loved Italian food...as long as it was cheese pizza or spaghetti.

"Wasn't it nice of Brendan to bring us dinner?" Hannah said before he could complain.

"Uh-huh." He sighed heavily and picked up his fork.

Hannah ate a bite of salad, savoring the garlic-balsamic dressing. It was just right to set off the eggplant parmigiana, and her frustration with Brendan faded—this was much better than macaroni and cheese.

"Isn't Danny eating salad?" Brendan asked.

"Not tonight."

She hadn't given Danny a serving, knowing he'd balk at eating the mildly bitter baby greens in addition to eggplant. And she couldn't blame him—children experienced flavors differently from adults, so foods that she loved didn't necessarily taste good to Danny. Normally she wanted him to try a bite of everything, but it was easier to keep things lower key in front of company.

Badger came trotting into the kitchen and stood at Danny's elbow. Hannah didn't allow Badger to be fed table scraps, but he remained hopeful…making her suspect that Danny was sneaking him bits when she wasn't watching.

"Badger, sit," she ordered.

The dog lay down, crossing one paw over the other, a picture of meek innocence.

"How is your new tenant working out so far?" Brendan asked.

"It's too early to say. He was irritable when he arrived, but that was probably from being in pain."

Brendan frowned. "I've read about the Hollister family—they're notorious. Let me know if you have any problems. If worse comes to worst, I'll look for a way to cancel the lease."

"I'm sure it won't get that bad."

"All right, but you may change your mind if his party-loving father shows up."

She couldn't change her mind. Having Jake Hollister as a tenant was going to ease some of her financial pressures, and it would be painful to give up the income now that she'd gotten the first check. She'd just have to deal with him as well as possible.

BARBI DROVE OUT of town, both excited and nervous about her first tutoring session. She hadn't taken a test since she was sixteen, and even when she was a kid she hadn't done so good on them—she froze when she saw a list of questions and her head wouldn't work. As for all that proper English and math, those things scared the crap out of her.

She got to Huckleberry Lodge and groaned when she saw a silver Lexus parked in front of the guesthouse. There weren't that many fancy cars in Mahalaton Lake. It had to be Brendan Townsend.

God, what a prig.

He was conventional about everything—even his pizzas always had the same three toppings. She'd bet that in bed it was missionary position all the way—some action on the breasts, a quick swipe on the thigh and wham, bam, thank you, ma'am. Sex was probably too earthy for him to do it right.

The first time she'd delivered a pizza to Brendan was on a hot day the previous summer, and she would never forget his expression when she'd arrived. She had been wearing skimpy shorts with a tube top and his eyes had narrowed with cool scorn. After that she'd started chewing gum whenever she brought food to his condo, making sure she snapped it loudly and blew at least two bubbles before he managed to pay her.

Not that she'd actually get mouthy while delivering a meal to him, but it was the sort of thing Brendan expected and she had to have a little fun. Besides, she'd grown up as the girl whose drunken father was in and out of jail for disorderly behavior, so there was no point in trying to fit in now. She might as well wear the clothes she liked and let the biddies gossip. And it wasn't as if she was *staying* in Mahalaton Lake, as much as she liked it here. She wanted to get away from any reminders of her father, and having her GED would make getting a good job easier.

Of course, Brendan didn't try to fit in, either. He wore a suit to everything, including the Founder's Day picnic and the fire department's monthly fund-raising dinners. Jeez, he'd been living in Mahalaton Lake for over a year; he should have loosened up by now. But there was one thing she *could* say for him—he tipped well.

Barbi debated for a minute before turning off the engine. She'd rather leave, but Hannah was expecting her and it would be rude. Besides, it was a chance to yank Brendan's chain—she wasn't delivering a pizza to him *now,* any more than when she saw him at one of the town's events.

Grinning, Barbi got out of her battered Chevy; she undid the buttons on her shirt and snugly tied the tails beneath her breasts for a nice display of cleavage. Let Mr. Big Shot Attorney get a load of *this*.

Glancing up, she spotted a man standing at a window of Huckleberry Lodge. She waved to him. He must have gotten an eyeful when her shirt was open, but it wasn't as if she had anything to be ashamed of—she'd stack her breasts up against any woman in Mahalaton Lake.

She trotted up the broad steps to Hannah's porch and knocked. It seemed strange not to be carrying a pizza box; she delivered one to Hannah and Danny practically every week. And when a crowd of week-end skiers were staying at the lodge, she sometimes delivered a stack of giant pies to them three nights in a row—skiing worked up an appetite.

"Hi," she said brightly when Brendan opened the door. "Whatcha doing here?"

"I brought dinner out for Hannah and Danny."

"Really? I didn't know I had competition—things must be slow at the office if you had to go into the delivery business. But I doubt you'll get my tips—you don't have my equipment." She wiggled her shoulders provocatively.

It was satisfying to see Brendan focus directly on her chest. He might not approve of her showing some skin, but he wasn't above getting his jollies at the sight. Men were predictable that way.

"For your information, I just…that is, Hannah and I…we had a meal together," he spluttered.

"Maybe I should come back another night."

"Nonsense." It was Hannah and she elbowed Brendan to one side. "Brendan is just leaving. I told him we were planning to watch a movie or something."

It was nice of Hannah to make up an explanation like that. Barbi didn't exactly *mind* people knowing she was studying for her GED, but she also didn't want to look idiotic being taught kid's stuff in front of Brendan that she should have learned fifteen years ago in high school. He was such a snot, he'd probably think it was hilarious.

Uneven footsteps sounded on the stairs below them and Hannah's face got tense. "Is there something you need, Mr. Hollister?" she asked.

"I just need to know where the spare lightbulbs are. The lamp in the living room blew."

Barbi turned around. It was the hunk she'd caught watching her earlier. *Yum.* Tall and trim, with hair so dark it was almost black, and intense brown eyes. Brendan might be sexy if he got serious help; this guy was pure heat without even trying.

"They're in the utility room," Hannah said in a tight voice. "I wanted to show you where everything is, but you refused a tour of the house. Remember?"

The hunk just shrugged.

"Hi, Mr. Hollister," Danny chirped, jumping down to the first step. "How're ya doing? Mommy said you didn't feel so good."

"I'm better today."

Danny smiled. *"Super."*

"Go on inside, Barbi. You, too, Danny," Hannah urged. She gave Brendan a kiss on the cheek. "Thanks for dinner. Maybe we can get together next week. Call me in a few days."

"I'll look forward to it."

He fixed his tie and checked the buttons on his coat before hurrying to his Lexus. Honestly, the guy was so stuffy and correct, Barbi didn't know how he could get by without a book of etiquette in his back pocket and a yardstick up his ass. Hannah was way too nice for him, but there weren't that many single men in Mahalaton Lake and she'd already been married to a louse. Brendan wasn't a louse, just dull.

Barbi winked at the hunk, and as she went into the

house, she could hear a low conversation between him and Hannah.

A minute later Hannah came in and closed the door. "Let's get started," she said. Her tone was light, but she sure looked flustered.

ON THE TUESDAY after Jake Hollister's arrival, Hannah knocked on the door of Huckleberry Lodge. She'd agreed to do the cleaning every Tuesday and Friday at one o'clock during the summer. Once the school year started, the time would shift to late afternoon.

"You don't have to knock," Jake said by way of greeting as he opened the door.

"In polite society, knocking is considered appropriate."

"I didn't grow up in polite society. That is, I should say traditional 'Western' polite society. They haven't always had doors in the places I've lived. Every culture has its customs about proper behavior—the trick is learning those customs."

"Have you made any effort to learn them here?"

Jake seemed genuinely startled. "I don't need to. I was born in Iceland, but I'm a U.S. citizen."

"Citizenship doesn't guarantee you know American customs. You don't get that kind of knowledge through an umbilical cord."

"I'm getting by just fine."

"Whatever."

Hannah bent over and picked up a stack of books

piled haphazardly on the floor near the native stone fireplace in the living room. Her great-aunt and uncle had loved books, and they were in abundance around the lodge, especially the classics and non-fiction.

She put the books on the built-in shelves flanking the fireplace and went into the kitchen. *Phew.* There was a pizza box on the sandstone counter by the stove, one on the floor, another on the window seat behind the breakfast nook and a fourth was on the table. The sink and nearby surfaces were covered with dirty dishes and cups and wadded-up napkins. A jar of raspberry jam was tipped over on its side and red syrup dripped from it onto the floor. An empty jar of peanut butter sat nearby.

Jake limped past her. He dug a slice of pizza from the box on the table, liberally sprinkled it with crushed red pepper flakes and chomped down on the crust end.

"Uh, have you eaten anything except pizza and peanut butter since you got here?" She set the jam jar upright and wiped up the mess with a wet cloth.

"I don't cook and Luigi's only delivers pizza. And that's only Friday through Sunday, as you've pointed out."

"Ask for Luigi when you phone and sweet-talk him into sending one of his other dishes at the same time you sweet-talk him into delivering Monday through Thursday."

"I don't sweet-talk well."

She widened her eyes in mock astonishment. "Really? That's hard to imagine when you're so charming and tactful."

Jake snorted and ignored her sarcasm.

Wrinkling her nose, Hannah got a plastic garbage bag from under the sink and began collecting trash. Huckleberry Lodge was equipped with the latest in kitchen appliances, yet her tenant was eating delivery pizza and peanut butter. She was appalled at his diet, but it was his concern; he was an adult, capable of choosing his own food.

"There's still half a pizza in here," she said, picking up the box from the floor and putting in her bag.

"It's old. Got it on Friday and wasn't that hungry."

"Then this one must be from Saturday," she said, peering into the box from the window seat. There were several pieces in that one, as well. "There's a refrigerator, you know. It's that large, rectangular thing over there." She pointed to the stainless steel commercial-grade refrigerator. "Amazingly, it keeps food at a safe temperature for future consumption."

"Very amusing. But I have an iron stomach after the way I've lived. Besides, I don't cook."

"There's also a stove, microwave and toaster oven—reheating doesn't require any culinary ability."

"Neither does ordering another pizza. Got two on Sunday and figured they'd last awhile. So don't throw those away." He gestured to the boxes on the table and countertop.

"Well, I guess it's a break from PB&Js."

"PB&Js?"

"Peanut-butter-and-jelly sandwiches. Seriously, how much time *have* you spent in the U.S. if you don't know that?" Hannah swept dried crusts of bread and wadded-up paper towels into her sack of trash.

"Almost none," Jake admitted. "I'm normally on assignment fifty weeks out of the year. And usually in remote areas. I have a small work studio in Costa Rica, but I'm hardly ever there, either."

Lord. Hannah couldn't imagine living like that, with no real home, just a suitcase, or whatever passed for a suitcase in his line of work. She glanced out the window at Mahala Lake, the water so blue it almost hurt her eyes. Except for the years she'd been at college, it was a sight she'd seen every day of her life, yet she never tired of it.

"Traveling can be fun, but I'm mostly a homebody," she said, raising her chin and practically daring him to say something *else* that was rude. Jake had made his opinion about staying in one place quite well-known.

"Yeah, I figured that out. The domestic stuff is okay if that's what you like, but home, marriage, kids—those things *end* my kind of career."

Hannah stared. "That isn't the first time you've mentioned something along those lines, and it's starting to sound like a warning. I don't need to be told to keep my distance. My ex-husband was a thrill seeker and I have no intention of making that mistake again. If I get married again, it's going to be to someone stable and caring who can put me and my son first. It certainly won't be to a man with one foot out the door and a habit of risking his neck."

"I didn't mean it that way," Jake protested. "It's on my mind, that's all. I talked to my former photography assistant this morning. We won't be working together any longer because he's getting married, and all he could talk about was the house they're buying and his great new job. He may be better off on his own, but he already *had* a great job. *With me*."

"You fired him because he's getting married? Is being single a rule in the photography business?"

Jake sank down on one of the chairs, rubbing his left leg. "I didn't fire him, but most spouses don't appreciate being left alone for months at a time, and Toby's fiancée is no exception. Vera must have given him an ultimatum after the accident and he caved under the pressure."

Hannah began putting cups in the top rack of the dishwasher, thinking about the mixed emotions on Jake's face when he'd mentioned Toby's enthusiasm for his new job…emotions too complicated to fathom. One thing was quite clear, however—Jake Hollister didn't understand people who wanted a home.

"Maybe your assistant didn't 'cave.' Maybe he made a choice," she offered finally.

Jake shook his head. "Toby liked the travel. He

complains about stuff, but that's just his way—he's the one who suggested going to the Gobi Desert three years ago. For Pete's sake, it's not as if he was cheating on Vera, and they talked on the satellite phone almost every day."

"A phone call is hardly the same as having someone with you. And if Toby loved the travel that much, he didn't have to quit."

"But he *is* quitting."

She rolled her eyes at Jake's sulky, little-boy tone.

"Well, your feelings about domesticity are hardly a secret," she informed him. "Whenever a reporter or an interviewer asks about marriage, you declare you're a confirmed bachelor."

"You've read about me?"

"Don't read anything into it. The rental agent for Huckleberry Lodge was excited about the idea of a celebrity living in the area. Lillian gave me copies of various articles and talked about you incessantly."

"I'm not a celebrity."

"You're the closest thing to it in Mahalaton Lake."

Hannah put detergent in the dishwasher and started it, uncomfortably aware of Jake watching her.

"Don't you have work to do?" she asked finally.

"Nothing important. I'm on a forced hiatus except for the fluff book I'm doing on the Cascades."

"Excuse me?" She turned and raised her eyebrows. *"Fluff?"*

"The Cascade Range has been done by half the nature photographers on the planet. It's boring."

Hannah's temper began to simmer again. This was her *home* he was insulting.

"The Cascade Mountains are among the most beautiful places in the world," she said crisply. "We have active volcanoes, varied animal life, gorgeous wildflowers…it's a scenic wonderland."

"But it's also commonplace." Jake made a dismissive gesture. "Nothing can compare to the sight of a polar bear in its natural habitat or the power of an Amur leopard climbing up a rock face with its prey."

"Oh? Have you ever heard the cry of a loon across the water? It's haunting. And how about the way dogwood blossoms seem to hang in midair, glowing in the low light of a forest? A place doesn't have to be remote to be breathtaking."

"Yeah, I'm sure it's nice."

Hannah could tell he wasn't convinced, but she hadn't expected to get through to him—he'd made up his mind and that was that. She took the bag of trash out to the cans behind the garage and headed back to find Jake sitting at the farmhouse table with a laptop computer in front of him.

Pressing her lips together, she continued putting the kitchen to rights. Removing the trash was a big improvement. It was even possible that the mess was more the result of him feeling lousy than of his truly being a slob; she'd find out over the next few months as his condition improved.

"By the way, where's your son?" Jake asked after a few minutes.

"With my parents. They went down to Portland for the day and I didn't think you wanted him here."

SHE'D SENT DANNY to spend the day with her parents? A twinge of guilt went through Jake. He wasn't a kid person, but he usually got along okay with them. It was just that first day he'd instantly envisioned having Danny underfoot all the time and hadn't wanted to encourage that. On the other hand, he hadn't expected to be so bored.

"You can bring him next time," he offered, surprising himself. "I don't mind."

"Can I get that in writing?" Hannah asked drily.

He grinned. Hannah Nolan wasn't what he'd expected as a landlady, but that was a good thing. He didn't need a comfortable motherly type, fussing over him and treating him like an invalid. Hannah would be more likely to kick him in the ass than fuss.

"Whatever you like. I'll have my lawyer contact your lawyer, and we'll do it right. If I had to guess, that guy who visited last week is a member of the bar. Conservative suit, no sense of humor, luxury car...what else could he be?"

She pressed her lips together and began wiping the sandstone countertops. Jake hadn't intended to let the place get so messy, but it was easy to let things go when just getting from one side of the house to the other was a pain. *Literally.* Yet even as the thought formed, he grimaced. He didn't like excuses; they stank worse than week-old fish.

"So is the guy you're dating the sensitive, vulnerable man you're looking for?" he asked.

"Brendan is a friend. And not that it's any of your business, but I didn't say I was looking for sensitive *or* vulnerable."

"My mistake."

Hannah tidied the sunroom before returning to the living room. He followed, to her obvious displeasure.

"I thought you were doing something on your computer."

"I've never had a housekeeper before. I should see how you do things."

She returned another stack of books to the bookcases by the fireplace. "I'm not your housekeeper. Our agreement specifies light cleaning twice a week, not to exceed two hours. You reminded me about the 'light' part when you arrived."

"Sure. But don't you think it's mostly a question of semantics?"

"You don't want to know what I think," Hannah muttered.

Jake tried not to smile. It wasn't nice of him to ruffle her feathers, but they were awfully fun to ruffle. He'd already stuck his foot into his mouth to the point she'd probably boot him out if she could get away with it. At least his lease gave him some protection.

Taking a dust mop from a closet, Hannah ran it over the hardwood floor and then dusted the flat surfaces. A citrus scent filled the air and he sniffed.

"What's that?"

"Lemon oil. It's good for the wood, but if you don't like it, I'll try to find something else."

"It's fine. Beats the smell of seal fat."

"Seal fat?" Hannah shuddered. "Where is *that* used on floors?"

"I'm not sure about floors, but the Inupiat have uses for it, including burning it in lamps. The village where I stayed this spring is quite traditional, and still consumes seal and caribou meat as its major food sources."

"I'm afraid seal is too exotic for me."

"It is for most people." He wrinkled his nose. "And to be honest, I prefer caribou. But seal isn't bad, and I could name several other more unappetizing dishes I've eaten. I won't go into the details."

The corner of Hannah's mouth twitched.

"On the other hand," he said reflectively, "when you're in an amazing place like Nepal or the Amazon basin, who cares what you're eating?"

"Actually, a lot of people do."

"They don't know what they're missing."

"You obviously don't know what you're missing about the Cascade Mountain Range, either," she returned promptly.

So that was still bothering her. Diplomacy wasn't one of his strengths, but he was usually more tactful.

Hannah set to work again, stripping the bed and putting on fresh sheets. The bathroom and guest powder room were scrubbed with a ruthless efficiency, and Jake could tell that her primary goal was to get out of Huckleberry Lodge as quickly as possible. After dusting and straightening the library, she finished by mopping the kitchen and bundling up the linens.

"That's all. I'll do these over at my place."

"Is there any way I could interest you in doing my personal laundry, as well?"

She smiled sweetly. "I'm afraid not. You have a top-of-the-line washing machine and dryer in the laundry room for that—I realize it probably doesn't measure up to pounding clothes on rocks and rinsing them in a cold river, but it will have to do. I'll see you on Friday."

As the door closed behind her, Jake began to laugh.

HANNAH DUMPED JAKE Hollister's sheets and towels on the floor of her laundry room and gave them a kick. *Jackass*. He'd baited her, but that wasn't the problem. It was his attitude about the Cascades she found truly infuriating.

If he acted that way in other parts of the world, he'd probably start a war one day. Actually, she was surprised he hadn't started one already.

Hadn't anyone ever told him he shouldn't insult someone's home? It was akin to telling somebody their baby was ugly, or that they were an idiot for choosing to live in a certain place.

She loved Mahalaton Lake and having her parents a few miles away. It was great to know people on the street and be a part of their lives. She felt connected here. As a teenager she'd thought about leaving, but not any longer. Yet apparently Jake Hollister was always thinking about the next place he was going.

Hannah loaded the towels into the washer. It was a good thing she was getting so much for renting the lodge. When Lillian had told her what Jake had offered, it had seemed absurdly high, but it made more sense now. With his appalling manners, greasing the wheels with money was probably the only way he could survive.

At least she wouldn't have to send Danny to her parents the next time she cleaned. It had hurt seeing the crushed expression on his face when he'd learned he wouldn't be "helping" in the big house. In the way children could instantly form a liking for someone, he had decided Jake Hollister was a kindred spirit. Even Jake's rudeness hadn't changed how he felt.

Hannah put detergent in the washing machine and started it. Her parents would soon be back with Danny and she wanted to fix them a meal.

Determinedly putting obnoxious photographers out of her mind, she began chopping vegetables.

Two hours later the scent of garlic and other spices filled the air and she was in better sprits. The front door opened and she heard Danny call, "Hi, Mommy!"

"Hi. Did you have a good time?"

"The best! We went to the zoo and saw the polar bears, just like the ones Mr. Hollister takes pictures of."

Her dad kissed her forehead. "Smells wonderful, sweetheart."

"It's Thai chicken. You and I will have to spice it up with chili garlic sauce since I made it mild for the wimps."

"I heard that," her mom called from the other room.

Hannah grinned.

"How was Mr. Hollister?" her father asked.

Her grin faded. "Fine, as far as I could tell. But he's a slob. No wonder he wanted someone to clean house. What a mess—jam dripping onto the kitchen floor, things thrown about, Great-Aunt Elkie's books all over the living room."

Hannah's mother hurried in, frowning. "Has he done any damage to the lodge or furnishings?"

"Not as far as I could tell. Honestly, though, I think the only things he's eaten since getting here are Luigi's pizza and peanut butter. Cold pizza, most of the time."

"Pizza is yummy," Danny said.

"I know, darling. But once a week is enough. That way it stays a treat. And we like it nice and hot, not cold and stale."

"Uh-huh. Poor Mr. Hollister."

Hannah nearly choked.

She did *not* feel sorry for Jake Hollister. He

seemed to delight in annoying her and she'd be lucky
to get through a month without him finding out how
loudly she could shriek.

JAKE WAS FIXING a peanut-butter sandwich when an
ambrosial smell invaded Huckleberry Lodge. He
went into the sunroom and looked out the windows
he'd left open. A blue SUV was parked in the driveway and he wondered if another boring suitor had
arrived to court Hannah.

But it was the fragrance coming from the guesthouse that commanded most of his attention. He
sniffed—lemongrass, coconut, garlic…it was as if
he'd died and gone to heaven. Whatever Hannah
was preparing reminded him of dishes he'd eaten
in Southeast Asia and beat the hell out of another
peanut-butter-and-jelly sandwich.

PB&J, he reminded himself.

And he could well imagine what his stubborn
landlady would say if he tried to wrangle an invitation to dinner. Something sharp and pithy, no doubt.
Perhaps he shouldn't have teased her so much—if
her cooking tasted as good as it smelled, it would
have been worth holding his tongue for a taste.

Paying for additional services—cooking and laundry and grocery shopping—was another possibility.
If he'd thought of it earlier, he might be eating something more interesting than a sandwich for dinner.

Danny, the little boy, came out on the large deck
of the guesthouse. He saw Jake and began waving.

Jake waved back halfheartedly, expecting the child to take it as an invitation and come barreling over to chatter his head off. Instead Danny settled down on a chair, head bent, looking at something, with his dog next to him.

Making a face, Jake closed the windows and returned to his sandwich. The bread was getting stale and he'd used the same knife to spread the peanut butter as he'd used on the pizza earlier, so everything tasted vaguely of pepperoni. As he'd told Hannah, he'd eaten much worse in the far-flung corners of the world, but then it had been spiced with exotic scenery and anticipation of the next great photo.

A year, he thought dismally.

That was how long the doctors had said it would take for him to recover and be able to work and travel the way he'd always worked and traveled. If he pushed himself too soon, he risked permanent disability.

Not that he had to stay in Mahalaton Lake the whole time, but it was the best way to photographically capture all four seasons for the book he'd agreed to do. So that meant a year of peanut butter and pizza and a feisty landlady with a small child. Hannah might be fun to tease and a treat to look at, but he'd rarely slept two *months* in the same bed, much less a year.

And since lovely Hannah was off-limits— obviously not being interested in brief liaisons—he had little to look forward to in *that* area, either... other than frustration and cold showers.

CHAPTER FOUR

"THAT SOUNDS GOOD," Hannah said to Gwen West-field as she scribbled notes on a pad.

They were planning the upcoming ice cream so-cial fund-raiser for the Mahalaton Rescue Squad, one of several fund-raisers held annually for the squad. The local community enjoyed the events, but they were also geared to bring in tourist dollars. It seemed only appropriate, since a good number of the squad's rescue calls were for visitors. Though not always.

Hannah shivered at the reminder of her high school boyfriend who'd pushed a climb too far—Collin had loved testing the limit in everything, and that time was his last. For months she'd woken up, unable to escape the horror of that day, hearing her own voice begging him not to go up that rock face alone, followed by her screams as he fell. Sometimes her heart still ached when she thought about how things might have turned out if Collin had lived.

He'd survived the fall, but only for a few hours, and all she could do was listen to him moaning and talking half-deliriously. Someone in the group had been carrying a satellite phone so they could call for help, but it had still taken too long for anyone to come. Back then they didn't have a local team trained in mountain rescues, which was why supporting the rescue squad was so important to her. After all...Collin might still be alive if help had arrived sooner.

Hannah sighed. It was painfully obvious that she had a weakness for restless risk takers. Steven had been a lot like Collin, with the same devil-may-care attitude and hidden demons. And she found Jake Hollister dangerously attractive as well, a response she was determined to squelch. Not that it mattered; he'd made it clear he wasn't interested in the things that mattered to her. *Insultingly* clear. And she was reasonably sure she hadn't revealed any sign of her attraction to him to justify a warning.

"I think we should try avocado ice cream," Gwen said eagerly. "I saw a recipe in a women's magazine while I was at the dentist's office."

Hannah resisted making a face. She liked trying new foods, but the people who lived in Mahalaton Lake were conservative in their tastes, and their summer visitors seemed to feel the same way. "I don't know if anyone is ready for something that different. Remember the garlic ice cream last year?"

"Oh. Right." Gwen looked crestfallen. She'd gone to California on vacation with her family and tasted garlic ice cream at the Gilroy Garlic Festival. Inspired, she'd made a gallon for the social, only to throw most of it out. It was one thing to sample garlic ice cream at a garlic festival, another to see it miles from the nearest garlic field. "Maybe I'll bring something else. Are you making your usual?"

"Yup. Two gallons of wild huckleberry." Every summer Hannah picked huckleberries in August and September, making jam with some and stowing the rest in the freezer to use throughout the next year, including for the June ice cream social.

"Everybody loves huckleberry."

"Make strawberry ice cream. Everybody loves that, too," Hannah suggested.

"But it's so ordinary." Gwen had moved to Mahalaton Lake five years ago when her husband, Randy, had been hired as their head of emergency services. Though a born New Yorker, she loved the town; she just got frustrated with the limited culinary tastes of most of the residents.

"Strawberry isn't ordinary, it's traditional," Hannah said firmly, writing *strawberry* next to Gwen's name on the ice cream sign-up sheet.

"I don't know. What if I try anise and—"

"How about pineapple sorbet?" Hannah suggested hastily.

"That sounds good," Gwen said, brightening.

"Besides, I just remembered that Luigi is donating a gallon of his homemade strawberry gelato."

"Okay. I can't compete with his gelato anyway."

Hannah crossed out *strawberry* under Gwen's name and wrote in *pineapple sorbet*.

She got up and refilled their coffee cups. They were meeting at her place, partly because there wasn't a single unoccupied surface in Gwen's home. Her husband always said that his wife had many fine qualities, but housekeeping wasn't one of them. The planning committee would meet again the next morning, so Hannah and Gwen were putting the final proposal together to save time.

"Thanks." Gwen poured cream in her coffee.

Hannah glanced out the window and saw Danny talking to Jake Hollister. Her mouth tightened. Before Jake had even arrived in Mahalaton Lake, Danny had heard a lot about the adventuring photographer—not from her, but from his friends and even her own parents. She didn't want her son developing hero worship for someone with his itchy feet.

"Is that the guy?" Gwen asked, leaning forward and peering out, as well.

They were sitting in the living room of the guesthouse, and the picture windows on both outside walls gave a sweeping view of Huckleberry Lodge and the lake beyond. Danny was chattering away with his usual exuberance, arms flying as he gestured wildly, while Jake leaned on the stair railing, holding a paper bag in his hand and occasionally nodding. Unless you were close enough to see the lines of pain carved around his eyes, you'd never guess he'd recently been in the hospital.

"Yup, Jake Hollister in the flesh."

"Mmm. Nice flesh, too. I wouldn't throw *him* out of bed for getting crumbs on the sheets."

"Does Randy do that?"

Gwen laughed. "Not since I nagged him out of the habit. Honestly, why do men feel the need to eat popcorn in bed?"

"Got me." Hannah hadn't been married long enough to have come to many conclusions about men, other than she didn't want to be married to the wrong one again. Her son was the only positive thing to come out of her marriage.

"Well, you're lucky to have such a cute guy living next door." All at once Gwen got a speculative expression on her face. "I wonder if he'd be interested in working on one of the fund-raisers for the rescue squad. He's so famous, it might attract more people than usual."

Hannah cringed, thinking how Jake might react to the idea. "He's got a reputation for being a loner, so I doubt he's a small-town, community-service-project sort of guy."

"Have you gotten to know him yet?"

She hesitated. "Not exactly. We've only spoken a few times. I'll be cleaning house over there twice a week."

"I hope he pays well. Not to be a hypocrite considering my own limitations as a housekeeper, but my sister claims some artists can be slobs."

Hannah mentally agreed, recalling the scattered pizza boxes and red jam dripping from Great-Aunt

Elkie's sandstone countertop. Her second cleaning session was that afternoon, and she dreaded thinking about what else he'd done to the place.

"Uh, the pay is okay."

But the company isn't, she added mutely. Luckily, she and Danny were probably the only ones in Mahalaton Lake who'd had to face his questionable manners. Barbi had obviously delivered pizza several times, but Jake's shiny new SUV hadn't moved since the day he'd arrived, so he hadn't gone into town and offended anyone there.

"I've been thinking," Gwen said. "If Mr. Hollister *did* agree to be involved, we could have a photo booth at the Christmas in August festival, or at one of the other fund-raisers. I bet people would pay a lot to have their portrait done by a famous photographer. It would be easy to do with computers and printers being so portable."

Hannah nearly choked on a mouthful of coffee. "He's not that kind of photographer, Gwen. His time in the Middle East was an anomaly. From everything I've read, he does extreme nature and wild-animal stuff, not people."

Gwen grinned. "What do you call my twins? Spending time with them is *definitely* taking a walk on the wild side."

"They're not so bad."

"Ha. Mrs. Gardiner refuses to have them both in her preschool class this fall. She claims they get into eight times as much trouble when they're together.

It's true, of course, but apparently it's the first time she's *ever* refused a student."

"She isn't as young as she used to be. As for the portraits, you're welcome to ask Jake to participate if you want to, but I prefer being left out of it. I...uh, don't want things to be awkward if he says no. You know, since he's living in the lodge."

Dealing with Jake would be tough enough without offending his artistic pride, and Hannah already had reason to think he was a snob when it came to his work. He'd called taking photos of the Cascades "fluff." Not to mention describing them as commonplace and boring—it was like saying anyone who lived here was commonplace and boring.

She couldn't imagine he'd explored the Cascade Mountains enough to know much about them. He'd just assumed that because they'd been well photographed, they weren't worth his precious time. Yet in her opinion, nobody had ever captured their unique spirit. However much she disliked Jake, he *was* a great photographer—if he wanted, he could do something amazing.

"I might approach him with the idea," Gwen said thoughtfully. "If only to make Randy jealous."

"I didn't think he got jealous."

"He doesn't. And it's kind of annoying."

Hannah shook her head. Gwen and Randy Westfield were the most mismatched couple she could imagine—and absolutely devoted to each other. Gwen was a willowy brunette beauty, while her husband was four inches shorter, stocky, sandy-haired and pleasant looking, rather than handsome. They had a wonderful marriage, with Randy gently amused at his wife's flights of fancy and Gwen gamely accepting the uncertainties of life with a husband in a high-risk job.

Hannah didn't think she could do it herself, but Gwen was proud of Randy and did everything possible to support his work. Of course, there was a big difference between someone who risked his life helping others, and someone who was just looking for an adrenaline rush like Collin and Jake Hollister.

"You wouldn't change a hair on Randy's balding head, and you know it," she said, pushing the thought away. She didn't actually *know* Jake was an adrenaline junkie, though the articles she'd read about him had suggested he had a near-death wish.

Gwen gave her a happy smile. "Nope, but it's fun to tease."

They went on making plans for the social, but Hannah's mind was only partly on the discussion. Jake had gone back into Huckleberry Lodge and Danny was throwing a stick for Badger to retrieve. He looked up and she motioned for him to come inside.

A minute later the door opened and Badger came bounding in ahead of Danny.

"Danny, what did I tell you about leaving Mr. Hollister alone?" Hannah asked him.

"It's okay, Mommy, he talked to me first. I brought

him a loaf of bread and he gave me five dollars to thank us." He handed her a bill. "Um, Badger and me are real hungry. Can we have a cheese sandwich? Please?"

Hannah put the money in her pocket. "It'll have to be cheese and apples since you gave Mr. Hollister our bread. Please talk to me before selling any more food to him. I'll fix lunch later." She gave Danny a plate of apple quarters and sliced cheese and returned to the dining room. "Can I get you anything, Gwen?"

"I'm fine. Randy asked if your mother is bringing her peach cobbler to the social. It's his favorite."

"Yes, and she's making vanilla ice cream."

"He'll be thrilled. He says it's even better than his mom makes." She looked at her watch. "Oops, better go. The babysitter can only take the boys in limited doses."

When Gwen had gone, Hannah sat down and looked at her list. She needed to go shopping, but it would have to wait. Being out of bread wasn't a big deal, and at least she now knew what had happened to the loaf in the garage freezer.

She was pretty sure the leftover Thai chicken she'd cooked on Tuesday had also traveled over to Huckleberry Lodge, thanks to Danny's generous heart. The plastic container was nowhere to be found, and her son was still at the age where he asked for food instead of trolling through the refrigerator like a hungry vacuum cleaner. However, he *was* capable of deciding to bring leftovers to their neighbor.

She'd considered speaking to Danny about it, but she liked that he was concerned for other people's well-being—even obnoxious photographers.

JAKE DROPPED TWO slices of the bread Danny Nolan had brought him into the toaster. Maybe he should have talked to Hannah before accepting it, but Danny had said it was okay. Besides, he'd given the youngster money, making him promise to get the cash to his mother.

When Hannah came over later he'd have to ask if she would take care of grocery shopping for him. Though considering her reaction when he'd teased her about doing his laundry, the answer would probably be no.

It was nice that Danny wasn't proving to be the problem Jake had expected. He'd encountered kids in his travels, of course. They were fascinated that a captured image could be seen instantly with the digital equipment he favored. Josie, on the other hand, despised the new technology, saying the old cameras and film were the true art. Jake didn't agree; it was simply a different *kind* of art. Still, he had to admit it was a pain having to recharge his camera batteries, especially in the remote parts of the world where he preferred working. He had a solar-powered charger, modified for his particular needs, but it wasn't as convenient as plugging into an electric outlet.

Well…Toby had taken care of charging batteries and shuffling equipment the past eight years. Working without him was going to mean changes; the question was whether to replace Toby or go solo again. Solo was probably best; he could never replace Toby, with all his cursing and complaining and unquestioned loyalty.

The toaster popped, and Jake smeared butter on both slices of bread. He sprinkled sugar and cinnamon over the top, only to hear the front doorbell ring before he could take a bite.

Frowning, he limped toward the front door. He'd told Hannah she could come in without knocking or ringing, though he didn't really expect her to do it. Jake opened the door, but instead of his landlady, he saw a broad-shouldered man holding an athletic bag with Lower Mahalaton Rehab Center emblazoned on the side.

"Mr. Hollister? I'm Owen Kershaw, your physical therapist, here for our eleven o'clock appointment."

Crap.

Jake belatedly remembered his first rehab session was that morning. He was tempted to say he didn't feel like company, but he'd never get better if he didn't work his ass off.

"Uh, hello. Please call me Jake."

Owen didn't try shaking hands, he marched in with his bag and a folding table and motioned toward the kitchen. "I noticed a room with lots of windows on that side of the house. Is there enough space to work in there?"

"Probably."

"Excellent. We'll have to be prompt about starting and ending our sessions. I scheduled extra time today because it's your first appointment, but from now on I'll need to leave shortly after twelve so I can be back at the clinic by one."

He walked toward the sunroom as Jake snorted. Why was the guy so uptight about coming to the lodge? He was getting paid well for the extra travel time.

Owen disappeared into the kitchen. "What is this?" he demanded a moment later.

Jake limped through the swinging door and saw the therapist pointing to the cinnamon toast with an accusing finger. "Breakfast."

"It's eleven o'clock. You haven't eaten yet?"

"What's the big deal?"

"Nutrition. The bread is fine—that particular brand is made from whole grain without a bunch of crap added to it. But sugar and butter won't help your body heal and rebuild muscle. You need protein and fruits and vegetables, as well as whole grains."

"Whatever." Jake grabbed the bread bag and the plate of toast and shoved them into the refrigerator. Okay, he'd known cinnamon toast wasn't the best meal in the world, but he could order a vegetarian pizza later in the day to make up for it. "Let's get busy."

Owen pulled something from his bag and handed it to him. "Eat this first. It's a protein bar."

Two hours later Jake was soaked with sweat and feeling as if he'd gone mountain climbing. He was also grateful for the protein bar, however hideous it had tasted. Not that the exercises had been as strenuous as hiking across an ice field loaded down with photographic equipment, but they were proof that he had a long way to go in his recovery.

"Excellent," Owen said, smiling for the first time. "Some of my patients find it difficult doing what I ask, but the real proof will be whether you do the exercises between our sessions."

"I'll do them." Jake wiped his face, perspiring as much from pain as from the workout. But he didn't want to take a pill; the damned painkillers messed with his head. The hot tub, on the other hand...

While he wasn't wild about many parts of the industrial world, the hot tub was a guilty pleasure. Sliding into the warm, swirling water when his body ached was one of the things he actually enjoyed here at Huckleberry Lodge. Sheltered from wind by Plexiglas on the railings, the private deck off the master bedroom still had a view of the lake, and at night, with the lights off, he could almost imagine he was in a natural hot spring, somewhere far away.

Through the window he saw Hannah come down her steps and cross to the lodge with Danny alongside. She was carrying a large bag, probably containing the sheets and towels she'd taken on Tuesday.

Jake locked gazes with her as they came up the back steps to the sunroom.

"Come in," he called.

Hannah opened the door and smiled when she saw Owen Kershaw. "Hi, Owen, remember me?"

The therapist grinned. "Hannah Nolan. Of course I remember. Your great-aunt was one of my favorite patients. What are you doing here?"

"This was Great-Aunt Elkie's house. She passed away after I graduated from college and left Huckleberry Lodge to me. I've leased it to Jake. Owen, this is my son, Danny."

"Hi, Danny." Owen shook hands with the youngster. "I have something for you," he said, and pulled something out of his athletic bag that looked like a tropical clown fish.

"That's just like Nemo," Danny declared.

"It's made from a special kind of sponge rubber. My patients squeeze them to build strength in their hands and arms," Owen explained, and Danny promptly began squeezing the toy with all his might.

"Does everybody know each other in Mahalaton Lake and Lower Mahalaton?" Jake asked.

Hannah shrugged. "No, but Owen works at the only rehab center in fifty miles—anybody who's ever needed physical therapy has gone there. My great-aunt broke her hip when I was sixteen and stayed at the center for several weeks, then we drove down for her physical therapy sessions. That was when she put in the hot tub."

"Hot tub?" Owen looked concerned. "I have questions about the chemicals they require, so just be sure to shower after using it."

Jake was glad the therapist hadn't tried to stop him. *No way* would he give up the hot tub. It might feel strange to enjoy something so far out of his chosen lifestyle, but it was better than the alternative.

"It doesn't use chemicals—it has one of those reverse osmosis cleaning systems. And it's serviced regularly," Hannah assured. "I see you're wearing a wedding ring. Do you have kids?"

The therapist's face lit up. "We've got two boys who run us ragged. They're four and five. And Cheryl is pregnant again. If you're interested, I'll bring pictures the next time I'm here."

"I'd love to see them."

Owen looked at his watch and picked up his bag and the folding table. "I'm late. It was a pleasure meeting you, Danny. Take care, Hannah."

"You, too."

"I'll be back at eleven on Tuesday," Owen said to Jake.

"Nemo?" Jake asked Hannah when the other man was gone.

"He's a character in an animated movie, about a little clown fish and its father. One of Danny's favorites."

"Nemo gets kidnapped and his dad goes looking for him through the *whole* ocean," Danny said. "Mommy, do you think my daddy is looking for me? Maybe he got lost and doesn't remember where we live."

Hannah's face froze. "Your father isn't... That is, he knows we're here in Mahalaton Lake. He just travels a lot. Now we need to start cleaning the house."

Danny stuck the toy in his pocket. "I'll get the trash. That's *my* job."

When he was gone, Hannah put her chin up with an air of defiance as she turned to Jake. "You said it was all right to bring him, and he likes to feel he's helping me."

Exhausted, Jake sank down on a chair. "It's fine. Does Danny ask about his father much?"

"He's starting to more and more. But how do you explain to a seven-year-old boy that his dad is a womanizing ba..." She stopped and visibly drew a breath. "Never mind."

"Sure. Oh, did Danny give you the money for the loaf of bread?"

A flicker of emotion crossed her face, though he couldn't guess the reason. "Yes."

"I appreciate him bringing it over. I started thinking about it afterward and realized I should have asked first. He also brought me some chicken. Thank you."

"Thank Danny. It was entirely his idea. Now, please excuse me, I have work to do."

Jake decided this wasn't the right time to ask about the grocery shopping. He slumped deeper in his chair and closed his eyes, his body throbbing with the effort he'd put into the therapy. But he refused to lie down. Given their testy relationship, he didn't want to appear weak in front of Hannah. Or maybe it was the age-old vanity of men in most societies, hating to appear less than virile in front of a woman. Especially such a beautiful woman.

There were noises around the house now. Domestic noises. Very different from what he'd hear in the highland villages of Nepal above Kathmandu, or deep in the Amazon. Yet it seemed as if there was a common rhythm to housework. Sweeping. Washing. Tidying. Even Danny's voice, asking his mother what else he could do, wasn't unlike the chatter of children in the dozens of cultures Jake had experienced from the day he was born.

It was better than the silence of the past few days, he thought, and far better than the echoes of the plane crash that still roared in his ears at the oddest moments.

THE TWO PIZZA boxes Jake had said to leave on Tuesday were on the kitchen floor, and Hannah stuffed them in a bag. Danny cheerfully took the bag out to the garbage cans.

Sugar was spilled across the counter and onto the floor as well, and she swept it up, thinking of what Gwen had said about some artists being slobs.

Maybe, maybe not.

However, it appeared that if something fell on

the floor, Jake simply left it there, and she found it hard to believe that was a common custom in other parts of the world. Of course, it *could* be because of his injuries—it might be hard to bend over and pick something up. But when she went into the bathroom and saw the mess on the countertops and sinks, Hannah decided to go with slob.

She scrubbed everything, keeping Andy Bedard's comments in mind about the need to keep everything sanitized. Andy was nice, a regular mother hen. And unlike some of the skiers who'd rented the lodge in the past, he and his guests always left things in good order.

After two hours, Hannah tied the dirty linens into a bundle, belatedly realizing she hadn't seen Danny in a while. She found him sitting cross-legged on the couch in the sunroom, listening to her tenant recount a story about trekking into the Australian outback. Danny's eyes were round with excitement as Jake described hanging over the water from a tree branch, taking photos of prowling crocodiles who'd like nothing better than to have him for lunch.

"Were you scared?" he asked.

Jake shrugged carelessly. "Not really."

"I bet they could bite me in half."

"Maybe not in half, but they've got really powerful jaws and can drag a grown man under—"

"Danny, I'm done. Can you take the laundry over to our house?" Hannah interrupted hastily.

"Okay," Danny agreed, though he looked torn.

When he'd clattered down the steps from the sunroom, Hannah turned to Jake. "Look, I appreciate your being friendly to my son, but he's prone to nightmares. Besides, a child his age doesn't need to know the details of how a crocodile could kill him."

"Hey, I saw my first wild croc when I was four," Jake said defensively, though he also seemed to be embarrassed. "It never gave me nightmares. And after that we spent several months on an African savannah while Josie photographed a lion pride."

"Josie?"

"My mother."

"Okay, fine. That was her decision. But I'm worried about Danny waking up at two in the morning, screaming bloody murder because he thinks a crocodile has climbed into his bed."

Jake winced. "Sorry. I don't know anything about kids."

"I understand that, but please keep in mind that certain things shouldn't be talked about in front of an impressionable child. Besides, I bet you *did* have nightmares—you just don't remember."

"If I did, they obviously didn't scar me for life."

Hannah clamped her mouth shut. Being scarred for life was a matter of opinion. Jake seemed to lead a solitary existence where taking high-risk photographs was more important than human contact. Perhaps she was biased, but even the greatest photograph in the world wasn't worth dying to get.

CHAPTER FIVE

IT WAS A QUIET Friday afternoon at Luigi's, and Barbi opened one of the books Hannah had given her to study. She chewed her lip, knowing she should give as much attention to math and proper English as other subjects, but history was a lot more interesting than adverbs and dangling participles.

"Good, you're studying," Luigi said with approval. He was a nice boss. If she could make enough money working for him to live on, it wouldn't be so important to get her GED.

Wrong, whispered a voice inside her head. She couldn't keep working for Luigi; she had to get out of Mahalaton Lake. When her father wasn't in jail for drunk and disorderly behavior or boozing it up at the bar, he was coming over to her place, demanding money or getting maudlin over her mother's death.

She tried not to carry more than twenty bucks in her wallet, but it helped to have a little cash because Vic got ugly if she didn't have *any*...especially when she'd been delivering pizza. Her father knew she ought to have tips on delivery nights, though he didn't know she'd started leaving most of them at the restaurant until she could get to the bank the next morning.

She *tried* to say no when he wanted money, but he'd just knock her down and go through her purse. She might be able to press charges against him, only how could she do that to her father?

And to be honest, she was scared to death of him.

Barbi looked at the bruises where Vic had grabbed her wrist the night before—he was a mean drunk. She shoved her bangles over the marks, her heart aching more than her sore wrist. It hadn't always been like this. Before her mom died, Vic had laughed a lot, worked steadily and only drank an occasional beer. But it was as if something inside him had broken when they'd buried her mother. Hell, he wasn't the *only* one who'd been hurt when Rachael Paulson died; he didn't have to dive into a vodka bottle and stop being a dad because of it.

Sighing, she turned a page of the history book. It was the section on the American Revolution and she needed to memorize the dates. Learning the information wasn't the problem, it was having her mind go blank when she took the test.

She was deep in the story of Benjamin Franklin's visit to Paris in 1776 when Luigi called to her.

"Two giant pies for Huckleberry Lodge, Barbara."

"Okay. Is one for Hannah and Danny?"

"Both are for Mr. Hollister. He never asks for any of my other dishes. No tortellini a'Luigi, or parmigiana, or even antipasto."

"Officially we only deliver pizza," Barbi reminded him as she lifted the insulated bag that kept the pizzas hot.

"He could ask," Luigi said with a sniff. He could get huffy about his cooking, though never in front of a customer—not that he got many complaints about the food. The winter skiers ate dozens of take-out and delivery pizzas every day, but they also crowded into the Tuscan dining room, declaring it the best Italian this side of Rome. The tourist trade was lighter in the summer, but they still stayed pretty busy.

Barbi drove out to Huckleberry Lodge and parked. Jake had told her to always just come in, so she pushed the front door open and called out, "Hey, it's me. I got your food."

"In here." He was in the sunroom, looking tired as he lifted hand weights, a sheen of sweat on his face and bare chest. She put the pizzas on a side table next to him. He extracted four twenties from the pocket of his jeans and handed them to her. "Keep the change."

"Ya sure, Jake? That's a pretty big tip." She asked every time he gave her a bunch of cash, because as much as she liked getting over thirty dollars, it almost seemed indecent to get that much for delivering two pizzas.

"It's worth every penny."

"I'd come even if you didn't tip me," Barbi said seriously. "That's my job."

Jake shrugged and flexed his leg in another exercise. "The lodge is several miles from town. It costs you extra in gas to drive out here, and you might lose tips from other customers."

She fidgeted for a second. "I've been thinking, you can ask Luigi for a dish from the regular menu if you want. I don't think he'd mind. He's real proud of his tortellini a'Luigi, and it's awful good."

"Yeah?" Jake seemed surprised. "Hannah mentioned making a special request, but I figured that was for locals."

"You're a local now. And don't tell Luigi I said so, but he's a teddy bear at heart. I bet he'd like you asking for something else."

"I'll keep that in mind. Pizza's just easy. Anyhow, keep the money."

"Okay, if you're sure. Just so you know, you can also give Luigi a credit card number if you want." She tucked the cash in the hip pouch she used to make change for customers and automatically checked her cell phone. Luigi always sent a text message when an order came in for a delivery pizza, but it had been a slow night.

A car drove up as Barbi walked out. It was Brendan's silver Lexus, and she loved his sour expression as he looked at her old Chevy. So it wasn't a Lexus. It was reliable, got decent gas mileage and didn't cost her a gazillion dollars to insure. Besides, she could do a bunch of the repairs herself. At a guess, Brendan had never *looked* beneath the hood of his Lexus, much less gotten his hands dirty changing the oil.

"Hiya, Brendan," she called as he got out. Wonder of wonders, he wasn't wearing a suit, but his dress pants and long-sleeved shirt weren't a big improvement.

"Barbi. Are you here to see Hannah?"

There was a whole bunch of criticism in the way he said her name. Usually she didn't let it bother her, but today it was especially annoying. Maybe it was the difference between Brendan and Jake Hollister. She enjoyed delivering food to Jake. He was sexy and gave humongous tips without being stuck-up about it or flirting with her. Brendan was an okay tipper, but he was so damned snooty she wanted to kick his butt.

"I'm working. What are *you* doing here?"

A look crossed his face, as if he thought she was being presumptuous. She hoped he'd say something about it so she could point out that he'd asked first.

"I'm taking Hannah and Danny out to dinner and a movie."

"I hope it's food a kid would like," she said. "You know, not stuffed peppers or eggplant."

A red flush crept up his neck. It was a rotten thing to say, since she knew he'd brought eggplant the night she'd come for her first tutoring session with Hannah. Danny had grumbled about it the entire evening. Poor kid, he didn't like Brendan any better than he liked eggplant.

"Not that it's your business, but I'm taking them to a Greek restaurant down in Lower Mahalaton," he replied stiffly.

"Don't push those grape-leaf things on him, either," she warned. "Danny enjoys things like plain cheese pizza and chicken. He wants ordinary salad with bits of carrots and cabbage, not beet greens or other fancy crap."

God forbid that Brendan ask *Danny* where he'd like to eat. For that matter, he probably hadn't talked to Hannah about it, either. Still, Barbi kept getting the feeling that beneath Brendan's high-and-mighty attitude, he might not be so bad; he might even be sexy with a little help.

Not that it mattered, since she was leaving Mahalaton Lake as soon as she could. Besides, he was hung up on Hannah.

"Children should be encouraged to expand their horizons." It sounded as if he was quoting something he'd read and she rolled her eyes.

"Give me a break," she said. "Danny's horizons are up to Hannah."

Brendan appeared uncomfortable again. "I'm not trying to step on Hannah's toes, if that's what you're implying."

"Okay, but what do you know about expanded horizons? You hardly wear anything but those stuffy suits. This is Mahalaton Lake, not Boston or Seattle. Hell, you look as though you just stopped to ask directions back to the city, not like you live here."

"That's ridiculous. There's nothing wrong with having certain standards for dressing and behaving."

"Standards?" She crossed her arms across her chest and nearly laughed when he focused on her cleavage. "What you really want is to stand out from the local lumberjacks and ski-lift operators. What's wrong—afraid you'll be mistaken for an everyday guy who works with his hands?"

His mouth dropped. "I'm not a snob. I respect people employed in those kinds of positions."

"Could have fooled me."

"It's true," he insisted. "My uncle has worked in the Miami maintenance department his entire life. He's a great guy."

"But you became a lawyer."

"What's wrong with that? I like the law. We've been lawyers for over two hundred years in my father's family. Townsend & Associates is a prestigious law firm back in Boston."

"Then why aren't you in Boston?"

"Because I'm here, that's why." His tone plainly said it was none of her business. "But it's a top firm. One of our ancestors even practiced law with John Adams."

"I'm not sure I'd brag about that," Barbi advised. "Didn't everybody in Boston get mad at John Adams for defending British soldiers on murder charges in 1770?"

Brendon's eyes widened. "How do you know that?"

"It's in the history books, or don't you think I can read?"

"I never said anything of the kind."

"You implied it. I bet you don't work for your family because you're too conservative."

Brendan scowled. "I happen to be far more liberal than my family."

"Ooh, that's scary. You won't even experiment with pizza. It's always the same—sausage, olives and onions."

"I suppose you have better ideas?"

"Pepperoni, mushrooms and artichoke hearts," she said promptly.

He wrinkled his nose. "*Ugh*. Artichoke hearts?"

"You don't know until you've tried it, which you obviously won't. Hell, try anything new. I bet you haven't even made friends with anyone except Hannah."

A door opening nearby distracted Barbi, and she saw Jake coming down the steps from the sunroom. He still seemed tired, but at the moment he was grinning broadly.

"Don't mind me," he called. "I'm just getting some fresh air."

"You need fresh air with all those windows?" Brendan gestured toward the sunroom, where most of the windows were wide-open.

Jake shrugged. "I'm used to being outside most of the time." He came forward and put out his hand.

"Hello, I'm Jake Hollister. We weren't formally introduced when you visited Hannah last week."

BRENDAN SHOOK THE newcomer's hand. "Brendan Townsend, attorney at law," he returned coolly. "I didn't realize people were that formal in the places you've lived."

"Every place has its customs. Even the United States, as Hannah has pointed out."

"Hannah is a *very* special friend of mine," Brendan warned, remembering that Hannah wasn't too happy with her new tenant. "I helped write her lease agreement paperwork and wouldn't like her to be dissatisfied about how things are working out here."

Jake smiled. "In some cultures, they don't waste time with veiled threats—they just say what they think. Others are too polite to say anything, no matter how they feel. I guess you're somewhere in the middle."

Brendan glared at Barbi when she laughed. She was impossible. And why had he told her about his family in Boston?

Once he *had* planned to join the family law practice—it was a Townsend tradition. Both his older sisters were partners, and he had four cousins who were either associates or partners, as well. Everybody had expected him to return, but when a prominent firm in Seattle had recruited him out of Harvard Law School, Brendan had accepted... much to his parents' dismay. Yet it was his move to

Mahalaton Lake that had appalled them the most. Townsends did *not* take breaks from big-city success—they were expected to die at their desks, not in their beds.

He'd never told anyone, but deep down he'd resented his father's work habits when he was a kid. Oliver Townsend had never attended a single school event for his children—even their high school and college graduation ceremonies had taken a backseat to the family law firm.

Brendan set his jaw at the memories. He'd been determined not to become like Oliver, yet it had happened anyway. It wasn't until he'd lost Maria that he'd woken up and seen what he was doing. He still wasn't sure that moving to Mahalaton Lake was the answer, but it was better than doing nothing.

"I wasn't making threats, I'm simply protecting Hannah's interests," he declared.

Hollister chuckled. "From what I've seen, Hannah can take care of herself."

"That's right. Oops, I gotta get back to Luigi's," Barbi said when her cell phone beeped. "Thanks again for the tip, Jake. See ya next time. Don't forget what I said about asking for something from the regular menu."

Brendan watched as she got into her faded yellow Chevy and drove off. He supposed it didn't matter where he lived, there would always be people who got on his nerves. It was the same for everyone. Barbi just happened to be one of those people for him.

"Hi, Brendan," Hannah called as she came out of her house a moment later, her cheeks flushed a healthy pink. "Was that Barbi I heard leaving?"

"Yeah, I ordered pizza," Jake explained before Brendan could say anything.

"Oh."

Hannah's expression when she looked down at Jake Hollister was distinctly wary. "Is there anything you need?" she asked him.

"Nope, I just wondered if you want to use the hot tub later. Danny mentioned you like it."

Hot tub? Brendan stiffened.

"I wouldn't dream of imposing," she said coolly.

"You're welcome to use it whenever you want."

Brendan saw an amused gleam in Jake Hollister's eye and for the first time in his life wanted to land a punch. Instead he grabbed the bouquet of flowers he'd brought and trotted up the steps to Hannah's porch. Starting a brawl was hardly the way to convince her that he was a decent guy who had nothing in common with her ex-husband. He figured her ex was the reason she was so cautious, wanting their relationship to move slowly.

"I love flowers, but you don't need to bring them every time," she said, letting him kiss her on the cheek.

"You deserve the best." He'd never forgotten his mother's delight whenever his father brought her a bouquet. Admittedly, that hadn't been very often, but she'd treated them as rare treasures. Maria had loved them as well, and he was grateful he'd taken the time to get them for her.

"Well, they're beautiful. Come in while Danny finishes getting ready."

Brendan followed, and once they were inside where they couldn't be overheard, cleared his throat. "I…uh, was wondering where you'd like to eat tonight. I made reservations at the Greek café in Lower Mahalaton, but it may not be the kind of food Danny enjoys."

Hannah blinked. "We've eaten there, so it should be fine. But it's nice of you to ask."

"Uh, sure." Yet he squirmed. The only reason he'd asked was because of Barbi's comments. Oh, he would have said something before they got to the restaurant, but by then, Hannah might have felt she couldn't object.

At least he'd already asked what movie Danny would like to see. Hannah had suggested they go to an old children's flick at the Lower Mahalaton Classics Theater. Dating a mother was a new experience for Brendan. Usually he'd avoided women with kids since it made dating more complicated, but that was before he'd moved to Mahalaton Lake and met Hannah.

"DANNY, HURRY UP. Brendan is here," Hannah called.

"Awright. Coming," he called back in a long-suffering tone.

She put the flowers in a vase and filled it with water. She hoped Brendan wouldn't realize what Danny's tone of voice meant. She also hoped he wouldn't realize that she'd forgotten they were going out tonight. When she'd seen him drive into the yard she'd hurriedly changed into something suitable, telling Danny to change, as well. Luckily Barbi and Jake had kept him talking long enough for her to get moderately put together.

Life sure was different now. At sixteen she'd lived for date night, carefully dressing and doing her makeup, always ready on time so Collin wouldn't have to wait when he arrived.

Collin.

Her mouth turned down. It was the second time she'd thought of him in just a few hours, and it was mostly because of Jake. He seemed casual about taking risks with his life...just the same as her high school sweetheart.

Hannah jumped as Brendan put his hand on her shoulder. "Is everything all right?" he asked. "You seem a million miles away."

"Yes, fine. Just admiring your flowers." She smiled, feeling guilty that she'd been thinking about a man other than the one taking her to dinner. "I'll see what's keeping Danny."

She found him playing a PlayStation game in his room.

"Do I hafta go?" he muttered. "Can't I just visit Jake?"

"*No.* Jake isn't a babysitter. Besides, Brendan planned this night for all of us. We're seeing a movie after we eat."

"I bet it's something dorky."

"It's a film called *Charlotte's Web.* I saw it when I was your age. Now turn the game off. Please."

Danny sulkily did as she asked and sat silently in the backseat of the car as they drove to Lower Mahalaton. Hannah knew he didn't like Brendan, but it wasn't as if they were getting married. They were just dating; they hadn't even gotten past a goodnight kiss.

Unfortunately Danny's dislike of Brendan had grown stronger since Jake Hollister's arrival. After all, how could a lawyer compete with an adventuring photographer? And it was no help that Brendan didn't understand small boys. Not that Jake understood them, either, but he had excitement on his side and the mysterious lure of the unknown.

But it wasn't just his stories; Jake *was* exciting. He'd done things most people just dreamed about, and from a feminine perspective, he was the sexiest guy she'd ever met. He also had the wounded-lion thing going for him—the strong warrior, injured in battle but not defeated. She'd have to be dead not to feel a zing around him.

It wasn't until they were at the theater that Danny cheered up, helped along by the big tub of buttered popcorn, soda and supersize candy bar that Brendan bought him.

"Gee, thanks," he said, his eyes gleaming.

"You're welcome. Would you like some, Hannah?"

"Uh, no, thanks, I'm still full from dinner." She wished Brendan had talked to her before buying the treats. And fate obviously wasn't on her side, because one of the previews of coming attractions was for the old movie *Crocodile Dundee*.

"Cool, Mommy. Can we see that?" Danny asked.

"We'll talk about it. *Later*," she said before Brendan could offer to take them.

Crocodile Dundee was rollicking good fun, but she wouldn't let Danny see it until he was older. For weeks after watching *Old Yeller* at a friend's house, he'd jumped in and out of bed for fear a rabid animal was hiding underneath, waiting to bite his feet if he got too close. He hadn't even wanted Badger to sleep in his room.

All at once, as if in response to her thoughts, Danny frowned. "Mommy, do crocodiles climb stairs?"

"No, they don't," Hannah assured, though she couldn't be positive one way or the other. On the other hand, she was quite certain there weren't any crocodiles in Mahalaton Lake.

Thankfully, the start of the movie kept Danny from asking anything else. She'd sat in the middle so Brendan wouldn't be in range of spilled soda pop or chocolate fingerprints, but it was nerve-racking to sit between them. Brendan wanted to hold her hand, which was sweet but inconvenient, and Danny had trouble juggling his bucket of popcorn, candy and soda. By the time the final credits rolled on the movie, she just wanted to crawl into bed, *alone,* though Brendan had hinted often enough that he'd welcome an invitation to join her there.

She missed sex, but life was a lot more complicated with her son in the next bedroom.

JAKE SPENT THE evening reading another book on the Cascade Range. He was impressed by the private library in Huckleberry Lodge. It contained a wide array of fiction and nonfiction, including dozens of books on the geology, fauna and plant life of the Cascades. Surely there would be something in one of them that would give him a flash of inspiration. Reading about the mountains wasn't the same as experiencing them, but his leg wasn't up to extended hiking yet, even around a place as tame as Washington.

This particular volume was about the volcanic history of the range. The eruption of Mount St. Helens in 1980 was well-known. And there had to be a million pictures of Mount Rainier—which according to his brother's wife was no longer considered a dormant volcano. Layne was a fount of information as a researcher for the regional magazine *The Puget Sound Babbitt,* though she was going on maternity leave any day now. Matt had laughed about it, saying that the pregnancy had been the only thing to convince her to take time off since their honeymoon.

Marriage, fatherhood…end of career, Jake thought dismally. But it probably wouldn't have as big of an impact on Matt, since he'd quit the party circuit a couple of years before getting married. Instead he was running a multibillion-dollar charitable foundation for his maternal grandfather.

Jake turned a page and saw a photo of Mount Rainier. It was part of the Seattle city skyline, and close enough that anyone there could visit for a day's outing. Maybe one of his own photo captions could be "America's Mount Vesuvius." But he dismissed it immediately. Somebody must have used that already, and he didn't like comparing one part of the world to another.

Jake looked out at the lake, calm now that the recreational boaters had quit for the day. Evergreens grew down to the shoreline, and a lone heron stood in the shallows, hunting for its dinner. Making a face at the pretty sight, he pulled a piece of pizza from the box on the coffee table. It was cold, yet his sour mood faded as he recalled the exchange between Barbi and Brendan Townsend. They were an incongruous pair—Barbi in her sassy clothes and Townsend with his buttoned-down mentality.

Barbi had visited Hannah several times over the past week, staying for an hour or two in the evening before leaving, so she obviously wasn't delivering meals from Luigi's. Maybe if she came out to Huckleberry Lodge often enough, there might be more opportunities to watch her and Brendan striking sparks off each other.

Jake rubbed his aching leg. The doctors had told him he was lucky not to have severed one of the major nerves, but it was badly bruised. Enough sensation had returned to show it should heal, but Dr. McGraw and Dr. Shiffman, the nerve specialist, had both said it would take at least a year. Nerves recovered slowly, and no amount of strength of will or faithful exercising could change that.

With a sigh, he tossed the book aside and got up. He stripped and stepped onto the private deck, turning on the hot tub's jets before sinking into the warm water. The swirling currents moved him back and forth, soothing his aches as he rested his head on the edge. All at once he chuckled, recalling Brendan Townsend's expression when Hannah was invited to use the hot tub. It would have been even funnier if the words *clothing optional* had been included in the invitation.

CHAPTER SIX

LATE ON MONDAY evening Hannah and Barbi were sitting on Silver Cottage's deck, enjoying the summer sunset as they discussed the types of questions that would come up on the GED exam.

"I should have told you, I'm never gonna pass," Barbi said, sounding discouraged. "It's so stupid. My head goes blank when I see a list of questions and I can't remember anything. You might as well stop wasting time on me."

"Blocking on tests is a common problem," Hannah assured her. "We'll do practice exams to help get you more comfortable. You're too smart to let this beat you."

The color brightened in Barbi's cheeks. "Smart?"

"Smart," Hannah repeated firmly. She was impressed with how much knowledge her friend had retained from her abbreviated school years, and she was picking up even more since she'd been studying. "And everyone admires how hard you work."

A shadow seemed to cross Barbi's face. "That's nice to know. Um, how was the family night out with Brendan?"

"Not bad, though Danny isn't wild about him, and it's even worse now that Jake Hollister is here."

"Why's that?"

"Well, neither of them is kid oriented, except Jake tells thrilling stories about exotic places he's actually seen, not just read about."

"Tough competition."

Hannah nodded. "And get this—Jake was telling Danny a story about photographing crocodiles on Friday afternoon, then at the theater that night, they were showing a preview for *Crocodile Dundee*. Now Danny wants to see it."

"Ooh, I love the scene where the crocodile tries to drag that blond woman into the water."

Hannah shot a quick glance into the house. She'd put Danny to bed at eight-thirty, but there was no guarantee he hadn't gotten up to ask for something.

"That's exactly the scene I don't want him to see," she said. "By the way, I was wondering if you're available to sell tickets at the ice cream social fundraiser on Sunday."

"Sure, I don't have to be at Luigi's until 4:00 p.m., and I love your huckleberry ice cream. But I thought Kim Barnes usually sold tickets."

"She does, but Mark's grandmother broke her leg waterskiing, so they both flew back to Florida yesterday."

"Luigi is right—retirement is dangerous."

Hannah grinned. "Hey, I hope *I* can go waterskiing when I'm seventy-four."

"Me, too." Barbi looked down at the book on her lap, her expression growing more serious. "Do you really think I can pass the test?"

"I'm *sure* you can," Hannah assured her gently.

She couldn't imagine what it must have been like for Barbi, losing her mother so young and having her father disintegrate into the town drunk. There were even rumors that Vic Paulson still knocked her around; he certainly got disruptive at the roadside bar on the edge of town. But whenever Hannah had tried to find out if there was a problem, Barbi shrugged it off.

She wouldn't have asked for her help at the ice cream social, except Barbi usually attended the town events, and however busy she was, it didn't seem right to assume she wouldn't want to be involved.

"I still wish you'd let me pay you for tutoring," Barbi said for the zillionth time since they'd started working together.

"Forget it. I'm enjoying the company."

Barbi frowned. "But Brendan must want to spend more time with you. He seems awful serious."

Hannah let out a long breath. "I don't know what *I* want with Brendan, much less what he has in mind. I'm not even sure he plans to stay in Mahalaton Lake. Once I might have been okay leaving, but this is where I want to live now."

"Was your ex-husband ever willing to move here?" Barbi asked curiously.

"He said he was, but I doubt he meant it."

Hannah didn't think Steven had planned to stay *married,* much less been honest about where they'd live and raise a family. Marriage was a game he'd played, and when he had gotten bored with the game, he'd wanted out. Of course, before then he had slept with any woman who'd have him and run up huge bills. She shivered, recalling his anger after they separated and he learned she'd canceled the credit cards. It was almost as if he'd truly expected to be able to keep spending money and just leave her with the bills; he certainly didn't pay any child support, though it was court mandated.

She was no longer even sure she'd loved him. She'd just wanted the romantic ideal she lost when Collin died on Mount Mahala. That kind of love was addictive. She *still* wanted it—she just didn't want it with someone who treated life like a game of roulette. And even if she could handle the stress herself, she didn't want her son to get attached to someone who could vanish from his life on a whim. Danny already wondered if he'd done something to make his father leave.

"I'll get sample tests for you to take," Hannah said, wanting to change the subject. "Just don't expect the same questions to be on the official exam."

"I won't. Uh, you haven't told Brendan about me not having a high school diploma, have you?"

"Of course not. That's your business."

"Good. He's snotty enough without knowing that."

Barbi pushed back from the table. "I'd better get going. I have to be at the bakery at 2:00 a.m."

"Is that a new job?"

"Yeah, I make the breads and stuff for them two mornings a week. See you Thursday."

Hannah walked her out, marveling at how matter-of-fact Barbi was about her varied jobs around town. She had a killer schedule, but hopefully some of that would change once she had her GED.

OWEN KERSHAW ARRIVED at eleven on Tuesday as promised and put Jake through a thorough therapy session.

"Cut back by half," he said when Jake explained how often he was doing his exercises. "I said you had to work hard, but your body is still healing. I've reviewed your medical file—don't forget that leg needed two surgeries to put it back together."

"I was *there*. How can I forget?"

"Your impatience is normal. But right now I'm the traffic cop, trying to keep you from going too slow or too fast. Your leg's range of motion should improve as the nerve heals, but you need to be careful. I know you don't want to use a cane, but it wouldn't be a bad idea."

"No."

"At least consider it." Owen began packing his equipment and Jake watched moodily.

Ordinarily one of his trademarks was patience. He could sit for hours watching a weather front develop over a mountain, waiting until that perfect moment to start shooting. Days or weeks could pass between sightings of a rare animal, and he knew his willingness to wait meant he'd get the photos no one else would. But this wasn't the same.

"You've made remarkable progress," Owen added. "The only reason you're doing so well now is because you were in prime physical condition at the time of the accident."

"They tell me that's why I survived," Jake muttered.

"Yes, I understand your side of the plane took the heaviest impact. You're lucky to be alive."

Ice formed in Jake's stomach and an image of Gordon's face, gray as he gasped for breath, flashed through his mind. "Luck is a matter of opinion. If you live, you live. If you die, that's it, you're dust. Everything is pure chance. I don't believe in karma or fate or any other metaphysical explanations for my existence."

"That's too bad." Hannah's voice came from the open door of the sunroom behind him.

He looked at her. "You believe in karma?"

"I believe in something beyond myself. Your work is technically brilliant, Jake, but how can you take the best photographs if you don't see the soul beyond the beauty? No wonder some of them seem a little cold to me."

"I didn't know you were a critic."

"Everyone is a critic. Or don't you care about how

the average person sees your work? Anyway, I'll be back later to clean, I just came over to say hi to Owen and see the pictures of his family."

"I'm glad you did," Owen said. He reached into his bag and pulled out an envelope. "I love to show them off."

Hannah laughed as she looked at the first shot. "I see you have two Picassos in the making."

"That's right. And I don't care what the package claims, finger paint stains fabric."

"Don't I know it." She looked at the second picture.

"That's Cheryl," Owen said. He tapped the next photo. "And there are the boys in their Halloween costumes. They both wanted to be Superman."

"Danny was Batman last year. I'm going to hate it if he starts wanting to dress up as the villain instead of a hero."

"Me, too."

Jake's eyes narrowed. Owen had made a point of saying he needed to leave promptly after their sessions. What was it with people wanting to look at snapshots of people they'd never met? It was a phenomenon he'd seen several times before—even getting trapped in the ritual once or twice himself. And Hannah had come over specifically to see them, so she wasn't just being polite.

She handed the pictures back. "You have a beautiful family, Owen. Cheryl is lucky to have you."

"I'm pretty fond of them." He checked his watch.

"I have to hustle to make my next appointment. See you soon."

"Drive safely."

When they were alone, Hannah smiled politely. "Sorry to intrude."

Jake shrugged. "You're coming over to clean anyway. How was your date on Friday with the lawyer? He seems too dull for you and Danny, but that's your business."

She scowled. "Brendan is a decent and responsible man."

"He's a lawyer."

"That doesn't make him dull."

"The lawyers I've met are all tediously conventional."

Hannah rolled her eyes. "How many could that be? I didn't realize yetis or African lions went to law school."

She had a point, however reluctant he might be to admit it. "By the way, has Danny had any nightmares about crocodiles?"

"None that he's told me about, though he's asked if they can climb stairs and wants to sleep with the lights on. I know you didn't mean any harm, but he has a vivid imagination. Besides, at his age he doesn't need to know the grisly details. He'll find out about them soon enough, along with all the other realities."

"What sort of realities are you talking about?"

"Never mind, that's not important. I just don't

want Danny to be forced to grow up too fast." She stopped and looked so sad that Jake frowned.

"Did you grow up too fast?"

Hannah shrugged silently, yet she crossed her arms over her body in a protective gesture that told him more than words.

"Is it possible you're being overprotective?" Jake asked carefully.

She shook her head. "No. We go hiking together and camping with my parents. I even let him swim in the lake as long as there's a responsible adult present. I want him to love the Cascades as much as I do."

Hiking, camping...Jake was surprised. Hannah didn't seem like the outdoorsy type. He'd figured she loved the mountains simply because it was where she lived.

"What about speed boating?"

She made a gagging gesture. "I wouldn't dare. We hate having them on the lake, but summer tourist traffic jumped once they were allowed. Dad goes out on a small motorboat to fish sometimes, but it's the putt-putt variety with oars as backup. Anyway, I'm going to see if Danny is done eating his lunch, and then we'll come over to clean."

Jake nodded and watched her leave. Her backside was just as attractive as her front, and he felt the usual stirring in his gut at the sight. She was a desirable woman, but while he wasn't opposed to a night or two of uncomplicated passion, he had a feeling that nothing would be uncomplicated with Hannah.

Barbi, on the other hand...?

Jake pictured her the way she'd looked on Sunday afternoon in low-riding jeans so tight it was a miracle she could sit down and a halter top that did nothing to conceal her ample charms. She was blond, blue-eyed and thoroughly appealing, but it was obviously Brendan Townsend who got her blood moving.

And Barbi didn't affect him the way Hannah did, which made absolutely no sense.

A few minutes later Hannah returned with Danny, who grinned widely. "Hi, Jake. How are you feeling?"

"Pretty good."

"I'm glad. I gotta get the trash. Talk to you when I'm done." He hurried toward the opposite side of the lodge.

"I'm going to get busy, too," Hannah said as she went through the kitchen into the living room, a laundry basket filled with neatly folded linens balanced on her hip.

Jake thought about their earlier conversation. She was obviously worried he'd tell Danny a story that would scare the kid, but he didn't know if that meant she was being overprotective or not. Jake was hardly an expert in child rearing—his upbringing with Josie had been unique, to say the least.

Admittedly, he hadn't learned to relate to other people effectively, but what he lacked in interpersonal skills, he made up for in experiences. By the time he was eighteen, he'd been on every continent on the planet and observed rare sights and animals that few people knew existed, much less would ever see. What was wrong with that?

Once again, domestic sounds filled the lodge. It was ironic that the highlights of his week were when Hannah came to clean with Danny. Normally Jake wouldn't want some kid and his mother hanging around, however shapely the mother might be, but he didn't have much to do aside from physical therapy, exercising and reading. Aside from Hannah's visits, his days had a monotonous rhythm, broken only by two or three short walks daily. He'd explored various trails leading out from the lodge, without bothering to take a camera, but eventually he'd start taking photos again.

Eventually?

Jake got up. There couldn't be anything eventual about his photography. It had been his passion since he was a boy. If nothing else, he wouldn't let the naysayers be right about him losing his touch. Money wasn't the issue—he'd made enough to live comfortably for the rest of his life, even without his trust fund. It was about the art. As for Hannah's comments about his photos seeming cold, it was just one person's opinion. It didn't mean she was right.

In the living room, he found Hannah putting away books, looking annoyed. Jake sat on the couch, realizing he shouldn't take so many volumes from the shelves without putting them back. It was just such a luxury having real books instead of his eReader.

Ebooks were great for traveling light, but he enjoyed turning real pages and the feel of a book in his hands.

"I'm impressed with how much material you have on the region," he said, trying to distract her.

"My great-aunt and uncle loved to read—most of these belonged to them. *So they're special to me.* And when Andy told me you'd be photographing the Cascades, I brought some of mine over, too."

He hadn't realized the books had sentimental value. There wasn't much room for sentimentality for someone who lived out of a backpack most of the time.

"That was considerate of you," he said politely.

She didn't look appeased. "Yeah, and then you called it a 'fluff' project."

Jake sighed. He *should* have been more tactful. "Judging by some of the tribal masks and other art around here, it looks as if your great-aunt and uncle also loved to travel."

Hannah nodded, her face softening. "They went to all sorts of places. Great-Aunt Elkie was so crazy about Japan they went back three times. I love reading her travel journals."

"You didn't get the travel bug from them?"

She blinked. "I wouldn't say that. They took me with them on several trips, and I especially remember the museums in Italy and all the Roman ruins. I hope to take Danny there one day."

"I suppose that's a start."

The smartphone in Jake's pocket rang, and he dug it out, expecting it to be Matt announcing he was a new father. Instead it was his eldest brother.

"Hey, Jake, how are you doing?" Aaron said when he answered.

"Fine. How about you?"

As Aaron chatted about his wife and kids, Jake watched Hannah continue putting books back into the shelves, apparently sorting them into a particular order.

"By the way, Skylar and I hope to visit you in August," Aaron said, catching Jake's full attention. "And I know Matt and Layne want to come, as well. Their baby will be here by then and it's a great chance for us all to see each other."

Jake froze. He couldn't imagine having *one* brother's family at the lodge, much less two. "Uh, I'm not sure how my landlady would feel about me having overnight visitors."

Hannah turned from the bookcase and began waving a hand for his attention, but he ignored her.

"We wouldn't stay with you," Aaron assured. "Between Lucy and a newborn, you'd never get any rest. I've reserved a house in town for the entire month, in case it works out."

"I guess. Uh, sure. I'll be working on my book, of course."

"We won't interfere. We'll talk more when the time gets closer and figure out a good week. I'm just glad you're doing better. It scared us when you were hurt."

"Thanks." While Jake wasn't sure how to handle the idea of two brothers and their wives and children descending on him, it was nice that they were concerned.

Hannah cleared her throat. *Loudly.*

"I'll let you go," Aaron said. "But let me know if you need anything."

"Sure." Jake disconnected and looked at Hannah, who was staring at him in apparent disbelief. *"What?"*

"Your landlady is standing right here. What do you mean, you don't know how I feel about overnight visitors? Your lease says no wild parties, there's nothing saying you can't have visitors. The only person I wouldn't be crazy about having here is your father, not with his reputation."

"It isn't that simple. That was my eldest brother. Aaron and another brother and their families want to come in August."

"There are five bedrooms and three bathrooms upstairs, but you don't want them staying here?"

"I'm not used to this family stuff. I don't see Josie all that often, much less Matt and Aaron or the others. It's nice they worry about what happened to me, but I'm okay now."

"You're still recovering. If you were my brother, I'd want to see you for myself."

Grim amusement shot through Jake. If Hannah

was his sister he wouldn't be uncomfortable at the sight of her in trim shorts and a T-shirt that showed off every curve. He'd had an image of schoolteachers as prim women in sensible clothes, but she'd shot that idea to hell in a hurry.

"The Hollisters aren't like other families," he reminded her.

"Fine. Just don't blame your lack of hospitality on your landlady." She grabbed an empty pizza box and carried it toward the kitchen.

"I don't understand. What's the big deal?" he called after her.

Hannah turned. "I was an only child and don't have many relatives. That's one of the reasons I hope to get married again and have more kids, so Danny won't be alone. But you're lucky enough to *have* a big family, and don't seem to care."

Jake rarely spoke about his family except in response to interviewers' questions, but he'd discovered that few people understood how complicated it was to be a Hollister.

"Hannah, I basically grew up as an only child, too," he explained patiently. "I didn't meet most of my half brothers and half sisters until I was an adult. There's no reason for us to be close."

"They're still family.... Oh, just forget it."

Jake watched her disappear through the kitchen door and frowned thoughtfully. Maybe he'd felt lonely growing up, but it had taught him to be self-reliant. And he *was* getting better acquainted with his siblings. Of course, while he'd made it to Aaron's wedding, he'd missed Matt's because he'd been photographing the rare Amur leopard in eastern Russia. Matt and Layne hadn't said they minded, but he also hadn't asked them how they felt.

HANNAH CRAMMED TWO pizza boxes from Luigi's into a garbage bag. Danny hurriedly took it out to the trash, no doubt anxious to finish up so he could hear more about Jake's exploits.

Tidying the kitchen took a while. Normally she would have methodically worked from one side of the lodge to the other, but she preferred to stay away from Jake whenever possible.

Several of the plastic containers she used for leftovers were in the sink and she sighed. She was trying to ignore Jake's effect on her…and the flow of food from Silver Cottage to Huckleberry Lodge. It was probably her own fault for mentioning Jake's poor diet in front of Danny, and in friendlier circumstances, she might have brought food to him, as well. Mahalaton Lake was the kind of town where people looked after each other.

Squaring her shoulders, Hannah marched through the living room to the master bedroom, *also* trying to ignore the way Danny was now sitting wide-eyed on the floor, listening to another one of Jake's stories. She understood why Jake was socially challenged given his upbringing, but after what she'd said earlier, surely he'd censor anything too frightening for a child.

The doors to the private deck were open, and Hannah stepped out to check the hot tub. Several towels were lying there and she picked them up, glad to see they weren't the nice ones from the bathroom. She kept a supply for the hot tub in a cupboard by the French doors.

She'd have to remind Jake to keep the doors and easy-access windows closed to discourage any curious critters from coming in and making a mess.

"Hannah, there's something I wanted to ask you about," Jake said when she headed back through the living room with her laundry basket.

"Yes?"

"I'm not crazy about towns big enough to have a traffic light, so I'd like to hire you to do my grocery shopping—I'll pay you fifty bucks plus the cost of the groceries, and you can do it when you're going for yourself."

"It's okay, isn't it, Mommy?" Danny asked. He was now lying on the floor, his legs up on the couch cushions.

"We'll talk about it."

"You *always* say that."

She gave Jake a cool look, wishing he hadn't asked in front of Danny. Of course, that might have been deliberate, knowing it would be harder to say no if her son wanted her to say yes.

Darn him anyway.

Things weren't working out the way Lillian had thought. As far as Hannah could tell, Jake hadn't left the lodge except for short walks. He was a slob, so it wasn't exactly *light* housekeeping, and he kept wanting more services from her, like doing his personal laundry and grocery shopping. She'd refused to do the laundry, but shopping wouldn't be so bad. And she could put the fifty dollars into a travel fund— she really *did* want to take Danny to Italy one day.

"Okay," she said slowly. "I usually shop once a week."

"That works for me. I have a list for the next time you go. I'll tell my business manager to increase the amount he sends every month and give you a check to cover things in the meantime."

He already had a list?

Obviously he'd assumed she'd agree, but the reminder of the monthly rent and cleaning fees kept her from saying anything. Jake was paying a huge amount to live at Huckleberry Lodge, and the extra fees for housekeeping, already paid a month in advance, were generous, as well. Nobody in Mahalaton Lake would pay her that much for changing beds and sweeping floors.

Of course, nobody would tell her son the type of stories that Jake was telling, either.

That was the worst part. Danny was fascinated by their tenant's tales of danger and adventure. And he'd even asked whether his dad was out there doing the same kinds of exciting things. But Hannah didn't want Danny to develop Steven's wanderlust, because beneath his charm, her ex-husband was a fundamentally unhappy person. And his adventures were largely at the expense of other people.

It would break her heart to see Danny like that—never content, always searching for something he could never find. Maybe she was just as overprotective as Jake had accused her of being, but he'd never been in her shoes.

CHAPTER SEVEN

LATE FRIDAY AFTERNOON Jake was sitting in the sunroom as usual and caught the scent of chicken, garlic and lemon wafting from Silver Cottage. It reminded him that Danny had said Brendan Townsend was coming over for dinner.

Swell.

The boring lawyer was getting a homemade dinner. And Jake knew it would be delicious from all the samples Danny had brought him of Hannah's cooking. For all of her prickly nature, she was great in the kitchen and seemed to favor cuisines from around the world. The flavorful leftovers were a welcome break from Italian food and peanut butter.

A particularly strong whiff of garlic came through the windows and Jake's stomach rumbled. He'd have to order something new off Luigi's regular menu.

A silver Lexus pulled in and parked as Jake was looking at the menu. The lawyer got out, the usual bouquet of flowers in hand. Danny opened the door and let him in, a sulky expression on his face.

Poor kid. He didn't like his mother's suitor, though he was also unhappy about missing another Friday-night pizza; he'd complained about it earlier that day. Jake fingered his smartphone…he needed to get food for himself, and ordering a pizza for the boy wouldn't be a big deal.

He dialed Luigi's, asking for an order of tortellini a'Luigi and a medium cheese pizza. Barbi walked in twenty-five minutes later wearing a skimpy halter top and close-fitting pants that ended just below her knees. It was disheartening to realize the sexy outfit did less for him than seeing Hannah in the more modest clothes she'd worn while cleaning the lodge. Being attracted to his schoolteacher landlady was the last thing he'd expected during his recuperation.

"Hiya, Jake."

"Hi, Barbi." He handed her money for the food and tip. "The pizza is for Silver Cottage. Will you take it over for me?"

"Yeah, but why are you getting pizza for Hannah and Danny when Brendan is here?"

"Danny was upset about missing pizza two Fridays in a row, so I thought it would be a nice surprise."

"Gotcha."

Barbi left with the box and walked up the steps to Silver Cottage. *Interesting.* There was an extra swing to her hips, and Jake didn't think it was for his benefit. She knocked and the door opened. It was Danny again, but Barbi said she had a delivery and Hannah appeared a split second ahead of Brendan.

"What is he doing, sending you a pizza?" Brendan

demanded, his voice bellowing across the space between the buildings.

"It's a cheese pizza, so I'm sure it's for Danny," Hannah said after checking the label on the box. She looked toward the sunroom, though with the afternoon sun shining on the windows, Jake knew she probably couldn't see him.

Brendan tried to hand the pizza back to Barbi, but she shook her head.

"Sorry, I can't do that. It's ordered and paid for," she declared politely. From her profile, Jake could tell she was smiling, most likely to annoy Brendan. The two seemed to clash over everything from the best toppings on a three-topping pizza to his conservative views. Plainly, some heat was hiding behind all that antagonism.

"This isn't funny, Barbi," Brendan insisted.

"I'm just doing my job."

Jake chuckled at her innocent tone. He didn't have to be an expert in human relations to see something *was* going on beneath the surface.

"Eat it yourself," Brendan insisted.

"I can't do that." Barbi said indignantly. "Besides, it's Danny's pizza, not mine. Jake wanted him to have it since he didn't get any last Friday."

"Yum," Danny cried. "It's okay, isn't it Mommy? Jake sent me a present."

"I…guess. Thanks, Barbi."

"No problem."

Barbi turned and winked in Jake's direction as

she descended the stairs, yet Jake was starting to feel odd about the whole thing. He'd wanted Danny to have the pizza, but maybe he was interfering in Hannah's life by sending Barbi over there.

Or maybe he was envious of Brendan, which seemed even worse.

BRENDAN TRIED NOT to let the pizza or the encounter with Barbi spoil his evening. The meal Hannah had cooked was delicious, and if Danny was used to getting pizza on Friday nights, then maybe it was best that his routine hadn't been disrupted again. The Hollister fellow simply delighted in being an irritant and had used Barbi to further his plan.

It was curious, though. Barbi had really seemed shocked when he'd suggested she keep the pizza for herself.

"Shall we take a walk down by the lake before dessert?" Hannah asked after the meal. "The trail goes along the shore and back into the trees part of the way."

She seemed restless, and though Brendan was more accustomed to working out on his treadmill than hiking a woodland trail, he nodded. "Sure."

"Come on, Danny," she called. "It's time for a walk."

Danny seemed to take it as a normal part of his day and they headed south, toward town. It was a pleasant evening and Brendan was glad to see Hannah relax as she stopped and pointed out various plants and birds to her son, seeing if he remembered what they were called.

"*Mooommy,* you asked about trillium *last* time," Danny said.

"Did I?"

"Uh-huh. Do you know what this is, Brendan?"

Brendan was startled by the youngster's question. While he appreciated the clean air and beauty of the small mountain town, he wasn't particularly knowledgeable about the vegetation. "I'm sorry, I don't."

"It's a huckleberry bush. That's what our lodge is named after. Mommy makes huckleberry jam and pancakes and stuff."

"That sounds good."

"It's *super fantabulous.*"

Hannah looked at the nearby bushes. "I think we're going to have a generous crop," she said. "Last year it was hard to get enough."

"I don't think I've ever eaten wild berries."

Her smile became strained again. "I pick wild fruit both in the mountains and over on the coast— things like blackberry, salal, Oregon grape…even salmonberries. We eat some, but I also use them in my classroom to teach about the environment."

"Oh."

"You aren't familiar with any of those except blackberries, are you?"

"Not really," he confessed. He'd grown up in a big city, so the idea of going outside and collecting food was foreign to him.

Hannah was watching Danny, who'd wandered farther along the trail and was playing with Badger. "I love these mountains. I love the *feel* of them," she murmured, almost as if to herself. "But I've never seen photographs that capture the way I see them. Jake Hollister is a brilliant photographer. He might be able to do it, but he thinks the project is beneath him."

Brendan fought a flash of jealousy, which was ridiculous. Hannah was *annoyed* with Jake Hollister, not expressing true admiration of his talent. Yet before he could say anything, she turned to him with a smile.

"Forget I said that. People are so excited to have a celebrity living in Mahalaton Lake, I'd hate for them to be disappointed."

"Of course. I'm just sorry you have to put up with his poor attitude."

"At least Danny likes him."

Brendan glanced at Hannah's son and wished he knew how to connect with a child. It shouldn't be this hard—after all, he used to be a kid himself. But that was a long time ago. And while he and Maria had talked about having a family in theory, they'd agreed to focus on their careers before making that kind of commitment.

Now it was too late, and he'd chucked his high-powered career to experience life at a slower pace. While there was usually enough legal work in Mahalaton Lake to keep him busy for a regular forty-hour week, he wasn't sure what to do with the rest of his time.

Barbi's comments about his not having friends popped into his head. Brendan hated to admit it, but she was right. Maybe he should call David Walther and see if he wanted to get together occasionally. David's wife was gone as well, and Maria would have liked seeing Brendan becoming friends with her father. If she *had* communicated with him in his dreams, concern for her father might have been the reason. Not that he believed in that sort of thing, but it was a nice thought.

"Er...I was wondering if you and Danny would like to do something tomorrow or the next day," he said. "We could go for a drive, or do anything you like."

"I'd love to, but I'm working on the ice cream social all weekend."

Brendan did his best to look understanding. He'd hoped that once the school year was out, he'd be able to see Hannah more often, but if she wasn't busy with Danny and her fund-raisers, she was doing some sort of project with Barbi.

"Danny," Hannah called. "Let's go back to the house for dessert."

"Okay, Mommy."

The trail was damp, and Brendan tried not to think about what it was doing to his good leather shoes. He'd learned a little more about Hannah on the walk, and that was worth muddy feet. Besides, he knew a great shoe-repair place in Seattle.

Seattle?

He halted in midstep, his brain chewing over something Barbi had said earlier. She'd made a flip remark about his suits, making it sound as if he had one foot in the city and the other on the Mahalaton Lake town limits. It wouldn't help his law practice if the local people didn't consider him one of them. Lately he *had* begun wearing more casual outfits at appropriate times, but Barbi obviously didn't think they were any better than his suits.

Brendan pushed the thought aside. Barbi Paulson was hardly an arbiter of good taste.

"Is something wrong?" Hannah asked, turning around.

"No. I was…um, wondering what makes the ground so springy," he hedged.

"Years of fallen hemlock needles. We're in a stand of old-growth western hemlock. The more open areas on either side were cleared by fires from light-ning strikes."

Brendan felt surprisingly mellow as they returned, yet his pleasant mood fled when he saw Jake Hollister heading toward them.

"Thanks for the pizza, Jake," Danny called.

"You're welcome."

"Fancy running into you here," Hollister drawled when they got closer.

Hannah rolled her eyes. "It's hardly a surprise

when we both live a few hundred yards away." She pointed to the camera hanging from a strap around his neck. "I see you're planning to take some pictures."

He shrugged. "I'm looking for the dogwood you mentioned. You made it sound interesting."

"It's late in the season for dogwood. You won't find any at this elevation."

"Do you know where some might still be blooming?"

"Maybe. I'll mark likely places on a map and put it under your door. Oh, by the way, when I was cleaning the master bedroom today I found the doors open to the private deck. You need to be careful, or animals will get in and make a mess."

"I'll keep it in mind. Enjoy the rest of your walk."

Brendan was tempted to add a stronger warning, but doubted his interference would be appreciated. One of the things he admired about Hannah was her independence, though it didn't mean he wouldn't like to take care of her now and then.

JAKE WATCHED HANNAH and her son and lawyer boyfriend disappear around a clump of silvery aspen. Then, dragging his thoughts away from the subtle swing of his landlady's hips, he took a few photos of the lake and forest, only to delete them. They were lousy, but he assured himself that it didn't mean anything—he'd taken his share of bad pictures over the years. Every photographer did.

A little inspiration would help, but inspiration was in short supply at the moment.

Still, a thought kept bouncing around in his brain about how to make his book work. Hannah's passionate love for the Cascades might be an angle he could exploit. She had the summer off from teaching, so maybe he could hire her to show him her favorite places and see what happened. It was an arrangement that would benefit them both—she could probably use the money, and he needed to prove he hadn't lost his edge.

Jake switched off the camera and walked the short distance back to Huckleberry Lodge. Brendan Townsend's Lexus was still outside the house, along with a familiar-looking SUV. He made a face. The lodge might be several miles out of town, but Hannah had her share of visitors, nonetheless.

"Mr. Hollister?" called someone from Silver Cottage's deck.

He looked up and saw an attractive brunette waving at him. "Yes?"

"I wanted to speak to—"

"Mama, I want *up,*" a childish voice interrupted.

"Not right now, darling." The woman looked back at Jake as the youngster jumped impatiently. "Maybe I should come down there." She emerged from Hannah's house a minute later. "Hi, I'm Gwen Westfield. My husband is the head of emergency services in Mahalaton Lake."

"Hello." Jake nodded warily and shook her hand.

"I'm working on a fund-raising booth for the Christmas in August street fair," she said. "I wondered if you'd consider taking portraits to help the town raise money for a new fire truck. We'd get photographic paper, and I have a printer and laptop, so you could print and sign the photos right there. All you'd have to do is bring your camera, and you could choose the times you wanted to work."

He stared.

Street fair? *Portraits?* He rarely took pictures with people *in* them, much less portraits. It might have been all right to do something like that for charity if he hadn't gotten hurt, but he'd just look desperate now. And if word got out that he was doing that kind of work, he could kiss any kind of adventure-based project goodbye. Nobody would ever take him seriously again—as much as he'd like to ignore the critics, he *did* care about his artistic reputation.

"I'm afraid that isn't possible," he said. "But I'd be happy to make a donation toward the truck."

She looked resigned. "Hannah didn't think you'd be interested, but I had to ask."

"I'll write you a check right now," Jake said.

"That's all right. You can do that at the festival." Gwen waved her hand. "I don't have my receipt book with me."

"Take it now," Hannah advised her friend, coming down the steps holding the hands of two small boys identical in appearance, right down to their skinned knees and freckled noses. "In case Jake doesn't go to the festival."

Jake didn't know whether to be grateful or annoyed. Gwen Westfield had assumed he wouldn't miss the town celebration while Hannah had probably guessed he wasn't likely to attend.

"Oh." Gwen blinked. "In that case, make it out to the MLFD Truck Fund."

He went inside the lodge and returned with the check. "Here you are."

Gwen's eyes widened as she looked at it. "Five thousand dollars? That's extremely generous."

"It's a good cause." Yet Jake knew he wasn't being generous; he was just avoiding an awkward situation. Between his trust fund and private income, he didn't have to worry about money, and it smoothed over situations like this.

"I'll give your receipt to Hannah the next time I see her, and she can get it to you."

"Whatever's convenient."

As she bundled her kids into the SUV, Brendan came out and kissed Hannah on the cheek. "Danny says his stomach hurts, so I'd better go. Thank you for dinner."

"You're welcome."

Hannah shot a harried glance at Jake before disappearing inside Silver Cottage. A minute later the lawyer's Lexus was gone and a sense of peace returned to the large clearing around the two buildings.

Jake smiled. It had turned out to be a fairly good

day—his leg didn't hurt as much, and he finally had a plan for attacking his project on the Cascades. But since Danny wasn't feeling well, he'd speak with Hannah another time about showing him around her favorite spots in the mountains.

As for Aaron and Matt's hopes to visit Mahalaton Lake later in the summer…it wouldn't have concerned Jake if it was just his brothers, but their wives and children?

It was just too much to take.

INSIDE THE HOUSE Hannah found Danny watching TV.

"I thought your tummy hurt."

"It's better now," he told her with an innocent expression on his face.

She wondered if he'd faked illness to get rid of Brendan, but he'd behaved most of the evening, so maybe it was better not to scold him. Besides, there *was* a stomach bug going around Mahalaton Lake.

A short time later Hannah was glad she hadn't said anything—one minute Danny was fine, the next he was violently ill. The worst seemed to be over after a couple of hours and he fell into an exhausted sleep around eleven.

Badger watched worriedly as Hannah cleaned up and put the soiled sheets and towels into the washing machine. She came back and checked Danny's forehead again.

"It's okay, boy," she assured the dog, and he lay

on the floor, seeming to understand he shouldn't be on the bed.

Only then did Hannah start thinking about what needed to be done the next day. She was supposed to set up for the ice cream social, make huckleberry ice cream and bake several batches of her peanut-butter chocolate-chip cookies.

Reluctantly, she fetched the phone and called her parents. They were always eager to help out, though she didn't like asking.

"Hannah, what's wrong? You're usually in bed by now," her mother asked when she answered. Unlike her daughter, Carrie was a night person, staying up until all hours of the morning while still managing to get up early, too.

"Danny has the stomach bug that's going around."

"Oh, dear. How is he doing?"

"Better for the moment, but I'm trying to figure out what to do about tomorrow. I'm supposed to be at Memorial Hall at 9:00 a.m. Is there any way that Dad could go in my place and help set up for the ice cream social? Everybody should have a list of what needs to be done."

"I'm sure he'll be happy to. What else can we do?"

Hannah recalled the grocery list she'd gotten from Jake earlier in the afternoon, but he'd have to wait. "Nothing. Danny will probably stay in bed sleeping or watching TV, so it'll be easy enough to take care of my baking, and I can do the shopping another day."

"Nonsense. I'll come over and watch him while you run to the store."

"I don't want to expose you to his germs."

"Don't worry about that. Besides, we both had it last week."

Hannah straightened. "Why didn't you tell me?" she demanded indignantly. She talked to her parents almost every day, and they'd said nothing about being sick.

Carrie laughed. "Because you worry too much. Trust me, Danny will be much better by tomorrow evening. But he probably won't be well enough to go on Sunday, so I'll watch him then, as well."

"You don't want to miss the ice cream social."

"I'd rather spend time with my grandson. I'll leave my contributions at Memorial Hall before coming out there."

"You won't enjoy being with Danny if he's missing the social," Hannah said drily. "He'll be a pain."

"I'll manage. Now get some rest yourself, and I'll see you in the morning."

"All right." Hannah put the phone down and checked on her son again. He wasn't seriously ill, but it was times like this that she was worried about living out of Mahalaton Lake. Yet she was still only a few minutes away from emergency services, so there wasn't any real need for concern.

Danny stirred restlessly and she brushed his forehead. He opened his eyes and looked at her fretfully.

"Mommy, don't turn the light off, a lion might jump on me."

Damn Jake, and damn his stories. Even so, Hannah couldn't deny they were exciting. She'd found herself listening a few times, lured by the exotic flavor of distant lands. Until Jake had become part of her life, she had forgotten how much fun it could be to travel, although the places she'd visited with her great-aunt and uncle bore little relationship to the remote corners of the world that he favored. And unlike Jake, she wanted a place to call home.

"I'll leave the light on, but there aren't any lions here in Mahalaton Lake. Have you been having bad dreams?"

"Uh-huh, but don't tell Jake. He never gets scared."

"Honey, I'm sure Jake gets scared, too."

"No, he doesn't," Danny insisted stubbornly. "And I wanna have adventures just like him."

Hannah tensed. She didn't think Jake was brave; she thought he was foolhardy. Between his stories and his press coverage, she'd gotten a clear picture of a man who was lucky he hadn't died years ago. She didn't want to lose her son, either to constant travel or some reckless act that killed him.

"There are all sorts of adventures," she said carefully. "You'll figure out what kinds are important to you when you're older."

"I like *his* kind." Danny stuck his lip out and rubbed his tummy. "But I don't like being sick."

"I know. Close your eyes and try to sleep. It'll be better soon."

"Okay."

She sat in the rocking chair by the bed and put her head back, thinking about the people Danny had exposed to his germs earlier that day. Gwen and her twin boys, Brendan, Barbi...Jake Hollister. Barbi had already been sick with the bug, but none of the others had as far as Hannah knew. And Jake was probably even more susceptible because he was still recovering from his injuries. However much he got on her nerves, she'd feel responsible if he caught anything.

Hannah let out a sigh. If she'd thought her tenant was a challenge before, wait until he was heaving in the bathroom because of her son.

CHAPTER EIGHT

JAKE GOT UP late on Saturday morning, having slept through the night for the first time in more than a week. Untroubled rest was rare these days. He'd often wake up around midnight and stay awake for hours, unable to stop thinking.

The possibility of being killed in a dangerous location was something he'd accepted long ago, but he hadn't really thought about getting injured in a way that might change his life. And he also hadn't thought about anyone else getting hurt, either. Now he'd nearly gotten Toby killed, and Gordon had died. It didn't matter that it was from a heart attack; the old bush pilot hadn't been near medical help when it was needed.

In a somber mood, Jake wandered into the kitchen and ate a slice of pizza from the box in the fridge, then stepped into the sunroom.

He looked over at Silver Cottage to see if anyone was stirring and saw Hannah on the deck, doing her yoga. Then he blinked and looked closer. *Not* Hannah, but someone who looked a good deal like her. The woman was older, but just as slim and shapely, with the same rich chestnut hair. An unaccustomed curiosity hit him.

Jake opened a window and leaned out. "Hi, I'm Jake Hollister."

The woman pressed her hands together before looking up. "Hello. I'm Carrie Nolan, Hannah's mother."

"Is she there?"

Carrie gracefully unfolded from the lotus position and stood. "Sorry, she's out shopping. Danny has a stomach bug, so I came over to stay with him. I hope you don't get it yourself—Hannah is concerned because he was there while she was cleaning yesterday."

Jake shrugged. "I never get sick."

Just banged up in plane crashes.

"Hannah doesn't, either. I think it's because she's a schoolteacher and is exposed to germs all year long. That's convenient when you're also a mother, but very annoying to the rest of us."

Jake grinned. He liked Carrie Nolan.

"Is there anything I can do for you?" she asked.

"No, I just wanted to talk to your daughter about something. It can wait."

"How about coming over for breakfast? Nothing fancy, I was just going to fix hot cereal."

Why not? He mostly ordered pizza from Luigi's, despite what Barbi had said about getting items from the regular menu, but he was getting tired of it. Funny, pizza had been his favorite treat as a kid.

He still remembered tasting it for the first time. Sully had met him and his mother on a layover in New York. It wasn't long after the disastrous climbing party on Sagarmatha, but Josie had brightened when she'd seen Sully waiting at the gate. They'd stayed two days, seeing the sights and sampling various New York restaurants, including one that served pizza. It was during that visit Jake had realized his mother's relationship with his father was more than ex-lover. Even now they still got together occasionally.

"I'd love breakfast."

Carrie met him at the front door, and she looked even more like Hannah close up, with only a few extra laugh lines and some strands of silver in her hair.

"Danny is asleep," she said in a hushed tone. "Go out on the deck. If he wakes up and hears you, he might come out. And even if you *do* have a tough constitution, it's best not to push it."

Jake glanced around as he went through to the French doors that opened onto the deck. Silver Cottage appeared to be similar to Huckleberry Lodge, with lots of natural wood and a rustic flavor that didn't sacrifice comfort. And the deck, while smaller than the one off the lodge, had an equally fine view of the lake and mountain beyond.

"I'm sorry Danny isn't feeling well," he said when Carrie brought out a tray with two steaming bowls.

"He's better today. The worst was last night, so

Hannah didn't get much rest. And of course she'll be baking cookies all afternoon and making huckleberry ice cream tomorrow morning for the ice cream social. Nothing stops my daughter."

"You mean people still have ice cream socials? I thought they went out of fashion a hundred years ago."

"Not quite. It's a Mahalaton Lake tradition and raises quite a bit of money for the rescue squad. Actually, there's some type of event almost every weekend during the summer. Hasn't Hannah mentioned them? She's on two or three fund-raising committees."

Jake tried to remember if Hannah had said anything about the community celebrations. There *had* been a brief comment, mostly as an explanation when he'd asked about her frequent visitors.

"Yeah, she said something about it. And I heard about the Christmas in August festival from someone named Gwen."

Carrie chuckled. "We love Christmas here, so we finally decided that once a year wasn't enough. Except for not having snow, Mahalaton Lake will look like an old-fashioned holiday card for over a week. We have visitors who come just for the festival."

"That's...uh, nice for the town," Jake commented awkwardly. Christmas wasn't celebrated in many of the different places where he'd grown up. He was aware of the religious aspect of the holiday, but the traditions surrounding it weren't part of his childhood.

He *did* wonder why Hannah hadn't told him about

the ice cream social, especially since it was happening so soon. She'd also assumed he wouldn't be interested in the festival. She was right, of course, but since local fund-raising activities seemed to be important to her, it was curious that she hadn't tried to convince him to attend. Or at least to donate money.

"I should have asked if the cereal was done enough," said Carrie. "We prefer it chewy, but some people like it cooked longer."

"It's fine."

The sound of a car caught Jake's attention. If it was Hannah, she probably wouldn't appreciate finding him on her deck, talking to her mother. He suppressed a grin; Hannah was an intriguing woman, full of interesting contradictions.

"Mom, how is Danny doing?" Hannah asked as she came out onto the deck. She spared Jake a brief glance, her mouth tightening.

"Mostly just sleeping, but he's been able to keep ginger ale and apple juice down. Jake and I just finished breakfast."

"I see that."

Carrie stood up. "Jake assured me that you don't need to worry about him getting the stomach flu because he never gets sick. Are you sure you don't want me to stay and help out with Danny while you're baking?"

"Thanks, but I'll be fine. I appreciate your coming over today."

"Anytime, you know that."

Hannah kissed Carrie's cheek, and side by side, their resemblance was even more startling. Jake recalled an old mountaineer saying that if you wanted to know what a woman would look like in twenty years, you needed to check out her mother. If Carrie Nolan was any indication, Hannah would just get more striking as she aged.

When her mother was gone, Hannah's expression turned chilly again. "I have your groceries in the car. I'll get them after I look in on Danny."

"Okay." Obviously, she didn't want him on her deck, much less in her house.

There were three paper bags in her trunk for him, and Jake insisted on carrying the two heaviest. He refused to be treated as if he was an invalid. In the kitchen Hannah automatically began putting the food away.

"It looks as if you got a few things that weren't on my list," he observed.

"Yeah, fresh food. Try it—you might like it." She ended by folding the paper sacks and stowing them in the pantry.

"That's all," she said. "I'll see you on Tuesday."

"Actually, I wanted to talk to you about that."

HANNAH NARROWED HER eyes. "Do you want to change the days I clean?"

"Not exactly. You love the Cascades, and I figured that since you aren't teaching this summer, I'd hire you to show me your favorite places in the mountains. We can start with the locations where you think dogwood trees may still be blooming."

"Even if I'm not teaching, I'm still busy."

"Weekends, sure, but not as much during the week. I'll pay you two hundred a day—double if it's overnight—and we can arrange the outings around your schedule. Danny can even come with us some of the time."

She clenched her fingers. She *was* busy, but how could she turn down the fee he was offering? Imagine, being paid to visit her favorite places *and* being able to bring Danny. She'd have to wait to do that, though, until she knew more about how Jake worked—Danny had trouble sitting still for long periods.

"Surely you won't earn enough on your book to justify paying me that kind of money," she said, stalling.

"I simply want it to be an artistic success. I'm not concerned about how much money the book makes."

No doubt having a wealthy father allowed him to not worry about how he would feed and clothe himself like most people.

"It's worth it to me," Jake added. "And since you don't think I have the right attitude about this project, this is your chance to convince me that the Cascades are something special."

It was a blatant challenge, and she ought to tell him to stuff it, but she couldn't. Hadn't she told Brendan that Jake was an incredible photographer?

And he *was* brilliant, even if his work often seemed sterile to her.

"Some of the places I love require a fair amount of hiking," she warned. "Are you up to it yet?"

"I'll manage." His tone didn't invite further discussion on the subject. "How about starting on Monday?"

Hannah sighed. She'd have to ask her mother to watch Danny again, but she didn't have any committee meetings that couldn't be rescheduled. "I should be able to work it out. I'll let you know tomorrow if I can't swing it. In the meantime, I have a sick son and dozens of cookies to bake."

She walked to the door, only to have Jake follow her.

"What?"

"I just wondered why you didn't say anything about the ice cream thing tomorrow."

"You mean you want to go?" Hannah asked, mildly shocked. She *would* have invited Jake to the community fund-raiser if she'd thought he was interested.

"*No*. That is, I'm not good in that sort of social situation."

"You've traveled all over the world, and yet you don't think you'd be comfortable at a small-town ice cream social?"

Jake shrugged. "I guess it's the way I was raised. We slept and ate with locals whenever possible, but Josie believed the best way to learn about a culture was to observe it, rather than to interact and taint it with our habits. I've mostly followed the same pattern since then."

"Joining in seems like a better way to know a culture. Didn't you get to play with any of the kids your age?"

He seemed even more uncomfortable. "Sometimes, but my mother didn't approve."

A curious sorrow went through Hannah…sorrow for the little boy who must have been terribly lonely, watching other people, but never really being a part of their lives.

"Well, if you decide you want to go to the social, it's at Memorial Hall on Main Street. You just head into town and keep going until you pass the city park. The hall is on the left. I'll even buy you a bowl of ice cream," she found herself offering.

"That's nice, but it still doesn't explain why you didn't mention the event."

Hannah nearly popped off a smart remark, but stopped herself. Jake was asking seriously, and he deserved a serious response. "Because the Cascades are my home and you insulted them. I didn't want my neighbors to be offended, as well. I realize you probably never stayed in a place long enough to have that kind of fondness for it, but home is important to most people, Jake. Maybe having to spend this time here is a chance to explore the culture of your own country."

A taut expression went across his face. "You're

right. I apologize for not being more courteous. It's just that photographing anything in the United States feels like…"

"Like what?"

"Surrender," he muttered. "I've always left more accessible places to photographers who weren't willing or able to go to the places that I could. Now doctors are telling *me* not to go to those places, either."

Hannah looked at the line of pain etched around his mouth. "Andy says you'll be all right, that it'll just take time."

"Yeah, I'm *expected* to make a full recovery, but nobody can offer guarantees. And they always have to remind me that I'm lucky to be alive. Or that I might have never walked again, though they could have just shot me if that had happened."

A sinking sensation went through Hannah as she remembered Collin's rambling words after he fell, saying he'd rather die than be in a wheelchair. She'd held his hand, praying for a miracle, as he'd slowly drifted away. Maybe that was why Jake had rubbed her wrong from the beginning. With his penchant for risking his neck, he reminded her of the worst hours of her life.

"Hey, are you okay?" Jake asked. "You look as if you're going to pass out."

"I… Yes, I'm fine. So that's what you've been so bothered about…that the doctors might be wrong about your leg."

"That's part of it."

"What happens if you don't fully recover?"

Jake set his jaw. "Then I'll go where I want anyway, and take my chances. I won't play their waiting game forever."

She swallowed, recalling something she'd heard him say to Owen. *If you live, you live. If you die, that's it, you're dust. Everything is pure chance.*

Maybe Jake took so many chances because he didn't believe in anything more than the here and now. Hannah had wondered the same thing about Collin; it was as if he was challenging the world to prove there was more to life than a bunch of biological reactions. But was that what Jake was doing, or had he simply never found something important enough to live for *beyond* his art?

"That's something you'll have to decide if the time ever comes," she said cautiously. "Um…I'll talk to you later."

Hannah hurried back to Silver Cottage. Danny was still asleep, and Badger lay at the foot of the bed, patiently waiting for his playmate to recover.

She slipped out of the room with a faint smile, but her humor faded as she thought about the things Jake had said. She hated the idea that he would be willing to throw his life away so casually.

It seemed as if everyone in Mahalaton Lake, resident and visitor alike, had turned out for the Sunday ice cream social, and Barbi spent a hectic two hours selling tickets before someone came to give her a break. Ticket in hand, she hurried to the ice cream serving table.

"Huckleberry, please."

"Sorry," Gwen said regretfully. "Every drop is gone. It went first thing. We have other flavors though—vanilla, chocolate, strawberry and pine-apple sorbet."

Before Barbi could think about her second choice, Hannah appeared.

"I saved some huckleberry for Barbi. I'll get it."

Barbi followed, appreciating Hannah's thought-fulness. The relative peace of the Memorial Hall kitchen was a pleasant contrast to the activity in the main room and on the veranda.

"Phew, it's been busy." Hannah opened the com-mercial freezer and pulled out a bowl with a gen-erous serving, handing it over with a plastic spoon. "There you go."

Barbi's mouth watered as she scooped up some ice cream. The rich, fruity flavor melted over her tongue and she closed her eyes in pleasure. "You make the best huckleberry ice cream. Every year it's the first to sell out."

"It's not hard to be best when you're the only one who makes it," Hannah said matter-of-factly. "The tourists want some because it's different and sounds like something you'd get on vacation, and the people in town want it because they love huckleberries and aren't willing to pick any themselves."

"One of the first tickets I sold was to Brendan. Did he have some?"

"He chose vanilla."

Barbi wasn't surprised. "Figures. That man has no imagination."

"He just has his own way of doing things."

"You aren't serious about him, are you?" For some reason the answer seemed awfully important.

"Right now we're just friends. I have to be careful because of Danny."

"Does he ever loosen up?"

"Well...*no,*" Hannah admitted with a laugh. "But he's bucking two hundred and fifty years of New England propriety, and that can't be easy."

"You mean he's a prig because of his uptight family. There's no law saying we *have* to turn out like our relatives, is there?"

"Of course not."

Barbi swallowed another bite of ice cream and tried to keep from looking at her friend. After so many years of being the daughter of the town drunk, she should be used to the notoriety. But all that would change when she moved away from Mahalaton Lake. Nobody would know about Vic and his temper or about her dropping out of high school.

Even so, the idea of going anywhere else scared the heck out of her, almost as much as Vic scared her when he was drunk.

She'd grown up in town and had friends like Hannah and Luigi here, even if a few people raised their eyebrows at the way she dressed. And it was a real pretty town, being at the edge of a lake with Mount Mahala in the background. Her mom used to say it was the closest to heaven you could get without actually meeting your maker.

"Uh, I better go back to the ticket table," Barbi said with a gulp. When she was nine and her mother died, she'd believed Rachael had gone to live with angels at the top of the mountain. But that was a long time ago, and it was awful hard to keep believing in angels, no matter how much she wanted to.

HANNAH HURRIED BACK into the main room in time to see Jake come through the doors. Her jaw dropped. He looked distinctly ill at ease and immediately raised the camera hanging around his neck to look through the viewfinder.

She walked over. "Hi. You made it."

"Er…yeah," he said, lowering his hands a few inches. "Will people mind the camera?"

"I don't think so, but why don't you just have a bowl of ice cream and enjoy yourself?" Hannah searched in her pocket and pulled out the advance sales ticket she'd bought for Danny before he had gotten sick. "Be my guest."

Jake peered through the viewfinder again. "Thank you, but I'm more comfortable taking pictures."

"You mean, as if you're chronicling a tribal ceremony?" she asked curiously.

"No. Josie used to take assignments to do pictorial cultural studies, but my work is strictly about nature. I only went to the Middle East to help out a colleague."

"Then why are you taking photos now?"

"Because it's what I do."

Jake's mouth was tense, and Hannah suspected the camera was mostly a shield between him and everyone else. From everything she'd seen, his reputation for being a loner was well deserved, so it was odd that he'd shown up at the fund-raiser.

"Well, keep the ticket in case you change your mind," she said, dropping it into his open camera case. She was about to excuse herself when she saw Brendan approaching with an annoyed expression on his face.

"Hey, Brendan. I thought you left," she said.

"I decided to come back. I hoped it wouldn't be as busy now, so we could talk."

He gave Jake a hard stare, and the two men measured each other like bulls at Pamplona. She sighed. What was it about the male psyche that they felt compelled to wrangle over a bone, even when the bone didn't belong to either one of them? For that matter, Jake didn't even *want* the bone. He'd made it quite clear that he wasn't interested in a relationship with *any* woman.

"How about tomorrow afternoon?" Hannah suggested. "I'm showing Jake a place where dogwood might still be blooming, but we won't get back late."

"You're *what?* Please excuse us, Hollister." Brendan dragged her a few feet away before she broke free.

"What is wrong with you?" she demanded.

"Sorry, it's just that…" Brendan gestured toward Jake. "I didn't realize you were cozy enough with your tenant to go anywhere with him."

"We aren't *cozy.* He wants me to guide him to my favorite places in the Cascades, that's all."

"There are professional guides, Hannah. He doesn't need an amateur showing him a few points of interest. Doesn't he have GPS? Or a map? Just circle the places he should go and send him on his way."

Her eyes narrowed. Having Brendan act this way was irritating, especially since he hadn't shown much interest in seeing the Cascades himself. Perhaps she needed to rethink their relationship. It was important to have shared values, but it was just as important to have shared interests.

"And what will people think if you're spending that much time together?" he whispered urgently. "Mahalaton Lake is a small town. You're the one who told me that everybody knows your business here. I won't have it."

Her eyebrows shot upward. "You have no say in what I do, Brendan. We aren't engaged. We aren't even dating exclusively. And even if we *had* gotten to that point, you *still* wouldn't have any right to object."

Brendan looked taken aback. "I'm sorry. I didn't realize… Can I still see you tomorrow?"

She let out a breath. "All right. But you can't stay long. Barbi is coming over at seven."

Turning on her heel, she hurried to the ice cream table, thoroughly frustrated. Her doubts about Brendan had been growing. Despite the surface things they had in common, they didn't talk about anything important. And though they'd been dating for a while, she felt nothing more than friendship for him…certainly nothing like the intense response she had to Jake.

But she couldn't think about it right now. Maybe later, when things were quiet…or when she wasn't so annoyed that he'd tried to forbid her to guide Jake around the Cascades.

HANNAH WAS SURPRISED when Jake handed her the keys to his SUV early Monday morning, inviting her to drive.

"It only makes sense," he said when she commented on it. "You know the area and I don't."

"All right."

Hannah got into the Jeep. The motor turned over quickly and she headed north around the lake. The place she had in mind was where she and her parents often camped. It was located partway up Mount Mahala and was often the last place to find dogwood blooming.

"Your mother says you're involved in several fund-raising committees," Jake mentioned after they'd driven awhile.

"A few. We have fund-raisers here for everything from classroom computers to stained-glass windows. I primarily focus on raising money for the rescue squad—that's what the ice cream social was for—though I support other emergency services like the new fire truck."

"I've mostly lived in places without modern amenities. It's good that Mahalaton Lake is upgrading."

"Not upgrading, *expanding*. We haven't used a horse-drawn, hand-pumped fire wagon for at least twenty years," she said wryly.

"That isn't what I meant." Yet from the look on Jake's face, it probably wasn't far off. Or maybe she was being too sensitive. His general ability to stick his foot in his mouth could also have something to do with it.

"We want to put in a second fire station and need the equipment," she explained. "Fire trucks are expensive, and the town budget can't afford one without community support. We're also hoping to add a second paramedic unit."

"Why is your primary focus the rescue squad?"

"Someone I cared about died in a mountain climbing accident a long time ago. I couldn't save him, but maybe I can have a small part in saving someone else." Hannah turned off the main road onto a forest service road. Few people traveled this road, since it led up and away from the lake and not toward one of the popular ski slopes.

"This person who died, was he family?"

"I...I once hoped he'd be." Though Hannah was sometimes sad for what she might have shared with Collin, she wondered now whether they would have had a future. Some people were like bonfires made of too-dry wood, burning themselves out in a wild blaze before they'd ever really lived. "We should talk about what you've seen of the Cascades, so I'll know what to show you," she said, deliberately changing the subject.

"I've seen Mount Rainier from Seattle, and from the interstate highway. And I drove up to Mahalaton Lake."

"You *do* realize the Cascade Mountain Range extends from Northern California into Canada, right?"

"I'm concentrating on the area north of the border between Oregon and Washington, not the whole range."

She wouldn't be able to show him everything north of Oregon, either. Even if she spent the entire summer guiding Jake around, it wouldn't be enough time to explore the entire region. At least he was okay with Danny going with them on some of the outings, which was one of the reasons she'd agreed. What better way to spend time with her son than showing him the mountains they lived in?

Jake glanced into the backseat at Badger. "Your dog is quite calm."

"He mostly chases after Danny, not wildlife," Hannah said. "I'm glad you were okay with him coming along. He enjoys outings."

She shifted uncomfortably, still wondering if Jake was up to a hike. From what she could tell, he was doing much better than when he'd first arrived at Huckleberry Lodge—not limping as much, and his color was better. But she was still a little tense about going on a wilderness hike with someone recovering from such serious injuries.

After they'd driven for another hour, she turned up a gravel road. The trees were even closer here, and sunlight filtered through the branches that met overhead. She still remembered seeing it when she was so small her legs didn't reach the floor of her dad's truck. And all at once she wasn't sure she should have brought Jake here, especially as the *first* place. If he mocked it, she'd probably want to strangle him.

"We've been camping here ever since I can remember," she said edgily. "I was a baby the first time we came. My dad packed everything in, including me, because my mother had a broken arm. It's about a mile, and mostly level. Is that too much for you to walk?"

"I told you, I'll be fine," he replied shortly.

"I'm only checking—you don't have to bite my head off."

Men and their egos. Would it kill him to let her know exactly how hard and far he should go? It wasn't as if she thought he was helpless.

After parking, she opened the rear door for Badger to jump out. He waited to see if she was going to attach the leash, and when she didn't, his entire body quivered with pleasure.

She dug out her cell phone and looked to see if it had a signal, though she wasn't hopeful. Outside of Mahalaton Lake reception was spotty, at best.

"Don't worry about that. I always carry a satellite phone," Jake said, giving a quick check to the contents of his own pack. He took out the phone. "I should have thought of it earlier. Call your mother and give her my number in case she needs to reach us."

Hannah hesitated. "Aren't satellite calls expensive?"

"I have no idea—my business manager pays the bills. Don't worry about it," he repeated.

She dialed Silver Cottage and made sure her mother got the number from the call display. "But only for emergencies," she explained hastily.

"I understand. By the way, Brendan phoned. He has the flu and won't be able to come out tonight. Poor guy, he sounded miserable," Carrie told her.

"Okay, thanks. I'll call him this evening and see how he's doing. See you in a few hours." Hannah disconnected quickly, feeling both relieved and guilty that Brendan was sick. Relieved, because this way she wouldn't have to make any decision about their relationship right away. And guilty, because he was a friend and she didn't enjoy knowing he was ill.

"What was that about?" Jake asked.

"Brendan has the stomach flu. I'm sure he didn't

get it from Danny—it's too soon—but I feel bad about it. He doesn't have any family in the area."

"Why don't you see if Barbi is available to take soda and stuff over to him?"

She considered the suggestion for a second, then shook her head. "Barbi works part-time jobs all over town. I can't ask her to do a favor for someone she doesn't like."

"You're unavailable to help Townsend because of me, and that makes it my responsibility," Jake said seriously. "If Barbi has a free hour, I'll pay her to fill in for you."

Hannah wavered. "All right," she agreed finally.

She got the number from her cell phone contacts list and Jake got in touch with Barbi, offering a generous sum for making a quick run to the grocery store and delivering the supplies to Brendan's condo.

"There. All taken care of," Jake said, tucking the satellite phone back into his pack.

Hannah swung her backpack over her shoulders. It was nice that Jake had offered to pay Barbi, and it showed more sensitivity than she'd expected. Still, she questioned whether he was genuinely concerned about her missing any commitments. Life was a game to him and he didn't stay in one place long enough for it to become real. The plane accident was probably the first time he'd been confronted with something he couldn't fix with his money or by moving on.

"You can find dogwood in both open and fairly

dense forests," she said after a few minutes, Badger trotting alongside her. She was trying to set a moderate pace that wouldn't tax Jake's body *or* wound his ego, and it wasn't easy. His face was expressionless, giving her no clue about whether they were going too quickly or too slowly.

"I've seen pictures in your books at the lodge. The written material says the white petals aren't actually part of the flower."

"Right, those are bracts. The blossoms are in the center, but it's hard not to think of the whole thing as the flower. They're beautiful everywhere they grow, but I especially love seeing them in the deep woods."

"You said that they glowed."

"They do. They just seem to hang there in midair, shimmering. Most of the year, dogwood is just part of the undercanopy of the woods, but in spring, it's like a jewel from an enchanted land."

"Uh-huh." Jake was mostly concentrating on walking, keeping his leg straight and the rest of his body cooperating. Six months ago he'd been able to hike all day carrying a heavy load; now it was a challenge to go a level mile with a light pack slung over his good shoulder. Still, he *was* improving.

He frowned as he thought about setting up a grocery run for Brendan Townsend. Normally he wouldn't get involved, but the conflicted expression on Hannah's face had bothered him. He suspected she had an overdeveloped sense of responsibility, maybe because of her late friend, or for some other reason.

As for Barbi Paulson, her first reaction to hearing about Brendan's illness had been concern, not "it serves him right" or some other invective. Then, as if she'd remembered she was supposed to despise Brendan, she'd popped off a smart remark. But smart remark or not, she was going to take a bag of groceries to him. She hadn't wanted to be paid, but Jake had quickly pointed out that she wouldn't want it to look as if she was doing Brendan Townsend any favors.

The sound of trickling water caught Jake's attention a short time later and he looked up to see a small stream shooting down through a crevice before setting into a series of woodland pools, the highest only a little bigger than a washbasin.

"Is this where you camp with your family?" he asked.

"There's a spot in a clearing near here that isn't crossed by any large animal trails. We have other sites as well, all around the lake and on Mount Mahala."

"As secluded as this?"

Hannah shrugged. "Pretty much. There are campgrounds available, but we prefer to get away by ourselves."

Jake drew a lungful of the clean, crisp air, taking in the scent of trees and growing things, and it was as if some of the life rushed back into him. He bent over the upper pool, intending to scoop a handful of water into his mouth, when Hannah stopped him.

"You might want to rethink that. It's glacial meltwater," she said. "The base of Meriwether Glacier is a ways up from here, but the water travels down so quickly, it doesn't have time to warm up that much."

Jake dipped a fingertip into the water. Hannah was right—it was icy. The hike had gotten him hot, and putting such cold water into his stomach wasn't a smart idea.

"Here."

She handed him an aluminum bottle from her backpack, taking one out for herself, as well. Badger got a drink, too, poured into her hand for him to lap from. It was disconcerting for Jake to realize that though he was a seasoned wilderness traveler, he hadn't thought to bring drinking water, while Hannah had.

"Thanks."

They sat on some rocks in a beam of sunshine, Jake surreptitiously rubbing his aching leg. Birds twittered, flitting back and forth in the trees above them, and he smiled faintly. He wasn't sure what he'd expected from his landlady's special places in the mountains, but this one was filled with peace... something he'd had precious little of since the crash. He looked at Hannah. Her eyes were closed and her body was swaying, almost as if listening to an inner music.

He opened his mouth.

"Please don't say anything awful," she murmured before he could speak.

"How did you know I was going to say something?"

"You drew your breath in a certain way. I belong to three fund-raising committees. It's a subtle skill, but I always know when someone is getting ready to say something, even when I'm not looking at them."

"Oh. And why would you think I'd say something awful?"

She looked at him. "Do you really have to ask?"

Probably not.

Jake took another drink rather than answering. He usually wasn't a complete ass when dealing with people. On average he was better than Toby, who complained a blue streak and wasn't always discreet.

Hannah rolled her shoulders and stood up. "If you're ready, the place where the dogwood may still be blooming isn't far from here."

He got up more slowly. "Of course I'm ready."

They crossed the stream and followed a narrow game trail. Shortly after, they emerged in a clearing where the large trees were still so thick only limited sparkles of sunlight found their way below. And in the midst of the green shadows, large white blossoms seemed eerily suspended in the air, exactly the way Hannah had described. The absence of other foliage on the branches intensified the sensation that the sight wasn't quite real.

Forgetting everything else, Jake unzipped his pack and took out one of his cameras.

CHAPTER NINE

FOLLOWING HER EARLY Monday morning shift at the bakery, Barbi pushed a cart down the supermarket aisle, unable to believe she was shopping for stuff to get Brendan Townsend through the flu. Still, he didn't have any family in Mahalaton Lake and Barbi knew what it felt like to be sick alone—not wanting to ask for help and feeling more alone because of it.

She had family in Mahalaton Lake, but Vic only came around when he wanted money or to cry on her shoulder about losing Rachael. She certainly couldn't call and ask him to get anything at the store for her, and she didn't like to ask friends...though both Luigi and Hannah had scolded her in the past for not letting them know when she was sick.

Barbi looked at the applesauce and picked out both a sweetened and unsweetened variety since she didn't know which one Brendan preferred. *And I don't care, either,* she thought defiantly. She added individual serving packs of Jell-O and a rice pudding she liked herself.

A few minutes later she walked up to Brendan's condo, a box of ginger-ale cans in one hand and a heavily loaded grocery bag in the other. She pressed the bell with her elbow and waited.

The door swung open and a bleary-eyed Brendan stared at her with a stupid expression on his handsome face. "I didn't order pizza." He looked ready to gag at the thought, and for once she was reasonably sure it didn't have anything to do with her clothes.

"Yeah, and it's Monday, too. Luigi's doesn't deliver on Mondays."

"I've got… Jeez." He clapped a hand to his mouth and retreated across his living room.

Unperturbed by the less-than-warm welcome, Barbi stepped inside and closed the door. The condo was nicely furnished, but dull, with only a few spots of color. And the kitchen was practically bare. Figured. She'd heard Brendan was well acquainted with the restaurants in both Mahalaton Lake and Lower Mahalaton.

She began stowing the groceries in the fridge, glad to see there wasn't any beer or wine inside. It wasn't that she had anything against booze, and Brendan's drinking habits had nothing to do with her, but she was still glad. She was debating whether or not he'd want his applesauce chilled when she heard footsteps behind her.

Brendan's hair was tousled, he was wearing ancient gray sweats and he looked entirely too miserable for words.

"When did you get sick?" she asked.

"Around 6:00 a.m."

"If it's any consolation," she said. "You'll feel better in a few hours. The worst part doesn't last long."

He brightened marginally. "You've had it already?"

"A couple of weeks ago."

"Oh. Why are you here?"

"Hannah was out of town for the day when she found out you were sick. She wanted me to get a few things for you. You know, bananas and soda and stuff."

Brendan looked nauseated again. "I'm never eating another bite as long as I live."

"Honest, by two or three this afternoon, you should be able to keep water down. Drink only a little bit at a time or you'll be sorry. I got club soda—it seems to work the best. In another couple of hours, try ginger ale. Otherwise you'll start getting wobbly."

"You mean more wobbly than I am now?" he asked wryly, resting against the wall for support.

Barbi's mouth twitched. "Yeah, more than now. Do you need me to do anything else, like a load of laundry?" she surprised herself by asking. But it was just because she felt sorry for the dope.

Brendan seemed equally surprised. "You can't be serious."

She shrugged and stuck out her chin. "I offered, didn't I?"

"I can't let you do that." But the protest was half-hearted at best.

He slumped farther down the wall and Barbi sighed. She had a couple of hours before her shift at Pat's Burger Hut, so she could look after a few things for him.

Besides, she knew how it felt to be sick and alone. Maybe Brendan wasn't going to die or anything, but she'd bet he felt pretty lonely and sorry for himself. At times like that it was nice to be reminded that someone...*anyone* cared.

"Come on, Prince Charming. You should be horizontal." She grabbed his arm and led him back to his bedroom.

She leaned him against the doorjamb as she quickly tidied the bed covers. When the sheets were pulled straight, he collapsed onto the mattress with a grunt, seeming barely aware of her presence.

Barbi looked around. There was an untidy pile of sheets flung in a corner of the room, along with towels and some dirty T-shirts. She gathered them up.

Unlike her shabby rental, the condo had personal laundry machines, and she filled the washer in Brendan's utility room. Otherwise the place was reasonably tidy, which was good, because she had no intention of doing more than a few basic chores.

She had the laundry neatly folded when she had to leave for work. Brendan had fallen asleep, so she put a bottle of club soda on his bedside table. Despite his dark stubble, he had a little-boy look that was endearing, but she stomped on the feeling.

A book was on the floor and she picked it up—

J. R. R. Tolkien's *The Hobbit*. Of all the Tolkien books about Middle Earth, *The Hobbit* was her favorite, and her brow creased with puzzlement as she put it next to the club-soda bottle.

If anything, she'd have expected to see the *Wall Street Journal* or a law text, but the book was dog-eared, plainly read over and over. It didn't fit. How could she and a fuddy-duddy like Brendan have anything in common?

And did it mean he wasn't such a lost cause after all?

HANNAH WATCHED JAKE'S focus narrow and intensify as he took picture after picture with a camera that made her pocket-size digital look like a toy. The rest of the world had vanished for him; the only thing he saw was the image through his viewfinder.

Sitting down, she leaned against a tree trunk with Badger resting his head on her leg, prepared for a long wait. She'd wanted Jake to see what she loved about the Cascades, so she couldn't complain.

There was a cathedral-like hush to the clearing, and she gazed upward. Even in sunlight, when a dogwood tree was blooming the branches faded into the background. But under the canopy of larger trees, the creamy-white bracts seemed to hang in the air, like butterflies.

Jake took another camera out of his pack, along with an ingenious gadget he unfolded into a tripod.

Some of his other equipment was more mysterious, but this was obviously something he found useful.

Shifting, Hannah stroked Badger's head and reluctantly began thinking about Brendan. When it got right down to it, she couldn't see him as a lover, no matter how perfect he should be for her. She couldn't fall in love on demand. It was a stubborn, illogical emotion, and she obviously hadn't got past her weakness for guys with a wild streak in their personality.

Like Jake Hollister.

Damn, that was depressing.

Hannah closed her eyes and tried to decide when she should talk to Brendan and break things off. Obviously not today. He had the flu and it wasn't fair to kick him when he was down. It was always possible he'd be relieved, but after his performance at the ice cream social, she doubted he'd be happy.

Still, she didn't think Brendan was in love with her. It was more the *idea* of them being together that he liked.

Okay, so she couldn't tell him today, and he ought to have an extra day to recover. Breaking up with someone was never a pleasant prospect, but she shouldn't wait any longer than necessary. Perhaps Wednesday or Thursday.

The noon hour arrived and Hannah's stomach grumbled. "Do you want some lunch?" she asked Jake, but he didn't seem to hear.

She opened the soft-sided cooler she'd put in her own pack and took out a chicken-salad sandwich, along with a bag of kibble for Badger. Jake hadn't said anything about food, but she'd put together a meal anyway.

His shopping list had been appalling—trail bars, trail mix, bread, peanut butter, jam of any flavor, cheese and dried fruit. In rebellion, she'd added bananas, apples, baby carrots and fresh milk and orange juice. He was living in a place where fresh foods were available. He didn't have to eat as though he were still in the wilderness. Of course, he also had cold pizza quite often, and whatever leftovers Danny could find in their fridge and bring to him.

Hannah finished an apple and wrapped up the core before getting up to stretch. Next trip she'd have to bring a book with her—just sitting and watching a genius work was interesting, but it got old after a while.

Jake obviously worked hard, but it did seem as if he mostly lived behind his camera, observing but not being a part of anything. A camera might not seem like a huge barrier, but she suspected it kept most people at arm's length. Jake probably preferred it that way.

Cooler in hand, she went over to stand directly in front of him. "Hey, do you want a sandwich?" she asked, speaking more loudly this time.

He dragged his attention away from his camera. "Do I want what?"

"Lunch."

"Oh. Sure." Jake unwrapped the sandwich she

handed him and bit into it absently, then his eyes widened. "There's curry in this."

"Yup, and chicken, celery and raisins."

"It's great."

The compliment sounded genuine, so she gave him a second sandwich and an apple before wandering back to her tree and dog, feeling sleepy. She was tempted to take a nap, but needed to keep track of the time. It looked as if Jake was capable of taking pictures until dark, and they'd agreed to get home in time for her to fix an early dinner for Danny.

By 2:00 p.m. Jake was finally showing signs of slowing down. "We'd better go," Hannah prompted, and this time she didn't need to stand in front of him to get his attention.

"Oh…yeah. Right."

He carefully stowed his equipment in his pack and they headed toward where they'd left the Jeep. In the clearing around the small stream, Jake caught her hand.

"Is something wrong?"

"I just want to thank you." He looked both exhausted and exhilarated as he bent and kissed her cheek.

Warmth curled through Hannah, and she swayed closer, though the kiss was so gentle, it couldn't be mistaken for anything *except* a thank-you. Before she could do anything too stupid, she stepped backward, wincing as she turned her ankle on a rock.

"I'm sorry, I shouldn't have done that," he said,

sounding genuinely contrite. "I get carried away when my work is going well."

"That...uh..." Hannah couldn't decide whether to be angry or shrug it off. "Thank me for what?"

"For showing me one of your special places, particularly after the things I've said about the Cascades. Taking pictures in that kind of light is a challenge, and I like challenges."

"I'm sure you've seen lots of places that challenge you."

He shrugged and an indefinable expression flitted across his face. "A few. Shall we go? You're probably anxious to talk to Brendan and see how he's doing. If you don't want to wait, call on my satellite phone."

"Thanks, but later is fine."

Hannah tried to smile, but she didn't want to think about Brendan at the moment. On the other hand, she didn't want to think about how it had felt when Jake kissed her, either. While he was attractive, she had no intention of getting involved with him. Between Collin and her ex-husband, her heart had been battered enough by reckless men for one lifetime.

Yet as they approached his Jeep, Hannah was struck by the absurdity of thinking about any type of encounter with Jake. He was determined to stay single and unencumbered by the things that were most important to her—family and children and other emotional ties.

"What are you grinning about?" he asked as she opened the back door for Badger to jump in.

"Was I grinning?"

"Yes."

"Maybe I'm just happy to be going home."

Jake didn't look convinced, but she didn't care. She reversed the route they'd taken that morning, and despite the bumpy dirt road, she noticed he was asleep before they'd gone very far. It was possible that a two-mile hike was more than he should have attempted, but he had to make his own decisions.

LATER THAT AFTERNOON Brendan reluctantly pried his eyes open and realized he hadn't gotten sick in at least forty minutes. That was something. And his mouth was dry to the point that he actually wanted a drink.

He reached for the bottle of club soda on the bedside table. The past few hours were a blur, but he remembered Barbi showing up at his door and staying awhile…though he had no idea *why* she'd stayed. She hadn't seemed the least bit horrified at seeing him look so disgusting, and had even offered reassurances that the worst would be over soon.

Swallowing tentatively, he waited for an immediate gag reflex, but the liquid settled mercifully in his tummy. He was about to drink some more, then remembered Barbi's advice to take it slowly.

He let his head fall back against the pillow and tried to remember when she'd left. He must have been asleep.

Ah, sleep... "Full of sweet dreams, and health, and

quiet breathing." An ironic smile twisted Brendan's lips as he thought of the old poem and the nightmares he'd had in place of sweet dreams. John Keats obviously hadn't been thinking about the stomach flu when he wrote those words.

Let's see…Barbi had brought him groceries because Hannah was out of town with Jake Hollister. Brendan groaned, recalling his idiotic behavior the day before. At least Hannah wasn't so angry that she didn't care he was sick.

And it was rather nice of Barbi to do something for him, no matter what the reason. She'd mentioned doing a load of laundry…. Brendan got up cautiously and found a neatly folded stack of towels, sheets and clothes on top of his dresser.

He briefly wondered why she hadn't put them away, but realized she'd respected his privacy by not going through his drawers and cupboards. That was nice. He hadn't thought a woman like Barbi would keep her nose out of places it didn't belong.

Yet even as the thought formed, Brendan frowned. It was unlikely he'd ever get along with Barbi Paulson, but she obviously wasn't a bad sort. Otherwise Hannah wouldn't be friends with her. He should have realized that before.

And exactly what *was* "a woman like her" anyhow?

He'd grown up in a world where Clothes Make the Man was a motto taken to an extreme degree. Proper dressing was expected of everyone in the

Townsend social circle. But nice clothes could hide some really nasty dirt, as he'd learned all too well during the summers he'd worked as an intern at the family firm.

So when it got right down to it, Barbi's colorful clothes didn't automatically say *anything* about what sort of person she might be. Maybe they were her armor, the same way his suits were for him.

But if that was the case, what was she protecting herself from?

BARBI CALLED HANNAH late in the afternoon to see if she should still come for a tutoring session that evening.

"Of course," Hannah assured her. "How did things go with Brendan? We talked for a minute after I got back, but he didn't say much. I think he's feeling pretty sorry for himself."

"With this bug, I can't blame him."

"It was really nice of you to go shopping for him."

"Not really. Remember, Jake was paying me." But Barbi squirmed because the pay hadn't included doing Brendan's laundry or tidying the condo, and she'd done it anyway. What else could you do when a guy was as sick as that?

"Be sure to collect when you get here. That guy throws money around as if it's so much tissue paper."

"It must be nice to be rich."

Hannah laughed. "I suppose. I'll see you later. Bring an appetite. I'm making a pot of soup."

"You don't need to feed me."

"I know I don't need to—I want to."

"Oh. Okay."

Barbi hung up and thought about what she'd said about being rich. It *would* be nice, but she'd settle for a place that didn't have Victor Paulson living there. Once upon a time she'd loved her father, but after over twenty years of dealing with his boozing and violence and self-pity, there wasn't much love left.

Maybe that made her a terrible person. People were supposed to love their parents. And she couldn't tell anyone how she felt; they probably wouldn't understand. Or maybe in a weird way she was protecting Vic, so nobody would know exactly how bad he'd become.

"MOMMY, WHY COULDN'T I go with you and Jake today?"

Hannah hung up the phone after talking to Barbi and looked down at her son. "Because you were sick a couple of days ago, and I need to be sure you're well. Besides, you get the wiggles and Jake needs to concentrate. Maybe you can go with us later in the summer." As much as Hannah wanted to include her son in the trips, now that she'd seen the way Jake worked, she wasn't sure it was a good idea.

"I'd be good. I like Jake."

"I know you do, but you can't go with us all the time anyway. Sometimes we'll be traveling too far, or hiking too much, so you'll need to go to Grandma and Grandpa's. They like seeing you, too. You also have day camp for a couple of weeks with all your friends. And then there's vacation Bible school at the church."

Danny sighed, looking torn. "Gosh, I'm busy."

She hid a grin. "Yes, you are. I'm going to fix chicken-and-rice soup for dinner now. Does that sound good?"

"Uh-huh, I'm tired of applesauce."

"I'll bet you are."

Humming to herself, Hannah put the soup together. She had two committee meetings in the morning. And she would clean Huckleberry Lodge in the afternoon.

Then on Wednesday she planned to take Jake down to Mount St. Helens and see what he made of it. The volcanic action of the Cascades wasn't always pretty, but it was part of life in the mountains. Of course, knowing Jake, he'd probably witnessed an *erupting* volcano up close and personal. But surely it would still be interesting for him to see the remains of Mount St. Helens and the way the land had begun to repair itself.

Jake had certainly seemed intrigued with the dogwood blossoms, or at least by the light surrounding them. It was doubtful that he could have faked that level of interest for several hours. Undoubtedly the photos would be brilliant, but she questioned whether he had captured what she loved about the trees in bloom, their white bracts heralding spring and summer. And maybe nobody could, because the way she saw them was filtered through years of memories.

She stepped too quickly away from the stove and felt a twinge from her twisted ankle. It was uncomfortable, but she'd gone for strenuous hikes on much worse. The hardest part was not being able to jump in the hot tub over at Huckleberry Lodge.

WHEN JAKE WOKE up it was after eight in the evening. He'd practically collapsed after getting into Huckleberry Lodge, and that was following a long sleep in the Jeep while Hannah drove. But at least he'd managed to hike two miles and work for several hours without falling flat on his face.

He rolled over on the sunroom couch, raised himself up on his elbows and looked out the open window. Barbi's car was there, and he saw both women on the deck outside Silver Cottage, talking with a stack of books between them on the patio table. But while he could hear almost everything discussed by Hannah's front door and in the compound between the two buildings, only whispers of sound came from the deck. The acoustics were different there, perhaps because it faced the lake.

Interesting. They were out there two or three times a week, always with books and talking intently. He considered going over to pay Barbi for her shopping and trip to Brendan's home, but she knew he was good for it and he didn't want to intrude.

Jake stretched and decided to go looking for dinner. Hannah had fed him a big lunch, but that had been hours ago and he was hungry again.

Yet as his gaze settled on his knapsack, Jake forgot about food. Some of the old excitement had come back to him while he was photographing the dogwood flowers. It hadn't been quite the same as before the plane crash, but it was something, and he'd relished feeling more like himself again.

Yet also not entirely like himself. He'd been concerned about Hannah's feelings in an unfamiliar way. He never got involved in people's lives, even to a small degree, but when he'd seen that odd look on her face when she learned about Brendan being ill...

Jake shook his head, deciding he was crazy. Making the arrangements for groceries was akin to offering assistance to a village while on his travels. His photography came first, but only a heartless jerk would refuse to pitch in when there was a damaging storm or earthquake. It didn't mean he was getting involved with Hannah.

He fired up his computer and got the SD cards from the cameras. The photographs appeared on the screen and he began evaluating them with a critical eye. Nothing unique, he decided, but a few captured that sense of a shimmering jewel hanging in the middle of a forest.

Jewel.

Jake snorted. The last thing he needed was to adopt Hannah's flights of fancy. He accepted nature for what it was—sometimes hard and cruel, sometimes stunningly beautiful, but all very real. Not that he hadn't encountered mystical and religious beliefs in the cultures he'd been exposed to over the years, but any immortality he might have would come from his photographs.

Yet even as he thought about it, Jake once again clicked on his Arctic folder and looked at the pictures of Gordon. He'd liked Gordon. Though they hadn't known each other for more than a few weeks, he still recalled his conversations with the old bush pilot and the way he could recite limericks and Robert Service's poems by the hour. And the hint of humor when he'd listened to Toby complain...

Jake frowned. Gordon's humor, however subtle, had been missing the day of the crash. Could *that* have been an indication of his approaching heart attack? It was possible there had been other signs as well...signs that were missed. Did that mean one of them should have noticed and insisted they stay in the village that day?

Someone like him, as the leader of the project?

Frustrated, Jake got up and yanked open the refrigerator. Maybe he should just get rid of the shots of Gordon, but the pilot's family might enjoy having the photographs. And he couldn't make crappy memories go away by pushing the delete key.

Jake's good mood crumbled.

Hell, one day of fair photography did *not* mean he'd gotten back on the right track.

CHAPTER TEN

"YOU'RE GOING TO Mount St. Helens with the photographer?" Hannah's father asked on Tuesday evening. "Don't you think that's a lot for one day?"

Hannah's mother had invited her and Danny over for dinner, and she was sitting next to her dad as he repaired a leaky utility sink in the garage.

"I'm just giving Jake Hollister a taste of the Cascades. How much he bites off is up to him."

Daniel Nolan chuckled. "I take it he still annoys you?"

"Sometimes." Yet she shifted uncomfortably, remembering the warmth she'd felt when Jake had kissed her cheek. *Platonically,* no less. "We had a decent outing yesterday, without any major debates, but when I went to clean at the lodge this afternoon, he was in a foul mood again. I think the hike on Monday may have been too much for him. He isn't the type to admit he was in pain, so he acted like a churlish bear."

"Watch it—that's your mother's description of me on a bad day."

"You couldn't come close to this guy. At least he

didn't upset Danny. They got to talking and Jake loosened up enough to tell him about the life cycle of the emperor penguin—apparently when he was nineteen he spent a winter in Antarctica taking pictures of them. I gotta tell you, his stories are a long way from *Happy Feet*."

"Say, that's a cute film."

"Aren't you the one who swore he'd never watch a cartoon?"

"That's before I had a grandson."

"You and Mom are alike." Hannah handed him a pipe wrench. "Why do the rules change for grandchildren?"

"They just do. Like Aunt Elkie used to say, 'load 'em up with sugar and send 'em home.'"

"She did that, didn't she?"

"Like clockwork."

Hannah smiled with the memories. Her great-aunt and uncle had taken the place of the grandparents she'd never known, and they'd spoiled her shamelessly. Funny how things could turn out—her dad had been raised in foster homes and her mom's parents had drowned in India when she was sixteen. Carrie had been sent to live with Elkie and Larry, falling instantly in love with a handsome local high school student named Daniel Nolan.

Her parents' story was probably why Hannah had so fiercely believed she and Collin would have a lifetime together. Carrie and Daniel were proof that sometimes teenagers *did* fall in love forever.

"I guess I can forgive you and Mom for indulging my son," Hannah said, taking a damaged piece of pipe from her father and giving him the replacement length.

Her dad could fix anything. He had the biggest contracting business in Mahalaton Lake, a business that he'd started at the same time he had set up shop as an architect. It had made sense in such a small town, and he liked being sure the best materials and workmanship were going into his building designs. Personally Hannah thought he'd done it out of self-preservation—being inside an office so many hours a day would have driven him crazy.

"Wait until you're a grandmother," he advised. "You'll love it."

"I love being a mom, too. I just hope I'm not making too many mistakes. After all, I'm the only one Danny can blame them on right now," she tried to say lightly.

"Mistakes are normal. Refusing to fix them isn't. I've had to replace a lot of floor joists and subflooring because people ignored a small leak in their toilet."

"Yeah, but what if you don't know there's a leak?"

Her father finished tightening the pipe and sat up. "What's bothering you, sweetheart?"

"Oh…I don't know." Hannah rubbed the back of her neck. She was worried about Danny hearing too many of Jake's tales, yet going overboard trying to stop it could cause problems, too. "Jake's exciting stories are causing sleep issues for Danny. They aren't serious yet, but they're also making him think more about his own father. He imagines that Steven is having the same kind of adventures and wants to go on them, too."

"And you're afraid that when Jake leaves, Danny will be upset, just like when Steven pops in and out."

"Yes."

"Hmm. Have you heard from Steven lately?"

"Not since that visit last fall." Her ex had buzzed in without warning, given Danny a video game and left before his son could get the box open. He hadn't been in the house for ten minutes. If he wasn't willing to be a father, even part-time, why couldn't he simply stay away? It wasn't fair to put Danny through such an emotional roller coaster.

Daniel wiped his hands and got up. "Your ex-husband is an ass, but we already knew that."

Hannah nodded. "*We* know it, but Danny loves him. Then he starts thinking he's done something wrong and that's why Steven doesn't come very often."

"He just loves the idea of having a father like his friends," Daniel said firmly. "How can you love someone you've only seen a few times in your entire life?"

"I don't know, I just don't want him getting hurt worse, and I *don't* want him turning out like Steven."

"Neither do we, sweetie. We'll just have to keep doing our best. Come on, let's go inside. I bet your mother has a cherry cobbler in the oven, and smelling cobbler while it's baking is half the pleasure of eating it."

Some of Hannah's tension eased, and she followed her dad into the house. The days were gone when he could make her problems go away just by being her daddy, but it still made her feel better to talk to him.

THE NEXT MORNING Jake watched Hannah as she drove the connecting roads to Mount St. Helens. After dropping Danny and Badger at her parents' home she'd grown silent and barely looked at him. Obviously she was still unhappy about his behavior the day before.

"All right," he said finally. "I wasn't in the best mood yesterday. I apologize."

"Yeah, well, a sidewinder would have been more pleasant to deal with."

"Uh…sidewinder?" Jake asked cautiously. It sounded familiar, but he couldn't place the name. "I don't know that particular term."

She shook her head. "It isn't a *term,* it's a poisonous snake. You must not have watched very many old Westerns when you were growing up. No wonder you don't know anything about the culture in your own country."

"We've been over this before," Jake protested. "My mother grew up in the U.S. She taught me."

"Okay, let's give you a quiz and see how you do.

What if I say something like, 'I'm releasing the flying monkeys.' What do you think of?"

"Well, in the first place there are no flying monkeys. There are some that *appear* to—"

Hannah made an exasperated sound. "It's a reference to *The Wizard of Oz* and the Wicked Witch of the West. Not an actual movie quote, but the flying monkeys are a big part of the movie."

"Oh." Jake had the feeling Hannah was going to beat him hands down in this game.

"Okay, next. 'Rosebud,'" she said in a low, tortured voice.

"You want flowers?"

"*Citizen Kane,* with Orson Welles. It's a movie supposedly based on William Randolph Hearst's rise to power in the newspaper business."

"Hey, I've heard of both movies."

"But you don't know them. Next one. 'This is what I call a timely interruption.' Uh…never mind, that's from *Captain Blood* and might be too obscure for most people. I know it because my great-aunt loved Errol Flynn and pirate movies."

Hannah was looking much more relaxed and Jake decided to sit back and enjoy himself. "Give me a quote that isn't so hard."

"'We'll always have Paris'?"

"Not a clue."

"*Casablanca.* That one is full of classic dialogue like, 'Louie, I think this is the beginning of a beautiful friendship.'" She was impersonating someone again, and while it sounded familiar, he was still clueless, until all at once it dawned on him.

"Humphrey Bogart," Jake said triumphantly. "I saw *Key Largo* a long time ago. Bogie and Bacall, right? Lauren Bacall has the sexiest voice. Nobody will ever match her."

"Thank you from all the women of the world," Hannah returned drily. "We love having standards we can't possibly live up to."

He grinned. "You started this."

"I suppose. There's a huge movie collection at the lodge. You haven't watched any of it?"

"Television isn't my thing. I don't even have one at my studio in Costa Rica. Before I go out on a location I download a stack of nonfiction books on my eReader. Along with my work, that keeps me pretty busy. And most of the places I've lived don't have television or movie theaters anyway."

"eReader? How do you recharge the battery?" Hannah asked curiously.

"With a handy little solar charger."

"Oh. Well, I approve of reading, but movies are one way to educate yourself about U.S. culture. You should watch some of the old classics...starting with *Casablanca*. I can make a basic list if you want, and I'm sure you can find recommendations on the internet. It's amazing how many things we say or read that have their roots in Hollywood."

Jake wondered how Hannah would react if he suggested she come over for a movie night.

Hannah turned the Jeep into a service station. "We'd better fill up."

"Sure." He took out his credit card and was looking at the instructions on the electronic pay station when Hannah pointed.

"Swipe your card that way through the slot, then follow the instructions on the screen. It'll probably ask for a billing zip code, so if you don't know it, you'll have to go inside and pay."

As they filled the tank, Jake noticed a fresh lattes sign in the window of the small store attached to the service station.

"Now, *there's* something I've noticed everywhere in this state...lattes and espresso. Washingtonians are obsessed with coffee, particularly in Seattle."

Hannah's eyes gleamed. "Yeah, let's get a cup."

"Let's say I watch the films you recommend," Jake said when they'd gotten their coffee and were back on the road. Hannah was sipping a mocha latte and he'd gotten a plain-Jane espresso—so called because he hadn't wanted sugar or special flavorings added. "Won't I sound as stuffy as your boyfriend if I start quoting old movies?"

Hannah's face looked strained again. "Uh...I wouldn't start quoting anything unless you're sure of the context, but wouldn't it be nice to understand some of them? You're right, though. We should add modern stuff—a few Pixar films, two or three kung fu flicks, the Harry Potter movies and *Sex in the City*."

Jake grinned. "Sex in the city? If that's the only place to have sex in this country, I'm going to be very disappointed."

"*Sex in the City* was a cable television series. There are still pop references to it, though it ended years ago."

"Good to know." Jake had enjoyed the game, but his head was starting to reel.

It was dawning on him that while he'd enjoyed a uniquely varied education as a child, he might have missed one or two things. It wasn't just movies or television programming—it was everything, such as fund-raisers and festivals. It was even gas pumps where you could pay your bill without talking to anyone.

All told, he probably hadn't spent more than a day or two at a time in the States in his entire life. And those visits had been rare. How did you catch up on thirty-four years of subtle meanings and references? Not that he needed to, Jake reminded himself hastily. His body was going to heal, and he'd return to doing the work he loved, in places where he loved to do it. And he could have spent his convalescence in Costa Rica or someplace else—it was just because of Matt and Andy that he'd ended up in Washington.

Nevertheless, he *did* feel out of step. It had never seemed to matter anywhere else in the world—he'd traveled to dozens of countries and knew he couldn't expect to understand that many places in depth. On the other hand, he hadn't realized how little he understood the country he'd always claimed as his own.

HANNAH HADN'T EXPECTED to enjoy the drive, considering the mood Jake had been in the previous day, but at the moment it wasn't turning out badly...even though his reminder about Brendan had dropped her stomach for a minute.

"Let's talk about Mount St. Helens," Jake suggested. "I've read about it in one of the books at the lodge. From what I understand, there was a minor eruption in 1980 that took off part of the peak and raised the level of the lake."

"It wasn't minor to the victims who died or their families," Hannah told him, trying not to be offended—there wasn't any point, Jake operated on a different plane than most people.

"Of course not," he agreed hastily.

"The eruption was fairly small from a geologic perspective, which is what the book must have meant," she acknowledged. "I mean, compared to the ancient self-destruction of Mazama that created Crater Lake in Oregon, Mount St. Helens was just a blip. But even so, it leveled thousands of acres of forest and took off more than thirteen hundred feet of the mountain."

"That would have been something to see."

"You mean photograph, don't you?"

"That's what I am—a photographer."

"Yeah, but can't you be *more* than that? I can't

imagine the heartache of watching the eruption and knowing people were dying. No offense, but it seems as if you only see the world through your camera lens."

From the corner of her eye she saw Jake frown, though he didn't respond.

Hannah turned onto forest road 99, explaining that 110,000 acres had been set aside as the Mount St. Helen's National Monument; the land itself was the monument. There was only limited access by car—roads skirted the area without crossing it. They were going to Windy Ridge on the northeast side, but they could return another day if he wanted to see one of the visitor centers or the Johnston Ridge Observatory.

"Some of the downed trees outside the monument have been salvaged for lumber. Then the area was replanted with seedlings," Hannah told him after they'd both been silent for a long while. "But inside the monument, nature is being allowed to take its course. Essentially the entire site is a laboratory where they're studying how nature restores itself."

"Uh-huh." Jake was focused on one of his cameras and Hannah was glad he wasn't watching as she swung around a curve she'd driven numerous times.

"Take a look."

He looked up absently and his eyes widened. The scenery around them had gone from lush forest to the stark, gray-white skeletons of trees. And spreading beyond them to the south and west were tree trunks lying on the ground as if cut down by a scythe and combed straight in patterns mirroring the direction the blast had flowed over the hills.

"When the mountain went it started with a huge avalanche, followed by a lateral pyroclastic flow," she explained, slowing the Jeep to a crawl. "Three hundred and fifty miles an hour, with molten rock and gases that pulverized everything in its path. Farther out, the flow slowed to around two hundred miles an hour, moving over the contours of the land, flattening trees, but not taking them with it."

"What about these?" Jake gestured to the tree skeletons that stood upright.

"This is where the force of the flow lessened and the rocks fell out. The heated gases went up, killing the trees, but not knocking them over. Do you want to stop and take pictures?"

"When we come back. You mentioned having to return by the same road."

"Yup. One way in, one way out. And just a reminder, there's always the chance of another eruption. We've had multiple periods of activity since 1980."

"Hmm." Once again Jake's face was unreadable. "But you brought me here anyway?"

"I checked the internet last night and there haven't been any recent grumbles that concern the scientists, not that you can always predict that sort of thing. The 1980 eruption was far more violent than anyone thought it would be."

JAKE LISTENED, LETTING the information Hannah was relaying run through his mind. She'd probably brought Danny and school groups here, telling them whatever she thought appropriate. Apparently the recovery of the devastated area was occurring more quickly than scientists had ever considered possible.

But life wasn't just creeping in from the edges. Pockets of life had survived in places no one had expected, sometimes protected under heavy snow cover or by the roots of uprooted trees. Gophers, sleeping protected underground at the time of the eruption, had brought up soil and seeds when they'd awakened. Islands of new life were being created by lupine plants, germinating in a hostile environment. Life...persistent, demanding, irrepressible.

Gordon popped into Jake's mind, and he wondered if the old bush pilot would ever stop lingering there. The possibility that he'd failed to recognize the pilot's imminent health crisis was the most disturbing of all. It was bad enough that he'd hired the man, which was what had put him in the plane in the first place.

At the viewpoint Hannah called Windy Ridge, they got out and gazed at the changed landscape, shaped by the explosion and its aftermath.

"This is what it looked like before." Hannah handed him an open book, and Jake stared at the image of a mountain and lake so pristine in their beauty, they hardly looked real.

"It doesn't look like the same place."

"It isn't," she said simply. "The bottom of *this* Spirit Lake is above the surface level of the old lake. A good deal of the missing mountain is down there. The eruption started with an avalanche. A three-hundred-foot wave was pushed ahead of it onto the surrounding mountains before washing back down with trees and debris into the new lake basin."

Spirit Lake.

Great name, he thought, looking at the water, where dead trees still floated on nearly a third of the surface. The shattered volcanic peak above looked as if it had been ripped open by giant, ruthless hands.

"Are you a park ranger, ma'am?" asked someone standing nearby in a group.

Hannah smiled pleasantly. "No, I'm a schoolteacher. Would you like to see some of the pictures I brought?"

They nodded and she passed the book around, telling them tidbits about the volcano as they compared the "before" picture to the changed vista they saw now.

"Hannah, how did it get the name of Spirit Lake?" Jake surprised himself by asking.

"I'm not sure, but there's a legend that a group of Native American fishermen drowned when a storm capsized their canoe. Supposedly the local tribes wouldn't come here after that because a strange moaning used to echo across the water."

"Ooh," one of the women said, shivering in

horrified delight. "I never heard that story and I've lived down in Oregon my whole life."

After they'd gone, Hannah tucked the book beneath her arm. "What are you thinking, Jake?"

"I'm wondering why you chose to bring me here."

"You mean because the volcano isn't as pretty as dogwood and rounded snowcapped summits?" She looked out at the slopes of the shattered peak. "This is part of what makes the Cascades. You can feel the mountains here, growing and changing. They're alive, just in a different way than we are."

His jaw tight, Jake prowled up and down the view point, trying to evaluate camera angles. "Can that part of volcano be climbed?" he asked, pointing to the area above the lake water.

"No, only the southern flank. I've done it. You can get to the top and back in a day. And they've opened a few other trails through the monument."

He was glad she hadn't pointed out that he wouldn't be mountain climbing for a while, *or* attempting any strenuous hiking trails through a hazardous area.

As for the volcanic monument, he'd have to see more from the other access points before he could decide how to photograph it. Some of his more powerful lenses would be needed to shoot places that couldn't be reached on foot. That was, *if* he included Mount St. Helens in his book. It would depend on whether he could get any photos that satisfied him.

Jake shot a quick look at Hannah as she talked

to a young couple who'd arrived a few minutes before. She loved her mountains, and he realized he should be listening...not so much for the information, but for her feelings and the way *she* saw the land around them.

It was an unsettling notion because he wasn't comfortable needing anyone from a creative standpoint. Or from any standpoint, for that matter.

"Where can we dig to find Mount St. Helens emeralds?" the woman asked as Jake stepped closer.

A pained expression crossed Hannah's face. "The emeralds are manufactured—they weren't formed by the volcano."

"We thought they blew out of the mountain when it erupted," the young man explained.

"No, though they're made with a small amount of ash collected outside the monument. Everything within the boundaries is protected, so even if there *were* emeralds here, you couldn't take them."

"Oh." The woman wrinkled her nose and looked at her companion. "Honey, if we leave now, we'll probably have time to go shopping at those factory-outlet places we saw on the freeway."

"I don't know if any of the outlet stores carry Mount St. Helens emeralds," Hannah warned quickly.

"No worries. Give me the Gap and I'm happy."

Hannah didn't say anything until they'd gotten in their bright red SUV and driven away.

"Okay, they may have watched a few *too* many

movies," she admitted, "though I can't think of any films where a volcano spits out gemstones. I wonder if they thought the emeralds were already cut and ready to be set in jewelry."

"It almost sounded like it."

"Well, I'll wait in the Jeep and read while you take pictures. I brought lunch, so let me know when you're hungry."

"Sure." Jake watched as she walked to the Jeep and got in.

He was already hungry, just not for food. The memory of telling Hannah about his opinions on marriage came back to him, and he sighed. While he hadn't consciously warned her off, it had probably been a *subconscious* warning. It was risky to be attracted to a woman the way he was attracted to Hannah, and working together was just making it worse.

Frustrated, he lifted his camera and began shooting a series of photos that weren't intended as art, but to help him plan and make decisions.

There *was* something evocative about the wreckage around him, triggering sensations he couldn't define. The land had been stripped naked—every rock, every hillock and small valley, every scar still revealed. But it wasn't the first time it had happened in the long geologic history of the mountains, and it wouldn't be the last.

How can you take the best photographs if you don't see the soul beyond the beauty?

Hannah's question echoed in Jake's mind, and he felt his jaw tighten. But it wasn't the criticism of his work that bothered him. She obviously operated from an emotional level, while he approached life analytically. Yet often there was an expression in her eyes, as if she knew something he didn't... which was a ridiculous thought.

He'd experienced dozens of cultures in his childhood, but Josie had made sure he didn't get caught up in their spiritual beliefs. It was understandable; while Josie had told him little about her childhood, he knew her parents had been religiously hidebound people who'd cared more about their moral principles than her well-being.

Forget it, he ordered. His art was the important thing.

Jake's camera pack was on his shoulder and he put a more powerful lens on than the one he'd been using. It was a toy compared to others he used, but still dramatically magnified the broken mountain peak.

There was a wisp of steam or smoke rising around the new cinder cone that was building in the center. The foundation of Mount St. Helens already lay on an older volcano, and one day this new one would probably rest on both.

Jake snapped several pictures and looked back down at Spirit Lake. As he stared, he thought he heard a few haunting chords of music, like a low moaning.

What the hell?

There were ancient stories everywhere he went, and while their roots might be based in historical fact, the myths accompanying them were not. Another low note sounded, and Jake looked back at the Jeep.

Hannah's head was bent over, though she frequently raised it and looked out at the mountain. He strode to the Jeep and opened the door. Soft flute music was coming from the SUV's speakers; the sounds he'd heard must have been the result of some odd trick of acoustics.

"Is something wrong?" Hannah asked, retrieving the paperback book she'd dropped out of surprise.

"Nothing. That is, I could hear the music. A little of it, at least."

"This CD is by one of my favorite musicians, R. Carlos Nakai. I heard someone playing a Native American flute up here when I was a teenager. But it wasn't for money or to entertain visitors—he said it was a song of healing for the land. Ever since then, I've tried to play something similar when I visit."

The muscles in his jaw tightened. "Do you honestly believe that stuff?"

"I'd rather believe in something than have nothing to hold on to." Her gaze was sad when she looked at him. "You've seen some of the most beautiful places in the world, Jake. How can you not believe in something greater than yourself when you see mountains falling away from you like waves, or trees that were already old when Charlemagne ruled France?"

"Why does it matter to you?"

"Because you remind me of someone I knew who died, terrified and certain that it was the absolute end. The strange thing was that Collin constantly courted death, even though he believed there was nothing but a blank void on the other side." Her voice caught.

"You're talking about your friend who died in the mountain-climbing accident."

"Yes."

"And you loved him."

"As much as a seventeen-year-old girl can love a boy."

Hell. He had never known a woman long enough to hear the details of her first love, and Hannah's story had ended far more tragically than most. No wonder she was so sensitive about people taking what she considered foolish risks.

"Losing him like that must have been awful," Jake said awkwardly. "Is that why you're so protective of Danny?"

"I'm protective of Danny because I'm his mother. Um, don't you have some pictures to take?"

Plainly, Hannah didn't want to talk any longer, which was fine with Jake. Death wasn't the most comfortable subject for someone who'd recently come close to dying himself.

"Yeah. But could you turn the music off? It's distracting."

"I don't see how you heard it out there, but I'll use headphones."

"Thanks."

Jake walked away, wondering what it was about Hannah that challenged him at every turn. He'd thought he had her figured out as just another bitter divorcée, but she was far more complicated.

At least he'd discovered where the music was coming from. But an hour later, at the far end of the parking lot, a few strains of eerie, haunting music sounded again in Jake's ear. He whirled around. A number of cars had come and gone, but they were alone again, and he was certain those notes couldn't have come from Hannah's headphones.

He pressed a finger to his temple. If he said something, she'd probably just remind him of the legend of Spirit Lake and the lost canoe of fishermen. Or maybe she'd claim it was the echo of the Native American flute music she had heard years ago… that it was the musician's healing song, lingering on the land.

But no matter how intriguing that sounded, it wasn't either one.

The musical notes were just his imagination— everyone had one, though his might be a little stunted. After all, what child needed an imagination when their playpen was an African savannah or the windswept reaches of the Himalayas?

CHAPTER ELEVEN

HANNAH TURNED THE pages of her novel, trying to focus on the plot rather than Jake Hollister. It was difficult to keep up with new releases and she was years behind.

On the other hand, she could recite almost everything from Dr. Seuss and *Where the Wild Things Are,* courtesy of bedtime reading with Danny. It was doubtful that Jake knew anything about the silly, fun Seuss rhymes with their clever bits of wisdom for children and adults alike.

Sighing, she looked up.

Jake was some distance away, shooting pictures of Mount St. Helens, but it wasn't with the same intensity he'd taken the photos of the dogwood blossoms. It didn't surprise her. People either understood what was special about the volcano, or they took a snapshot and hurried on to visit the Seattle Space Needle or see the majesty of Mount Rainier...or in some cases, to visit the Gap.

Not that Hannah didn't love Mount Rainier. It was the king of the Cascades, so beautiful it was almost unearthly, surrounded by flowered meadows and ancient forests. She'd picked huckleberries on its lower slopes, taken the rigorous trek to its summit as a teenager and explored miles and miles of its trails.

Each peak in the mountain range had its own beauty, even the ravaged form of Mount St. Helens. And it was a reminder of the volcanic roots of the mountains, a stark reminder of nature's power.

Usually the vast grandeur made her problems seem less significant, but today Hannah couldn't get Brendan out of her mind for more than a few minutes.

Sighing, she put her book down and took out her cell phone. She couldn't delay talking to Brendan forever, and unpleasant tasks just got harder the longer they were put off.

"Townsend Law Office," the secretary answered.

"Hi, Renee, it's Hannah Nolan. Is Brendan available?"

"Sure, his appointment just left."

"Hannah," Brendan exclaimed a moment later. "I'm glad you called. I feel terrible about Sunday—I don't know what came over me. And then you were still so nice to have Barbi come over to help when I was sick."

"Uh, yeah. Are you available for lunch tomorrow? We should talk."

A short silence followed. "That sounds ominous. Why don't you go ahead and say what you want to say right now?"

Hannah squirmed. "If that's what you prefer. The

thing is, the more we get to know each other, the fewer things we seem to have in common."

"If this is about hiking and wild berries and such, I can learn."

"But you're not interested in it. And it's not only that. You're a great guy, you just aren't the right one for me, and I would hate for you to develop expectations that aren't going anywhere."

There was a second silence, much longer this time.

"Are you sure?" he asked finally.

"Yes. I'd like to stay friends, but I'll understand if you don't feel the same."

"Of course I want to be friends. But…uh, I'd better go now. I have another client coming in. Goodbye," Brendan said quickly, then disconnected.

As Hannah dropped her phone in her backpack, she wished he'd gotten angry. But he was too much of a gentleman. Now she felt guilty for letting things drag on when in her heart of hearts she'd known for weeks that nothing could happen between them. There should have been *some* excitement when she saw Brendan…a little tingle when he kissed her, with the promise of more to develop. Instead everything had remained very polite and cordial.

Hannah got out of the Jeep and stretched.

It was late in the morning now, and the number of cars in the Windy Ridge parking area had increased. A park ranger had arrived as well and was talking to a group. Normally she'd hurry over to hear anything new there was to learn, but she was too edgy.

Jake turned around as she approached.

"Hi. Are you getting hungry?" she asked. "It's been hours since breakfast."

"I could eat."

Because of the cool breeze, they sat in the Jeep. Hannah hadn't expected to go hiking today, so she'd prepared an old-fashioned picnic with fried chicken and potato salad.

"This is really good," Jake said as he ate. He'd sniffed the potato salad suspiciously—apparently never having tasted it before—eaten a tentative bite and was now wolfing it down. In Hannah's world, potato salad wasn't exotic, but exotic was really a matter of perspective. "By the way, I'll have my business manager reimburse you for the meals. I didn't think about food for these trips."

"No need. I have to eat, too, and I made enough for my parents and Danny."

"I usually just have trail mix when I'm working."

"That's what I figured." Hannah wiped her hands on a napkin. She handed him a container of brownies and peeled a banana for herself.

Jake ate a brownie, reminding her of a little boy as he licked a streak of chocolate frosting from his finger.

"I've been thinking," he said, taking a second brownie. "Since climbing isn't allowed on this side of the volcano, I'll have to bring specialized equipment to take some of the pictures here. So if you want to head back to Mahalaton Lake, it's fine with me. I'll shoot placeholder photos as we drive."

"I don't mind pulling over whenever you want, but what do you mean by placeholder?"

"That's just what I call them. Basically, they're general location photos that don't aim for high quality, but help me plan an extended day of shooting. I can come back on a weekend when you're at one of your community events."

"In that case, I'll leave my maps in the Jeep." She always carried a full set of maps in case there was a road problem and she needed an alternate route. The GPS on her smartphone was a great tool, but it was nice to look at a map and get a mental picture of where she needed to go.

"Thanks."

Hannah tucked the food containers away and drove out of the parking lot, going well below the speed limit so Jake could get the pictures he'd planned.

When he'd finally settled back and was dealing with the SD cards, she glanced at him. "I've been wondering if you're getting the pictures you want. I mean, with me needing to leave by a certain time to be home for Danny. If this isn't working out the way you want, we can always quit."

"What do you mean?"

"You, me…going on these outings together. And just so you know, there *are* professional guides available in Mahalaton Lake. They take groups into the back country in all seasons of the year."

"Why would I want to stop going with you?"

Hannah shrugged and concentrated on driving. It was Jake Hollister's business how he spent his money, and all the fees he was paying were putting her way ahead on her finances.

THAT EVENING HANNAH sat in the kitchen, talking on the phone to Wendy Schell, who was vice president of the Mahalaton Lake Fire Department auxiliary. A water pipe had broken at the church where the MLFD's annual pancake supper was traditionally served, and anyone would have thought the world was coming to an end. Wendy had a talent for overreacting.

"Wendy, one of my dad's construction crews is at the church right now doing the repairs. It's going to be all right," she said for the third time.

"But I saw how much water there was, and the dinner is just three days away. We've got signs and flyers all over town. I don't see how we can change locations," Wendy wailed.

"Dad said everything will be back to normal sometime tomorrow."

"But there'll be damage to the floor."

"Nope, Dad says it shouldn't be a problem."

"But—"

"No buts," Hannah cut her off hastily. *"It's fine."*

Though she was a member of the MLFD auxiliary, she wasn't on the committee for their monthly suppers. But Gwen was away visiting her family for a few days and had told Wendy to call Hannah's cell "if anything comes up."

"All right," Wendy said, though obviously reluctant to let the subject go. "You're such a dear. I don't know what I would have done without you."

Hannah bit her lip to keep from saying something inappropriate. "You would have managed. I'll talk to you tomorrow."

She disconnected before the other woman could rev herself up again. Wendy was in her sixties, widowed with no children and hungry to feel needed. Most people in Mahalaton Lake tried to be understanding of her desperate desire for attention, but it could be difficult to deal with nonetheless.

Rubbing the tight muscles at the back of her neck, Hannah checked on Danny. He was sound asleep with Badger lying at the foot of the bed.

"Stay, boy," she whispered when the retriever lifted his head.

Putting the cell in her pocket, she went across the yard to Huckleberry Lodge. She wouldn't feel comfortable about going anywhere with Jake until Wendy was convinced there was no more drama to milk from the situation…or until Gwen got home, which was supposed to be by early afternoon the next day.

Yet even as the thought came, Hannah scolded herself. Wendy wasn't a bad person, she was just insecure.

Hannah knocked and waited, but didn't get a response. She was halfway back to Silver Cottage to write a note when she heard Jake's voice.

"Hannah, is something wrong?"

She turned around.

Lord, he was only wearing a towel wrapped around his hips. Her stomach instantly clenched with awareness. "Uh, not really, but I need to cancel our plans for tomorrow."

"You sound tense. Come in for a minute while I dry off. I was in the hot tub." He disappeared back into the lodge without giving her a chance to refuse.

Hannah sat on the living room couch and tried not to think about how tempting Jake's bare chest had looked in the sunset. She didn't actually *know* he hadn't been wearing anything beneath the towel. On the other hand, the deck off the master bedroom was private enough for nude hot-tubbing, and with his background, Jake wasn't likely hung up on modesty.

It was a tantalizing thought and much easier than thinking about the calls she'd probably get in the morning from Wendy. It was too bad she'd never felt the same tingle from imagining Brendan nude in a hot tub...or any other place. Jake just had a natural zing, the kind that made women do irrational things.

"Hey." Jake eased onto the couch next to her, now

fully covered by drawstring sweatpants and a faded University of Washington Huskies T-shirt.

Hannah raised an eyebrow. "I wouldn't have taken you for a football fan."

"I'm not. My brother's wife thought I should have comfortable things to wear while I was recovering, so she raided his closet."

"That was nice of her. Didn't he mind?"

"I don't think Matt minds anything Layne does." Jake sounded slightly baffled by his brother's attitude, but Hannah thought it was endearing.

"So what's happened about tomorrow?" Jake asked.

"It's a long story and not very interesting. By the way, I'm sorry I brought up my old boyfriend again. I could tell it bothered you."

"That's all right. I deserved it after being such a grouch yesterday. You got to me with that flute thing, too."

"What bothered you about it?" she asked.

He shrugged. "It's the way I was raised. That stuff about a healing song for a land sounds nice, but I don't believe in that sort of thing and it gets awkward. Do *you* believe the land can be healed with music?"

"I don't dismiss the possibility. And there's something about Native American flute music that reaches inside a person."

"True." Yet Jake almost looked angry, and she sighed. Apparently she was right; he had a whole lot of demons to work out. Maybe it was natural to start questioning your life and the meaning of everything after almost dying.

The cell phone in her pocket rang and she pulled it out, expecting to see Wendy's name on the screen, but it showed D. Nolan. "Hey, Dad, how's it going?"

"We just finished. There wasn't that much water, so everything should dry quickly."

"I figured Wendy was exaggerating. You'd better get home before she shows up and has another meltdown. Oh, and thank Mom again for watching Danny for me today."

"Will do. Sleep well, sweetheart."

Hannah put the phone back in her pocket and looked at Jake.

"Was that the problem with tomorrow getting worked out?" he asked.

"A lot of it. The annoying part is still there."

"That's too bad."

He stroked her hair, an intense, yearning expression on his face, and warmth curled through her body. Without thinking, she leaned forward and kissed him.

JAKE DREW A swift breath and cupped Hannah's jaw, savoring the taste of her mouth.

There was little softness in the places where he'd grown up, often in remote campsites, or when it was feasible, staying with a willing villager. Josie had always been proud that she had made it in a hard world that most men couldn't handle, and she'd taught him to be self-reliant. But he had to admit, there was something to be said for hot tubs and women with skin like silk.

And Hannah smelled wonderful. He'd noticed it before, but close up, her sweet scent was intoxicating.

The soft leather cushions of the couch whispered beneath them as he pulled her to him, stroking his tongue into her mouth. Hannah was clouding his thoughts, making it hard to be logical and think about anything except sex...and the thought of sex with her made him dizzy.

Hell, he'd had his share of women. It was amazing how many of them wanted to sleep with someone who had a small amount of fame and a whole lot of money. Finding a temporary partner was never a problem when he was through with one of his projects. But Hannah wasn't like the women who were dazzled by his reputation and money, which made the idea of being with her that much more appealing. *And dangerous*. He didn't want to hurt her any more than he was willing to give up the life he'd chosen.

Hannah's hands skimmed around his waist and under his T-shirt. Her fingers splayed wide on the bare skin beneath and he groaned.

Telling himself he shouldn't—that he *really* shouldn't—he traced the shape of her breasts and teased her nipples, even as he deepened the kiss.

Tasting, searching, the demands of his body out-weighing the cool logic in his brain.

All at once Hannah's hands were no longer under his shirt. They were pressed against his shoulders.

Reluctantly, with his senses demanding he continue what they'd started, he lifted his head.

"I need to get back to Danny," she said, her voice sounding almost normal. "I don't want him to wake up and be alone."

Danny. Her kid. Right.

"No problem."

Jake eased away, hoping she wouldn't look down. The sweatpants he was wearing would do nothing to hide his arousal, and while he wasn't ashamed of it, they *were* planning several overnight trips around the state. From what he'd seen, Hannah had excellent survival skills. If she thought she'd have to fend off unwelcome advances, she'd probably tell him to find someone else to take him around the Cascades.

But he didn't *want* someone else to do it—he wanted Hannah. The way she talked about the mountains of her childhood...he still didn't know if looking through her eyes was the answer to his lack of artistic inspiration, but it was a damn sight better than not trying anything at all.

Hannah left quickly and Jake let out a heavy breath, coming to an unsurprising conclusion—however much fun it was to tease Hannah, kissing her was much more fun.

HANNAH SPENT A sleepless night. What had possessed her to kiss Jake? And she couldn't fool herself; she'd initiated the kiss…one that had become far hotter than anything she'd shared with Brendan.

Obviously, she hadn't resolved her weakness for restless men with intimacy and commitment issues.

The sun was rising as Hannah went out on the porch and tried to concentrate on yoga, wishing she had her mother's focus. Then she might be able to get the opposite sex out of her mind altogether.

The poignant cry of a loon rippled across the water, and it was still so rare to hear one, Hannah stopped chanting and listened. Loons had almost vanished from Mahala Lake after speedboats were allowed, but several nesting pairs had returned after strict rules were introduced regarding where and when the boats could be used. Now all was peaceful again.

Except for Jake Hollister.

Hannah tried to focus, but after a half hour she gave up and sat gazing at the lake. It was a typical mountain summer morning, cold enough to make a jacket welcome, yet already showing signs of a warm day ahead.

She glanced at Huckleberry Lodge. Simple kisses shouldn't warrant sleepless night or major soul-searching. She wasn't sixteen any longer and trying to figure out who she was and where she fit in the world. Yet here she was, still thinking about it.

She'd slipped because of the expression on Jake's

face, Hannah decided—that melancholy, lonely expression that suggested he was more than just a pompous genius with a camera. She couldn't imagine what it must have been like growing up without a stable home, wandering from country to country, never really being part of anything...just observing it. What she should remember was that Jake had chosen to maintain that life after becoming an adult, so he couldn't have found it that difficult.

Gritting her teeth, Hannah got up and went inside.

She refused to let her heart get broken by another man who wasn't going to stay put. Even more important, she couldn't let Danny get hurt. It was rough enough having a father who didn't care. He didn't need Jake Hollister breezing in and out of his life like a kamikaze moth. Besides, if Jake did have a death wish, he would be the *last* role model she wanted for her son.

In the kitchen she saw the clock click over to seven o'clock, and almost at the same instant, her cell phone rang.

"Hello, Wendy," she answered, resigned.

"I know it's early, Hannah, but have you talked to your father about the repairs? I thought we could go over to assess the damage together."

"I meant to call last night, but something came up. The repairs are done and Dad said there wasn't much water, so there's no damage to assess. We're all set for Saturday."

"Oh."

"Gotta go," Hannah said brightly. "Remember, Gwen will be back this afternoon. *Bye*."

She sagged against the counter as Badger padded around the corner, his tail waving gently.

"Hi, boy."

Danny appeared next, sleepily rubbing his eyes. "Mommy, I like going to Grandma's, but can't I go with you and Jake today?" He sat on a chair in the breakfast nook, yawning.

"We aren't going after all. I may need to do some work for the pancake supper."

"I looove pancakes for breakfast, too." Danny looked at her hopefully.

"Me, too. But why don't we have French toast this morning since we're eating pancakes on Saturday?"

"Yummy."

Hannah grinned. French toast was their special Sunday breakfast, so getting it during the week was a treat. She got out the ingredients while Danny put a coat over his pj's and took Badger outside to play fetch.

Twenty minutes later she was getting ready to call him back inside when the door opened.

"Mommy, Jake says he never ate French toast before."

Hannah spun around and saw Jake standing ten feet away, still wearing his old sweatpants and Huskies T-shirt.

"I'm *sure* you've eaten French toast," she said firmly.

"No, never. I've had toast in France, of course,

but Danny tells me it isn't the same thing." There was a hint of laughter in his face and she glared. Clearly everything was back to normal as far as *he* was concerned.

Danny took off his jacket and dragged Jake to the breakfast nook table. "He can have some of mine."

Yeah, right. Hannah piled the golden slices of French toast on plates and put them in front of Jake and her son.

"You put butter all over and stick your fork in a bunch of places so it gets in the holes. That's maple syrup, and that's huckleberry," Danny explained, pointing to the two steaming pitchers she'd put on the table. "Mommy made it, but *I* helped pick the berries." He busily began jabbing his toast with his fork.

"I've never had huckleberry syrup, either." Jake poured a small amount over a forkful of French toast and popped it into his mouth. "Wow."

"Some people think huckleberries are the best berries in the world," Hannah said. She poured another glass of orange juice and put it on the table, along with a cup of coffee.

"You'll have to show them to me. Photos of indigenous food sources might be interesting for the book."

She smiled tightly. Things were getting complicated. On one hand, Jake was paying her to show him the Cascades, and she really wanted to convince him how wonderful they were. On the other hand, she'd kissed him and she couldn't pretend it was a platonic thank-you kiss like the one he'd planted on *her* cheek.

"I can show you huckleberries," Danny offered. "Wanna go after breakfast?"

"Sure, and I'll tell you about the grizzly bears I photographed in Canada. They like berries, though they're meat eaters, too. I've seen claw marks on trees that were twice as high as my head. Their claws are *huge*—longer than your fingers and really powerful." Jake spread his fingers and made a slashing motion through the air.

"Whoa." Danny's eyes were as round as saucers and he seemed barely aware of the French toast he was shoving in his mouth.

"We'll *all* go to see a huckleberry patch," Hannah said hastily, reminded for the umpteenth time that Jake's stories weren't the kind of tales she wanted her son hearing. She *especially* didn't like him hearing them when she wasn't around to put brakes on the gory details. And it wouldn't do any good to tell Danny that his father wasn't having those kinds of adventures, or that if he was, it was probably at someone else's expense.

Jake cocked his head at her. "I thought you couldn't go anywhere."

"I just need to be available *in case* something happens, so I can't go far. The vice president of the fire department auxiliary is very…" She shot a look at Danny, knowing anything she said about Wendy could be innocently repeated. "Um, she's very concerned because we had a broken pipe last night at the church where the pancake supper is being held on Saturday."

Hannah cracked more eggs into a bowl and whisked in sugar and cream before dropping several slices of bread into the frothy mixture.

"Why isn't it the vice president's problem?"

"That's the way things work in Mahalaton Lake. My dad is a contractor and he got called to do the repairs. I'm acting as liaison because Wendy is... excitable."

"Oh. I get it."

"Grandpa builds stuff," Danny said. "I have a fort and a tree house with real water over at Grandma and Grandpa's."

"Real water?"

"He means *running* water," Hannah clarified. She forked eight slices of egg-drenched bread onto the griddle to cook. "Dad installed a small faucet and drain in both the tree house and fort, which also has a fireplace, electricity and half bath."

"Really roughing it, huh?"

"It's useful for Cub Scouts meetings. You only saw the front of my parents' house when we dropped Danny off yesterday, but they have a good piece of land in the back. The south lake trail ends at their place—by road it's four miles, but only two on foot."

"Mommy can walk there, but my legs aren't long

enough," Danny added. "Do you wanna go to the pancake supper with us, Jake? The firemen make pancakes as big as my head."

Hannah flipped the French toast on the griddle, fairly confident Jake would turn down the invitation. It was unsettling having him in her kitchen, looking so sleepy and gorgeous, but she was trying to act normal.

"As big as your head? Uh, sure, that sounds like fun."

She gripped the handle of her spatula and turned around, trying not to show her disbelief. *Fun?* Jake had come to the ice cream social, and then spent the entire time with a camera up to his eyes. That wasn't fun—that was someone who needed a barrier between himself and the rest of the world.

Jake grinned as if reading her mind. "It'll be a cultural experience—not that I really need one. I presume it's another fund-raiser."

"The volunteer firemen do a supper every month—spaghetti, chicken pot pie, chili, that sort of stuff." Hannah dropped several more slices of French toast on his plate and another on Danny's, then sat down with a couple for herself. "Some of them are also on the rescue squad."

"Is that staffed by volunteers, too?"

"Yes. We have a handful of professional firefighters, but no budget for a specially trained rescue squad. Our head of emergency services is an expert climber, though, and a helicopter pilot. I'm not sure how, but Randy talked the ski lodge into donating a helicopter to the town a few years ago."

"Altruism?"

"Possibly. Or motivated self-interest. Their promotional materials talk about Mahalaton Lake's 'superior emergency services.'"

"Sounds as if you've had something to do with them being superior," Jake commented.

Hannah shrugged and swallowed some coffee, hoping the caffeine would kick-start her brain. If she'd been thinking clearly, she might have been able to head off Danny's invitation to the pancake supper. Now Jake would tell him about grizzly bears with scimitar claws and the ability to leap over tall pine trees in a single bound...at least that was how Danny would probably hear it.

She wasn't sure what to think. Since meeting Jake, Danny was having some bad dreams and wanted to sleep with the lights on, which was no surprise considering the excitement level of their neighbor's stories. But it wasn't unusual for children to have a little trouble adjusting to something new. It didn't mean they shouldn't experience new things. She was protective, but not *that* protective.

Jake Hollister was an opportunity for Danny to hear firsthand about places and things he'd probably never see for himself. It didn't necessarily mean Danny would take after his father.

JAKE CAREFULLY MOPPED up the remaining syrup on his plate with the last of his French toast. He hadn't been able to resist Danny's description of the breakfast his mom was preparing. And the huckleberry syrup was every bit as delicious as the kid had said.

He was even more impressed when Hannah and Danny led him to a huckleberry patch an hour later. The berries, mostly located on the underside of the branches, were tiny. Unless they grew to five times their current size, they'd be a major pain to pick.

"How much bigger do they get?" he asked.

"A few get to the size of small blueberries, but mostly they're smaller than a pea. And since they ripen over a long period of time, green berries will be mixed with ripe ones. There should be a few early ones ripe now." Hannah bent and searched and after a minute held out her hand—five small, purple berries rested on her palm. "Try them."

Jake popped the berries in his mouth and a sweet tangy flavor spread across his tongue. "I've tasted wild berries all over the world, and those have to be the best."

"And there are blossoms on the same bush where I found the ripe berries."

He bent and peered at the branches. A delicate, pale pink lantern-like blossom was hanging in a cluster of the green berries. "How many does it take to make a bottle of syrup?"

"A fair amount. I make jam and syrup when I pick

them, but also keep bags of berries in the freezer for homemade ice cream and baking."

Jake searched among the bushes, then lay down on the ground and focused his camera up into the branches. Photographing flowers and berries was hardly his forte, but at the moment he couldn't trek into the wilder parts of the Cascades. He needed to take advantage of the images he *could* capture.

With an effort, he shut his mind to everything except the delicate blossoms, hanging together with both green and purple berries. And the taste of them, rich and bursting with flavor...and the promise of becoming syrup poured over French toast.

That was what he needed to capture—the story behind the blossom. It was a new thing for him, and he wondered if that was partly what Hannah had meant when she'd talked about seeing the soul behind the beauty. Places and things didn't have souls...but they *did* have stories.

CHAPTER TWELVE

BRENDAN STOPPED BY Luigi's late Saturday afternoon to thank Barbi for coming over when he was sick.

"Ciao," Luigi greeted him. "Do you need a menu?"

"I'm just here to see Barbi."

"Barbara is in the dining room."

The restaurant was divided into two parts, one side being more like a traditional pizza parlor and the other providing a more elegant atmosphere. Brendan stepped into the Tuscan-style dining room and saw Barbi setting out silverware on the tablecloths. She seemed astonished to see him...probably as astonished as *he'd* been when she showed up at his door.

"Yeah, Brendan?"

"I want to thank you again for coming over when I was sick. It was a really decent thing to do."

She plunked down a saltshaker. "Don't sound so surprised. Besides, I told you it was for Hannah, 'cause she was out of town."

"But I still appreciate it. And then you did my laundry...though, well, I'm not sure why."

"You were sick." Barbi stuck her chin out as if daring him to question it further.

Brendan nearly smiled. He'd been sick, all right. Positively disgusting. There weren't too many women who would have stuck around him in such a mess, tidying up and making sure he had fresh towels and sheets.

"Barbara," Luigi said from the door. "That pizza is ready to deliver."

She hurried past Brendan without looking at him again, and he caught the whiff of a light, fresh fragrance. It was nice. Heavy scents gave him a headache. One of the first things he'd noticed about Hannah was that she didn't wear much perfume, either.

Not that it mattered now that she'd broken things off with him. If only he could talk to her about it, maybe he could change her mind.

"Is there anything else, Mr. Townsend?" Luigi asked when they were alone.

Brendan shook his head. "Sorry, but I'm eating at the pancake supper tonight."

"It is for a very good cause."

"I imagine it hurts your business when there's a community dinner on a Saturday."

The restaurateur made a dismissive gesture. "We'll have a light night, and get more business than usual tomorrow. At least for pizza. And if not, there is always the next day."

Brendan left, thinking again about the difference between Mahalaton Lake and the city. He couldn't imagine a businessperson in Seattle or Boston being so philosophical about lost trade.

The pancake supper was being hosted by the Grace Community Church, and the parking lot was partially filled when he arrived. He'd intended to call David Walther and suggest they go together, but having the flu had put him behind at the office. Ironically, it had been one of his busiest weeks legally.

He paid for his meal and added an extra donation, then stood to one side, thinking it was too bad Barbi couldn't be there. He'd attended several of the town's events over the past fourteen months and usually saw her there, as well. Sometimes it seemed as if he'd been in Mahalaton Lake forever, and sometimes it was as if he'd only just moved. One thing was sure, though, the dreams he had about Maria in Seattle, the ones with her telling him to come here, had never returned. He didn't know what to make of those dreams, even though they'd changed the course of his life.

"Hello, Mr. Townsend," said Cora Baldwin. She was married to one of his clients, and she gestured to a table along the wall where a line of men were poised with electric griddles, pitchers of pancake batter and spatulas. "The start of the line is over there. It's all-you-can-eat, so enjoy."

"Thanks, Cora. But please call me Brendan." Even after living here for over a year, he had the worst time getting people to use his first name. Doctors, pastors and even the mayor seemed to be addressed informally...everybody except him.

Cora smiled pleasantly as she walked away, but he had a dismal conviction he'd remain "Mr. Townsend" to her. Was it because he hadn't been born in Mahalaton Lake and still didn't quite belong? Glancing down, Brendan assessed his appearance...suit, vest, tie, shoes shined appropriately. Very proper, the way he'd been taught to dress in a family conscious of its public image in Boston. Of course, he wasn't *in* Boston, as Barbi had once pointed out.

Still mulling it over in his head, he looked around to see if there was anyone else he could sit with... and saw Hannah arrive with Danny and her parents, along with Jake Hollister.

He sighed. If Hollister hadn't been there, he might have tried to talk to her again, but not under these circumstances.

HANNAH GOT INTO the food line with her parents, Danny and Jake and watched the fireman cook their pancakes. Half the fun of the supper was seeing the guys in their aprons and hats, expertly making large, fluffy pancakes on the electric griddles. Several could even flip them high in the air.

"Isn't Brendan eating with us?" her mother asked in a low voice, looking across the social hall.

"No." Hannah's tone didn't invite further discussion. She'd broken up with Brendan because he was the wrong man for her, but she didn't want Jake to start imagining he'd had anything to do with it... especially after that kiss. Next thing she knew he'd be warning her off again.

"I see."

"Here you go, Hannah." Randy Westfield handed her a plate at the same time her family and Jake were getting theirs. "Be sure to come back for more."

"Thanks. Is Gwen around?"

"She's probably in the kitchen with Wendy."

"How is Wendy doing?"

Randy's face looked pained. "The same as usual."

"That bad, huh?" Hannah gave him a sympathetic smile and went over to sit next to Danny. Across the table, Jake appeared uneasy. While he had a plate of pancakes in front of him, his camera was around his neck, and as she watched, he lifted it to look through the viewfinder.

"You might want to put that away, at least until after you eat," she advised. "You don't want to get syrup on your equipment."

"Oh, yes," Carrie added. "Somehow it ends up on everything."

Jake hastily tucked the camera in his bag—his professional equipment was probably more important to him than breathing.

Hannah smiled determinedly. She loved the department's monthly suppers. They'd been part of her childhood, and she wanted them to be fond memories for her son, as well.

BRENDAN SIGHED AS he looked at Hannah tucking a napkin under Danny's chin. He'd really blown things with her and didn't know if there was any hope of fixing it. Perhaps he should just leave and get a meal elsewhere.

"Ready to eat?"

Startled, Brendan looked down and saw Barbi Paulson. She put her arm in his, and it felt good not to be standing alone like an awkward dodo bird.

"I thought you were working."

"Luigi always gives me time to come over and eat at the MLFD suppers."

"That's nice."

"Did you have a fight with Hannah?" she asked, looking over to where the Nolans and Jake Hollister were sitting.

"You could say that. I did something dumb at the ice cream social," he found himself admitting. It was more than that, but being an ass that day couldn't have helped.

"I'm sure she'll forgive you," Barbi assured him. "Let's get our pancakes."

Since it was early, there still wasn't a line at the cook table. The firemen teased Barbi when she wanted a pile of silver dollar-size pancakes, but it was friendly banter, rather than flirting.

"Three regular cakes," Brendan said when asked.

But the cakes weren't "regular"—they were thick and fluffy and wider than tortillas.

Barbi led the way to the opposite side of the social hall from where Hannah was sitting with her family. Butter and syrup sat on each table, along with cups and insulated carafes of coffee.

"In case you didn't come to the MLFD pancake supper last year, there's hot chocolate and tea over on the beverage table," Barbi explained, carefully dotting butter on each of her small pancakes.

"Coffee is fine. They sure do a nice meal."

She dribbled syrup onto her plate. "Uh-huh. Next time they're serving spaghetti. It's strictly firehouse cooking. Whenever the auxiliary tries to fancy things up, the guys won't let 'em."

"Doesn't Mahalaton Lake have any female fire-fighters?"

"No, but there *are* women on the rescue squad. My mom always wanted my—" She stopped abruptly and stuffed a small pancake into her mouth.

Brendan didn't think she'd ever mentioned her mother. Then again, he was pretty sure she'd never mentioned her family, period. He cut a neat wedge from his own stack of pancakes and chewed it down. "Ohmigod, these are great," he exclaimed, looking at his plate in surprise.

"Ohmigod?" Barbi cocked an eyebrow. "Such language, Mr. Townsend. Are you certain you're from Boston?"

He grinned, some of his mood lifting. "I escaped, remember?"

"What did you have to do, gnaw off your leg irons?"

"Something like that. When you're a Townsend, you're supposed to get a law degree, join the family firm and die at your desk. No detours."

"Sounds awful."

Yeah, it did. And it wasn't as if he'd made a hugely better choice by going to Seattle. There he'd been assigned to corporate cases and had hated helping rich companies get richer while dodging every environmental and safety regulation they could legally avoid. The only good thing in his life had been Maria, and she'd been more career focused than him.

But in Mahalaton Lake he helped families set up trusts so their children could be protected. He wrote wills and advised on myriad issues that were often as simple as honest property-line disagreements.

Hell, he finally liked his profession.

"Whatcha thinking about?" Barbi licked a drop of syrup from the corner of her mouth and Brendan shifted, his shorts becoming snug. She was a very attractive woman when she wasn't mouthing off.

"I'm thinking Boston isn't so bad, but I like practicing law in a small town."

"Then why do you act as if you're up there on Mount Mahala, and the rest of us are below you?"

"I don't.... That's not how I feel," he said indignantly.

"It's how you act. A suit at a pancake supper, are you serious?"

Brendan looked down at himself. He'd wondered earlier if his formal attire was why Cora Baldwin wouldn't use his first name. Things in Mahalaton Lake were much more complicated than he expected—even his clothes seemed to be an issue.

"I'm getting more food. You coming?" Barbi asked suddenly.

"Uh, sure." He followed and once again the firemen patiently made her more bite-size pancakes, along with his three large ones. By the time he'd cleaned his plate again, he was stuffed.

"I need exercise," he groaned.

Barbi stood up. "I have the perfect thing."

Brendan's eyes widened as she tugged him into the hallway. "Take off your jacket," she ordered.

Okay, they were in a church. There was no way she planned to seduce him...though in another setting he might be willing. He took off his coat.

"Now your tie and vest."

Confused, he did as she asked. Briskly she hung the garments on a clothing rack that looked as if it had been screwed together from sections of old galvanized pipe. Then she unbuttoned the cuffs on his sleeves.

"Roll your sleeves up above your elbows."

"Barbi—"

"Do you want to fit in better or not? Volunteering to help will make everyone feel as if you're one of them."

Brendan thought about the standards he'd been determined to keep...without ever truly considering if they were worth keeping. He rolled up both sleeves as she undid several buttons at his neck.

Barbi stepped back and regarded him critically.

"Not bad," she pronounced. Grabbing his hand, she took him into the bustling church kitchen through yet another door. "Hi, everyone," she called. "I brought fresh meat for you. I gotta go deliver pizzas, but Brendan wants to help. He'll empty trash, wash pans, carry those heavy coffeepots...whatever you need."

A chorus of pleased exclamations sounded around the kitchen, and he turned, feeling almost panicked. *"Barbi."*

"Just do what they tell you."

With that minuscule bit of advice, she shoved him toward the smiling women working around the sink and countertops and disappeared.

BARBI HURRIED BACK to Luigi's, knowing she'd stayed longer at the pancake supper than she should have. But seeing Brendan there, looking so alone and out of place, had made her sad.

She wasn't sure what to make of him.

They still argued, but lately he didn't seem as snooty as he used to. What didn't make sense was why he'd moved to Mahalaton Lake in the first place.

He was a big-city guy and determined to do things a certain way. Not that she knew much about cities, but something that worked for Boston and Seattle wasn't necessarily right for a small mountain town. Didn't he get that? Maybe she shouldn't have pushed him into volunteering, but it was hard for people not to feel friendly when they were all getting splashed by the same soapy dishwater.

"Sorry I'm late," she called as she raced into the restaurant kitchen.

Luigi shook his head. "Nobody ordered pizza except the crew on duty at the fire station. I told them you would come when you finished eating pancakes. How could they object?"

She grinned, yet every time Luigi was so decent to her, it made the idea of leaving Mahalaton Lake that much harder. And now there was Brendan, who wasn't nearly such a pain in the butt as she'd thought.

Luigi quickly assembled two pizzas, and when they were baked, Barbi cut and put them into boxes.

"Tell them no charge," he said.

"They'll insist. You know the fellas. No free rides."

Luigi looked annoyed and grumbled under his breath as she hurried out again.

LATER THAT EVENING Jake stood in the library reading the titles of the movies on the shelves. While he'd noticed there was a large DVD collection there, he hadn't paid a whole lot of attention before Hannah's "quiz" on movie quotes. He could count on one hand the number of times he'd been to the cinema, though he'd seen native dances and rituals all over the world.

Jake supposed that was what the pancake supper was…a native ritual. A delicious ritual that thoroughly trumped doughy pancakes made over a campfire. The way Hannah had savored the sweet syrup and buttery flavor…

He groaned and walked the length of Huckleberry Lodge several times, trying to make the ache in his groin go away. There was nothing like nature's most primal drive to make you feel alive, but it had left him with a pain that hot tubs and physical therapy couldn't help.

Under the surface, Hannah was a woman with passions and depths he could only guess at. He suspected her ex-husband had sensed the same thing, but had been too shallow and impatient to stick around to explore them. Not that *he* was thinking of doing that, either, Jake assured himself. Soon he'd return to work, doing his photography the way he'd originally set out to do it…*alone,* with no distractions.

And it was just as well.

What if Toby had been killed in that crash? It would be another reason to feel guilty, and it was bad enough thinking about Gordon. Nonetheless, it would feel strange after years of silent laughter at Toby's grumbling.

Jake stepped onto the lodge's main deck and

looked down at the water. As with Spirit Lake, this one lay under the shadow of a volcano, but Mount Mahala was one of the less active peaks in the range.

Spirit Lake.

The name alone… A light prickle went across his shoulders. Perhaps he wasn't as immune to superstition as he wanted to believe. Though he was loath to admit it, he *did* understand what Hannah had been saying up at Mount St. Helens…about feeling something mysterious and powerful in the presence of an extraordinary work of nature.

And she'd struck a chord in him when she'd spoken about her boyfriend's death. It was true—believing in nothing was cold comfort in the face of imminent mortality. However uncomfortable it had been, it was nice that she'd been willing to share such a painful memory to help him understand how she felt. It also helped that she wasn't a religious fanatic, like some of the people he'd met over the years; she just seemed open to the idea of something more.

Jake leaned on the deck railing, struck by the uncomfortable thought that for all his travels and experience, he might actually be rather narrow-minded.

Hannah and Danny, with Badger at their heels, came out of Silver Cottage and walked along the shore before taking the northern forest path. They went out every evening, and sometimes he caught faint snatches of their conversation…Hannah telling her son stories about the land and animals and trees, with a sprinkling of Native American legends and myths.

Jake was about to go back inside when he heard a sharp canine yelp in the distance. Adrenaline shot through him and he hurried down the steps. The Cascades might seem tame to him, but there *were* dangers. Jake was a hundred yards up the path when Danny appeared, running for all he was worth.

"Danny, what happened?"

The kid streaked past without a word.

Almost at the same moment Jake caught the strong whiff of skunk. His pulse slowed with relief. Getting sprayed by a skunk was revolting, but not dangerous.

A couple of minutes later Hannah appeared with a miserable-looking Badger, now on a leash. "Don't get too close," she called. "Badger darted in and saved Danny from the worst of it, but he got the works, including some in his eyes. It temporarily blinded him."

Jake walked ahead of her on the trail, focusing on his gait because it wouldn't help if he fell and hurt himself.

At Silver Cottage they found Danny in the outdoor shower between the double garage doors, his clothes in a pile next to him, scrubbing for all he was worth.

"Now he wants a bath," Hannah murmured.

Jake held out a hand to take Badger's leash. The animal's eyes were watering and he blinked painfully.

"That's nice of you," Hannah said, "but this is my problem."

"I'm helping," he insisted. "I'll start with the dog while you take care of Danny."

Hannah hesitated for only an instant, then gave him the leash and opened the garage. On shelves along the far wall were rows of tomato juice in tall cans and containers of carbolic soap. Obviously, it wasn't the first time they'd run into the business end of a skunk.

With his leg still so unsteady, Jake couldn't chance lifting the large golden retriever into the outdoor washtub by the shower, but Badger seemed to understand and leaped in with only a small amount of guidance.

"Mommy, it's *gross*," Danny yelped.

"I know. Keep your eyes closed and keep scrubbing."

She opened several cans of the tomato juice, then turned the water off and poured it over him as the first salvo, while Jake did the same with Badger and began working the juice through the dog's thick fur.

"Hey, Danny, I haven't told you about the time I climbed the Matterhorn when I was fourteen," Jake said conversationally.

"I climbed it, too," the youngster informed him. "Sorta. In the bobsleds at Disneyland."

"I've never been to Disneyland, but I understand the rides can be scary."

"I wasn't scared," Danny said stoutly. "And I told Mommy you're *never* afraid, not even of a crocodile. Next time I see a bear I'm gonna show him I'm real brave, too. I'll whack him on the nose and tell him to get out of my way."

"No, you won't," Hannah said sharply. "You'll do exactly what I taught you to do."

Jake got a sinking sensation. He was in the habit of discussing his hazardous experiences with interviewers who wanted a good sound bite, but he hadn't thought about how they would come across to a child.

"Danny, when I told you I wasn't scared taking pictures of the crocodiles, it's because I was in a tree where they couldn't get to me," he said carefully, "but I *would* have been scared if I was on the ground with them. I've been scared lots of times."

The youngster's eyes opened wide. "Really?"

"Yes. I've done some dangerous things, but it's to get pictures of places and animals that…uh…people might never get to see for themselves. It's never been to prove I'm brave or anything. That would be dumb. Do you understand?"

"I guess."

Fortunately Danny was declared de-skunked a short while later and sent into Silver Cottage to get warm, which left both Jake and Hannah to work on Badger.

"Thank you for that," Hannah said quietly as they poured more tomato juice on the animal's fur.

"I didn't want Badger to wait," Jake replied, deliberately misunderstanding. "He was suffering. But he may need to spend a few nights in the garage. The odor doesn't seem to be getting better."

Hannah shook her head. "I can't do that—he'd never understand. Besides, I think our clothes are contaminated and that's partly what we're smelling."

Damned if she wasn't right. "I'm not modest," Jake said, stripping down to his shorts. He dropped his clothes into the old washing machine in the garage where Hannah had put Danny's things.

HANNAH'S BREATH LEFT her in a rush. He was really… *gorgeous,* despite the scars—both old and new—that she was trying not to look at.

Hell.

She turned her back and pulled off her own clothes, grabbing an ancient T-shirt of her father's that she kept on the shelf with the skunk supplies. With a quick flip she pulled it over her head, though her wet skin didn't let it shimmy downward as easily as she would have liked. Nevertheless, by the time she turned around, the hem had settled below her hips.

"Spoilsport," Jake jeered, though he didn't appear to have been watching. He was working another application of tomato juice into Badger's fur. "I can't believe how cooperative he's being."

"I'm sure he understands we're trying to help. And I know he deliberately got between Danny and the skunk. Good boy," she praised the retriever. Badger's tail thumped on either side of the washtub as he wagged it.

With their contaminated clothes no longer adding to the ambience, a last thorough washing of Badger's fur seemed to do the trick. A slight odor lingered, but it was livable. Hannah toweled him, still offering praise for his heroism before looking up.

"Um, thanks for the help. I could have managed, but it was easier with an extra pair of hands. And I also appreciate you being honest with Danny about sometimes getting scared," she said determinedly.

Jake finished drying himself off. "No thanks needed. It was the truth. I'm going to jump in the hot tub now. Maybe you and Danny should join me. There's no better way to get warm."

The offer was appealing, but Hannah shook her head. "I should go tuck Danny into bed."

"Maybe you could come by yourself…for a little while." He dropped the towel he was using and gave her a wicked smile. He walked toward Huckleberry Lodge, unconcerned about his near nudity, and she let out a breath.

She was hardly a virgin to get flustered at the sight of a man's body, but her pulse was definitely jumping.

CHAPTER THIRTEEN

NORMALLY HANNAH COULD relax on Sunday after-noons, but between the adventures with the skunk and being behind on everything else, she had a busy day.

Her outings with Jake were pleasant over the next few days. He really seemed to listen as she talked about the land and the meaning it held for her...the sense of creation in the volcanically ac-tive mountains and the varied plants and animals. Of course, maybe it helped that she didn't mention healing songs for the land or anything that smacked of metaphysical beliefs.

Sometimes it felt as if they didn't agree on a single thing. And that shouldn't matter to her. She wanted to get married and have more children and to pro-tect her son while Jake just wanted to get back to his wandering ways. But somehow it *did* matter—maybe because she couldn't remember ever feeling so drawn to someone.

Still, Jake *had* talked seriously to Danny about fear and bravery and having good reasons for doing something dangerous. It wasn't that Hannah didn't believe in ever taking risks, she just didn't believe in being foolish.

On Thursday morning the air was fresh and cool following a rainstorm the night before. She ran over to clean the lodge after dropping Danny at his day camp and tutoring Barbi, who'd come out to Silver Cottage early following one of her night shifts. Hannah frowned, remembering how edgy Barbi had been. And she'd seemed on the verge of asking something a few times.

The cleaning schedule was another thing that was getting shifted around to allow for the photographic outings, along with Hannah's meetings and the tasks she had to get done for upcoming fund-raisers. Even Jake's Friday physical-therapy sessions had gotten rescheduled to Thursdays, and she often ended up cleaning at the same time Owen was there.

"Come in, I can't get up," Jake called as she knocked on the door.

Alarmed, Hannah hurried inside and found him lying on the couch.

"What's wrong?"

"Nothing, I just…" He gestured and to her astonishment, she saw a scrawny adolescent kitten draped across his leg, sound asleep. "Last night I kept hearing something cry. I thought it was just the rain or a strange bird, but I finally walked up toward the main road and found this guy under a bush. He's exhausted."

"Poor thing."

Hannah loved cats, and she knelt by the couch to examine the stray more closely. It was a tuxedo cat, black on top with a white blaze on its face, a white belly and tidy white paws—or they would be white once they were licked clean. Right now its fur was still grubby, though she could see evidence that he'd recently attempted to wash himself.

"He's mostly skin and bones," she murmured.

"Yeah. I fed him milk and a can of tuna I found on one of the pantry shelves. I'll buy cat food later, along with a litter box."

She blinked. Jake wouldn't shop for himself, but he'd go get supplies for a half-starved cat?

"You're keeping him?"

"Just until he's stronger and I find him a good home," he said brusquely. "I couldn't leave him out there."

"Of course not, but he'll need to stay inside. There are wild animals in the area that would enjoy having him for dinner."

"I'll keep him in." Jake stroked the cat's bony head, and its tail twitched in response.

"I have some things at the house you can use until you get to a store," she said, standing. "I'll be right back."

At Silver Cottage she collected a cardboard box lid and a bag of cat litter she kept on hand for winter traction, along with several cans of albacore and chicken. Seeming to guess that something was up,

Badger followed her back to the lodge. He walked around the couch and Jake glared.

"Go away."

"Badger likes cats," Hannah said softly. "Watch."

The kitten woke up as the dog nosed him, arching its back and spitting, but Badger patiently began licking him from head to toe until the spits turned into purring.

"He's a mother hen," she explained. "I'll set up a litter box in the laundry room, but you'll have to teach the cat to use it."

"He's already using some rags in there. How come you have cat litter?"

"I carry it in the car during the winter to throw under the wheels for better grip in ice or snow."

"You ought to have a four-wheel-drive vehicle."

She shrugged, not about to explain the realities of living on a teacher's salary…again. "I'll start the cleaning. Have you thought about what you'd like to see this afternoon after your therapy session?"

"Uh, no, but I'll look at that list you made up."

Hannah began collecting the trash around the lodge and noticed the kitten had abandoned Jake's leg to curl up against Badger's stomach. Its fur was soaked, but much cleaner.

"I don't see why you don't go to Lower Mahalaton for your therapy," Hannah said as she wiped the countertops in the kitchen.

Jake opened the refrigerator and took out a carton of orange juice. "It's easier to have Owen come here."

"For you, maybe."

"Hell, I'm paying a premium, including for his travel time. The rehab center comes out way ahead."

"It isn't just a question of money. Driving up to Mahalaton Lake means he doesn't have time to work with as many patients, and that's a shame because he's a great therapist."

"I know—my sister-in-law researched it for me."

"Is that the one who's going to have a baby?"

Jake took a swig of orange juice. "She had it, actually. Matt phoned Monday evening."

Hannah turned around. "Boy or girl?"

"Uh, boy."

"And…?"

"And what?"

She made an exasperated sound. "What's his name? How much does he weigh and how long is he? When were your sister-in-law and nephew expected to come home from the hospital…? You know, the usual details when someone has a baby."

"Oh. Matt said something about all that, but I don't remember. The kid's name is William, I know that much. Named after Layne's uncle. They're calling him Will."

"You sent her flowers, right?"

Jake blinked. Obviously, he hadn't.

Hannah pulled out the Mahalaton Lake phone book. "Here. If there weren't any complications, they should be home from the hospital by now. You can arrange for flowers with the local florist shop.

Send something really pretty. If Layne is anything like me, she needs to feel special after giving birth. Of course, in her case she's got a husband, and that'll help."

"Then your husband wasn't…"

"He was long gone by the time Danny was born," she said reluctantly. "Steven didn't see Danny until he was two. And only a few times since then." There was no point in pretending her ex was any prize.

"Then why does Danny talk about his father so much?"

"Because his friends all have daddies and he wonders if *he's* the reason Steven isn't here. I try to reassure him, but the fear is still there, deep down."

"That's crazy," Jake said, sounding indignant. "I'm not a kid person and *I* like Danny."

"Emotions aren't logical. And besides, he brings you our leftovers." Hannah held up a bag filled with leftover containers that she'd collected to return to Silver Cottage.

Jake looked embarrassed. "That has nothing to do with me liking him."

"He may not know that. You were rude the day you got here, but now you tell him stories…which only started when he began bringing food over."

"Crap."

"Danny was worried you weren't getting enough to eat. But in the back of his mind he may wonder if the food is the reason you started being nicer to him. Now, call the florist before Owen gets here, or place an online order."

Hannah went across the lodge into the master bedroom and began making up the bed. The place wasn't as messy as usual, but Jake hadn't been home as much, either.

"Hi, Owen," she called as she headed for the utility area with a bundle of laundry. He'd arrived and was checking the range of motion in Jake's leg.

"Hey, Hannah."

She filled the washing machine with towels and sheets and automatically began folding a batch of Jake's clothes that were sitting in the dryer. Then stopped, scowling. She wasn't doing his personal laundry. Not now, not ever. She'd washed the sweatpants and T-shirt contaminated by the skunk's spray, but that was different.

Hmm...the skunk.

Sighing, Hannah finished folding the clothes. There was nothing dangerous about skunk spray, but helping to scrub it out of Badger's fur had gone above and beyond the normal responsibilities of a tenant. She owed Jake a few favors.

The sheets and towels were tumbling in the dryer when Owen left, and she'd gone into the sunroom to discuss where they were going that afternoon when there was a knock on the front door.

"Maybe Owen left something," she said, getting up to answer. But instead it was an elderly couple she'd never met.

"Is this where Jake Hollister lives?" asked the woman. "We're his grandparents. I'm Ruth Mac-Donald, and this is my husband, Dean."

"It's nice to meet you. Please come in."

Jake's grandfather was using a walker for support, and Hannah got them settled in the living room before returning to the sunroom.

"Jake, your grandparents are here. Mr. and Mrs. MacDonald."

Instead of looking pleased, Jake scowled. "What in hell are *they* doing in Washington?"

"Uh…visiting? They're in the other room. Let me know if you need anything, I'll be next door."

"Don't leave."

JAKE COULD SEE Hannah was confused by his response, but it was nothing compared to how *he* felt. He'd never even met the MacDonalds. Josie had left home on her eighteenth birthday and never returned—rarely even visiting the States. One of the few things she'd said of her parents was that they'd smothered her with religious dogma.

He went into the living room with Hannah and saw a woman who resembled Josie, though older, and a man with a deeply lined face. They smiled tentatively at him.

"Can I get you anything?" Hannah asked, obviously trying to smooth the uncomfortable moment. "Coffee, perhaps?"

Ruth lifted her hands, then dropped them. "We don't want to be a bother."

"It's no bother." Hannah vanished before Jake could stop her.

"Goodness, you look just like your pictures," Ruth said following an uneasy silence.

"Yes…" Dean put a hand on his walker, trying to stand. "Oh, this hip," he muttered. "Broke it a couple of months ago."

"Don't get up. I'm sorry you were hurt," Jake said awkwardly, sitting across from them.

"It's nothing, but we've been concerned about you. The stories about the accident…" His grandfather's eyes blinked with the ready tears of old age. "They were quite alarming. It's a blessing to see you looking healthy."

"I'm doing well."

"We're grateful for it," Ruth said. She fidgeted with the purse on her lap. "That young woman is so sweet…is she a friend?"

"Huckleberry Lodge belongs to Hannah. I'm renting it from her. She lives next door."

"It's good you aren't out here alone."

"I can take care of myself." Jake's sharp words seemed to echo in the room, and he wished Hannah would come back. She understood people; she'd know how to talk to the MacDonalds. It wasn't as though he wanted to be rude. He just didn't have a clue what to say.

"Of...of course you can take care of yourself. Please, that wasn't what I meant."

"Don't mind Jake, his bark is worse than his bite," Hannah advised as she came through the kitchen door and put a tray with cups and a plate of cookies on the coffee table. "I had a thermos of coffee already made at my house. I hope it won't be too unusual for you—it has New Mexico piñon nuts in it."

Ruth looked as if she'd been drowning and Hannah had thrown her a lifeline. "I'm sure it's delicious," she said eagerly.

"Where are you folks from?" Hannah asked after she'd served everyone.

"Minnesota." His grandmother bit into a cookie and a smile spread across her face. "These are wonderful. Most peanut-butter cookies are too sweet."

"And not peanut buttery enough," Hannah agreed. "You're welcome to the recipe. I have a copy of our church cookbook I can give you—most of my recipes are in there."

"Thank you." Ruth appeared enchanted.

"It's nice of you to visit all the way from Minnesota."

"We heard Jake was staying in the U.S. during his convalescence and wanted to see him when we had the chance."

"Just a quick visit—we're going back to Portland tonight. That's where we flew in," Dean explained. "We wanted to come earlier, but the doctor wouldn't allow it so soon after my hip surgery."

"We're terribly proud of you, Jake," Ruth added. "And of Josephine, of course. I love looking at her pictures. I feel as if I'm right there with her, seeing those amazing places."

Dean nodded. "Your mother has a true artist's eye, Jake. And it started early. She was fascinated by an ancient box camera I had when she was growing up. The pictures she could get with that thing… remarkable."

Jake's head spun as both Ruth and Dean continued to speak of his mother's work with a knowledge that went beyond an occasional glimpse in a magazine.

"I can't think what it must have been like to stand on the top of Mount Everest. Imagine, our daughter being able to do something like that," Ruth said.

Jake nodded, recalling Josie's determination to climb Sagarmatha after the failed attempt when he was eight. She'd succeeded the year he was in the Antarctic. She hadn't told him she was going, she'd just done it. His mouth tightened as he also remembered his frustration at learning she'd challenged the mountain again.

Hell.

What had made him think of that?

Two hours later Ruth looked at her watch. "We'd better go, dear. Our plane leaves early in the morning."

"Quite right." Dean struggled to his feet.

"Here is our phone number and…uh, address." Ruth tentatively handed Jake a small piece of paper.

"You're welcome to visit whenever you like. It sounds silly, but Josephine's room is still there, just the way she left it."

"I'll keep that in mind."

Jake wondered if he should urge the MacDonalds to stay longer, but they were strangers to him. Josie had only mentioned her parents a handful of times when he was a boy, and never positively. But these people hadn't condemned her lifestyle or spouted religious homilies. They seemed wistfully proud of her accomplishments.

"I'll run over to my house and get the cookbook," Hannah said. She met them at their rented sedan and helped get his grandfather settled in the passenger's seat.

Jake didn't know what was expected of him, but he wasn't ready for hugs and kisses, so it was Hannah who got a hug from Ruth and planted a kiss on Dean's cheek.

"It was lovely meeting you," she declared. "Drive safely."

She waved until the car had disappeared from view, then turned to him with a puzzled frown on her face. "I don't get it, Jake. Why didn't you invite them to stay the night?"

"They're strangers to me."

"But they're your grandparents. And they're older, so they'll be exhausted after driving up here and back in a day."

"That doesn't mean they aren't strangers. So they

came to see me. They were probably just curious. Besides, you heard what they said—they have an early flight tomorrow."

Hannah looked disappointed and it bothered him more than he wanted to admit.

"I can't believe you're just dismissing this. Are you so disconnected from people you can't understand how hard it must have been for them, coming to see a grandson they've never met? They couldn't be sure how you'd respond, but they still took the chance."

"It's not that simple. Josie told me about her parents. She didn't have a happy childhood."

"I'm not saying your mother was wrong, but why don't you make up your own mind? Maybe they've changed. Or maybe they have a different perspective on things than Josie. Oh…never mind. I have sheets and towels to fold."

She went back into Huckleberry Lodge and Jake sighed. What was the answer? The MacDonalds hadn't been pushy or said anything negative or preachy, but that didn't mean his mother was wrong.

He went inside and found Hannah in the laundry room.

"Hannah, can we just forget about the MacDonalds right now? I'll think about what you said, but at the moment I've got too much to handle without adding anything else."

"Fine." She shook out a towel and folded it neatly. "There's a craft fair in the park by Memorial Hall tomorrow and the next day. I have to be there on Saturday to sell coffee and cookies for the rescue squad and won't have much time to visit the other booths. So I'd like to go tomorrow morning. If you come with me, you could get a gift for Layne and your new nephew. Besides, the ten percent of the proceeds from the booths are going to the rescue squad."

He sighed. It was hard to argue with a good cause.

"All right...maybe we could go first thing, then find somewhere I can work in the afternoon."

Jake still didn't feel any urgency about his Cascade photographic project, but he *had* to start getting something accomplished. If he didn't get the summer photos taken, he would have to stay that much longer the following year. The possibility didn't sound as alarming as it once might have...but that was the problem. He didn't want to get stuck in one place out of inertia.

"I know a spot where avalanche lilies should be blooming."

Another flower? Well, hell. He'd taken shots of dogwood and huckleberries; he might as well do avalanche lilies, whatever those were. And it was better than sitting around, worrying if his career might be over.

"Whatever."

One of her eyebrows shot up at his unenthusiastic tone.

"Um...good. *Fine,*" he added quickly.

HANNAH THOUGHT ABOUT Jake the entire time she was baking cookies that evening for Saturday. How could he have so little concern for his family? And the worst part was knowing that it mattered to her because she was starting to care about him. Not that she was in love with Jake, but he wasn't quite the arrogant, self-centered man he'd seemed when he first arrived in Mahalaton Lake.

"Mommy, don't you like the present I made at camp?" Danny asked when she tucked him into bed.

"I love your bracelet, but I didn't want to mess it up making cookies. I'm wearing the necklace, though." She pointed to the brightly colored string of beads around her neck.

He yawned. "Can I keep the light on?"

"Sure. Did you have another bad dream last night?"

"Uh-huh. But Jake was in it, and he chased the lions away with a stick."

Hannah's throat was tight as she returned to the kitchen and pulled the last batch of cookies from the oven. In a few short weeks Jake had touched practically every aspect of their lives. Her son was even dreaming about him. And while Jake had admitted he got scared, Danny obviously still saw him as a hero.

She stepped out on the deck, telling herself she was restless because she and Danny hadn't gone for their usual evening walk. Danny and Badger were getting their enthusiasm back for hiking the forest trails—though the memory of the skunk lingered in more ways than one—but she'd been busy baking.

Jake was down by the lakeshore and Hannah leaned on the railing to watch. He had a camera on a tripod, with a lens so huge it looked like a telescope and needed its own support. This past week, she'd seen him out often in the evenings, taking pictures. When it wasn't cloudy, the glaciers on Mount Mahala reflected the setting sun with a fiery glow. And when the surface of the lake was calm, there was a perfect reflection of the snowcapped mountain on the water.

Some evenings Jake's camera was pointed along the shore, rather than the mountain, perhaps in search of great blue herons or other wildlife. With luck he would spot a loon. They were rare, but Hannah had seen one near the lodge, swimming with its young, and she was hopeful more nesting pairs would find the lake.

As if sensing her gaze, Jake turned around and looked toward Silver Cottage. She straightened and stepped back from the railing.

While it was unlikely he wanted to talk, she didn't want to take the chance. She was having trouble reconciling the man who'd gone out in the rain to rescue a lost kitten with the one who'd been so cold to his grandparents.

The anxious, yearning expressions of the Mac-Donalds kept coming back to her. Whatever mistakes they'd made in the past, they were paying a high price now…in a daughter they never saw, and a grandson they hadn't met until today.

THE NEXT DAY at the craft fair Jake wasn't surprised when Hannah immediately headed for the Mahalaton Rescue Squad booth with a box of her peanut-butter chocolate-chip cookies. He'd offered to buy them, but she'd refused, saying it was important for the entire community to be involved in supporting the squad.

Gwen was there and she smiled at them both. "Thanks, Hannah. And the raffle tickets for your huckleberry syrup are selling well." She looked at Jake determinedly. "By the way, is there any chance I can interest you in donating a signed picture of Mount Mahala for us to raffle off? It's for the rescue squad—near and dear to Hannah's heart."

Jake wasn't sure if there was a subtext to her words, but he remembered what Hannah had said about community involvement. And since he was satisfied with some of the photographs he'd taken in the past week, donating one to a raffle wouldn't be embarrassing.

"Sure. I'll have a couple of prints made and get them framed."

Gwen's smile brightened to megawatt proportions. She clearly hadn't expected him to agree. "That's wonderful. We'll advertise and start selling the tickets immediately. It can be one of the big prizes we award at the end of the Christmas in August festival. Hannah, if I could borrow you for a second...?"

While the two women were conferring, Jake walked around and looked at the crafts being sold, though he avoided the booths offering photographs for sale. It was dicey, whether they were amateurs selling a few photos or genuine professionals. He didn't have anything against either one, but it was uncomfortable when someone recognized him and wanted an opinion of their work. There was also always the risk of being unconsciously influenced by someone else's work.

Stopping at a stand featuring wood carvings, he examined two trains, complete with circular tracks they could be pushed around. One was cheerfully coated with hard enamel paint, the other was natural, with different colors and types of wood forming the parts.

"Are these children's toys?" he asked the man sitting there.

"Yup, though I've sold a number of sets to railroad buffs."

"I'll take both," Jake decided. Danny would probably enjoy having one, and the other could go to his new nephew. It would be a few years before Will could play with it, but it was unique and plainly made by an expert craftsman. "Is there any chance I can pay to have the painted set shipped to Seattle?"

"I sell my work over the internet, so we're set up for shipping. But it can't go out until Monday."

"That's fine." Jake gave him Matt's address as the man's wife wrapped the second train set for him to take.

The wood-carver glanced at Jake's credit card. "Say, you must be the fellow renting Hannah's place."

"That's right," Jake acknowledged.

"My buddies at the fire station told me you gave a large donation to the truck fund."

"It's nothing compared to what firemen do."

"We still appreciate the support. I used to volunteer down there, but got a bum leg now. Busted it one too many times." The man thumped his knee and Jake's stomach twisted. His own leg was getting better, but the reminder that some injuries didn't heal well still sent a cold chill down his back.

"Uh, yeah." He signed his name on the credit card slip and took the two large bags containing the train set he'd gotten for Danny, only to turn around and see Hannah standing behind him.

"Hi, Vince," she greeted the wood-carver.

"Morning, Hannah. I was just thanking Mr. Hollister for his contribution to the fire truck fund."

"As I said, it's nothing. Hannah, are you done looking around?" Jake asked brusquely.

HANNAH ROLLED HER eyes as Jake hurried her away. "What's bugging you *now?*"

"Nothing."

Yeah, I believe that, she thought as they got in his Jeep. He was driving, and she directed him to go south. The quickest access roads to Mount Mahala were on its southeast flank, which was the most popular part of the mountain for skiers.

"It's nice that you're donating a photo to the raffle," she said when they were getting close to the place she'd chosen, figuring he'd had more than enough time to cool off. "You've already made generous donations to the rescue squad, not just to the new fire truck."

"I just…" He shrugged. "The Inupiat who came and pulled us from the plane wouldn't accept anything. I guess this is one way of repaying their help."

"Andy told me they used dogsleds to move you."

"Look, Hannah, I really don't want to talk about it." He sounded angry again and she sighed.

"I've noticed the stories you tell Danny are rarely about Alaska. Don't you think it might help to talk about what happened? Not to Danny, but to an adult?"

"What do you know about it? You stay here in your safe world and want your son to do the same thing."

Hannah tried not to get angry, knowing why Jake had gone on the attack.

"At least I don't have a near-death wish," she said calmly. She no longer thought it was true, but since

Jake obviously had some unresolved issues, surely he'd be better off dealing with them.

"I don't care what anybody's told you, I *don't* have a death wish."

"I said *near*-death wish. And while I appreciate what you said to Danny, most people *don't* risk their life every day unless they're policemen or rescue workers. Are those risks the trade-off for living behind your camera most of the time? I've known two adrenaline junkies, and both needed the exhilaration of danger to feel alive."

The small road they were driving ended in a trailhead, and Jake jerked to a stop.

"You don't know anything about me," he countered furiously. "I'm living life on my own terms, rather than according to the dictates of society. But your life is *all* about societal conventions, especially when it comes to boyfriends. How are *you* going to feel alive with a man who's shocked by someone like Barbi Paulson simply because she doesn't fit his concept of the proper woman? He's obviously attracted to her, and I'm sure Barbi feels the same, but I doubt it'll go anywhere."

"Barbi and *Brendan?*"

Jake snorted. "Yeah. Maybe I do hide behind my camera a lot of the time, but at least *I've* seen the sparks between Barbi and that stuffed shirt. If you have any concern for either of them, you ought to be encouraging a relationship, instead of hanging on to a man who's wrong for you."

"I'm not *hanging on* to anyone. I broke things off with him the day we went to Mount St. Helens."

The news seemed to take the wind out of Jake's sails. Honestly, he made her brain frizz. She could try blaming it on having a weakness for a certain type of man, but the longer she knew Jake, the more she could see he didn't fit into any category.

"It's about time. Though I could point out that you wouldn't even commit to the 'safe' man you were dating. Doesn't real love involve risk, too?"

Hannah got out of the Jeep, her temper simmering despite her efforts to control it. Whether it was the argument or the fresh air, Jake looked more intense than she'd ever seen him, and a sharp twinge went through her gut. Maybe that was her fate, a weakness for men who looked at the horizon, instead of what was around them. It might even make her an adrenaline junkie, too, only for a different kind of thrill.

"You don't know anything about love," Hannah returned coolly. "Look at how you behaved toward your grandparents."

"And you know nothing about the MacDonalds. My mother had a miserable childhood with their religious fanaticism and judgmental attitudes. She made sure I wasn't exposed to it myself."

"That's for sure," Hannah muttered. His mother

had made sure Jake didn't believe in anything, including family and commitment and having a home.

And she didn't care. She really didn't, she told herself as Jake glared, impossibly handsome and desirable and exciting. And she still didn't care when he grabbed her shoulders and kissed her...though she was too busy kissing him back to think about it.

JAKE GASPED A few minutes later when he came up for air. Hannah was half lying on the hood of the Jeep, her legs wrapped around his hips. Her shirt was unbuttoned and bra unhooked, and she looked like a sun goddess in the dappled light coming through the trees.

The woman drove him insane.

Death-wish accusations had never bothered him before. People could say what they liked; that didn't make it true. The only thing that had ever mattered was his photography. Granted, he took chances getting his pictures and it was exciting to see things that few people, if any, had ever seen. But that was the point—it was a great feeling to share those sights with the world. Couldn't she understand that?

"I'm glad we got *that* out of our systems," she said politely, though her eyes still glittered with emotion.

Jake helped her sit upright and tried to ignore the pressure behind the zipper on his jeans, knowing he hadn't gotten anything out of his system. But he wasn't going to argue the point, because sex with Hannah might be the riskiest thing he could ever do.

After all, it was women like Hannah who convinced men like him to give up the lives they'd chosen.

CHAPTER FOURTEEN

SHORTLY BEFORE NOON on Saturday, Barbi hurried down to the craft fair by Memorial Hall and found herself looking for Brendan. He'd been alone each time they'd run into each other lately and, while she still sassed him, the heart had gone out of it. He wasn't a bad guy, he just needed loosening up.

"Morning, Hannah," she said at the rescue squad booth. "I'll take a cup of coffee and some peanut-butter cookies. The ones you make with the chocolate chips."

Hannah looked pale, as if she hadn't slept, but she smiled and put her order on the counter. "You can't beat peanut butter and chocolate."

"Nope." Barbi put cream in her cup and stirred it. She wanted to ask Hannah if it was okay to make a move on Brendan. After all, Hannah didn't seem to care that much about him. But asking if it was okay to make a move on her boyfriend seemed so awkward.

She opened her mouth, only to close it when a group of tourists stopped at the booth, wanting information about the rescue squad.

Barbi waved goodbye and wandered to a quieter side of the park. Sitting under a tree, she tried to ignore the squirrel doing its best to convince her he was starving. "They're *cookies*. Sugar isn't good for you," she said.

The squirrel twittered and stood on his hind legs, displaying a sizable set of equipment.

"I bet you're popular with the lady squirrels."

He flicked his tail.

"What's that?" asked a voice, startling both her and the squirrel, who dashed up a tree.

Barbi looked up at Brendan. "Nothing. I'm just admiring a well-hung squirrel."

"Ah." A hint of red crept up his neck, but he sat down and opened a pizza box between them. "I know you're probably tired of pizza, but I don't want to eat alone. Help yourself."

"Don't you want to eat with Hannah?"

He shrugged, a funny expression on his face. "She's busy."

Barbi looked down at the pizza and blinked. Instead of his usual toppings of sausage, olives and onions, it was her favorite—pepperoni, mushrooms and artichoke hearts.

"You said artichoke hearts sounded awful."

"Thought I'd give them a try." Brendan bit into a slice and a smile grew across his face. "Not bad."

She hid her own smile as she took a bite. "You know, you never told me why you moved to Mahalaton Lake, or why you didn't go to work for your family."

Brendan stopped eating and stared into the distance. "I didn't go back to Boston because I couldn't fail there. I suppose that doesn't make any sense."

"Naw, I get it. Nobody would care if you were good or bad in Boston, just that you were a Townsend. So that's why you went to Seattle."

"Yeah. I had to prove myself in Seattle, just like anyone else. And I did succeed. I became a partner and was really moving fast, then someone I cared about at the firm died of a brain aneurysm. There were symptoms, but Maria wouldn't take the time to see a doctor. After she was gone I decided there had to be more to life than a stack of legal briefs and a high-profile client list."

"Looking for what it all means, huh?"

"I don't know about that. I just couldn't stay. That is, at first I cut back my hours, but the firm didn't approve. Maria grew up in Mahalaton Lake, so I decided to try to sort things out here. David Walther was her father."

"I remember Maria," Barbi said. "She was a year ahead of me in school and was the captain of the debate team."

Brendan smiled. "Yeah, Maria loved to argue. She used to say that Mahalaton Lake was big enough that you didn't have to be around people you didn't like, and small enough that you could know a lot of your neighbors. But I've got to admit, a population of three thousand people seems awful small after

Seattle. And I don't know if I'm getting my head in the right place anyway."

"Well, if you want to do *that,* you should stop being so stuck-up."

"I'm *not* stuck-up."

"Maybe not, but you act that way. Ease up and ditch the suit. Most of the time you look like a stuffy Perry Mason."

Brendan shook his finger at her. "Don't diss my hero. Perry was never wrong."

Barbi laughed. She still liked giving him a hard time, though it was getting difficult to ignore the buzz low in her abdomen whenever they were together. And it was pretty classy that he'd been willing to make such a huge change in his life when his friend died.

It must have been tough leaving Seattle like that. Just the *idea* of moving to another town scared the bejesus out of her. But it was the only way she knew to get away from Vic.

BRENDAN TOSSED A piece of crust to the "well-hung" squirrel that had cautiously returned and was gazing at them with a bright, eager gaze. And he had to admit, it *was* well hung. Barbi was outrageous, but it was fun listening to her, even if he couldn't make himself join in. Too bad he hadn't figured it out earlier.

She also had a good head on her shoulders. He hadn't exactly thought about his move to Mahalaton

Lake as a search for meaning, but that was what it boiled down to. Maria's death had made him want to change his life, yet all he'd done was change his geography, without really figuring out what else he needed.

"Have some dessert." Barbi held out a plate of cookies and Brendan took one. He recognized them as one of Hannah's specialties, but didn't say anything.

"Thanks. You were right about the pizza toppings, but don't say you told me so."

"Me?" Barbi batted her eyelashes and he laughed.

It was strange. He was more comfortable than he'd ever been in his life, even though he was sitting on the ground and becoming aroused at the sight of his companion. Barbi was unabashed about showing off her figure, and while her eye-popping clothes had turned him off in the past, he'd found her more and more appealing over the past few weeks.

After all, clothes were just clothes. Who she was was far more important.

LATE SATURDAY AFTERNOON Jake sat on the deck, holding the slip of paper his grandmother had given him in one hand and his smartphone in the other.

The MacDonalds had seemed like nice people, and they'd never suggested that he could have come to visit them, instead of the other way around. Which was true, except he'd never considered it after the things his mother had said.

It was unpleasant to think Josie might have turned her back on two people who genuinely cared about her...and him. They'd certainly cared enough to travel from Minnesota, a trip that couldn't have been easy considering their age and Dean's health.

Why don't you make up your own mind about them?

Hannah's words kept echoing in his head. She was right. He shouldn't just accept Josie's version of things. As much as he loved his mother, she was a hard person to understand—*eccentric* didn't begin to describe her.

Actually, there were a number of things he needed to think through. Until meeting Hannah, he'd never fully looked at how different his life had been from other people's. That didn't mean he should change it, but there might be other options to consider.

Slowly Jake dialed the phone number on the paper. He waited as the phone rang once, twice, then heard Ruth's voice say, "Hello?"

"Hi, it's Jake. I...um, just wanted to be sure you got home safely," he said.

A shocked intake of breath came over the line. "That's so thoughtful. We're fine. We had a smooth flight and the airline provided wheelchair service for Dean."

"Good. Not too tired, I hope?"

"No...just glad to have seen you."

"I'm glad, too," Jake said, meaning it. "I'd better let you go now, but we'll talk soon."

Ruth said goodbye and he turned the phone off. Strangely, he wished he could talk to Hannah about it, but they weren't on the best of terms at the moment.

HANNAH AVOIDED JAKE all weekend, debating whether she should call off the plans they'd made for Monday—a two-night trip to Mount Baker and across the North Cascades Highway. But since Jake had canceled his Tuesday therapy session to accommodate the trip, she left Danny and Badger with her parents on Sunday evening, and stepped out of Silver Cottage just as the sun was rising on Monday.

The Mount Baker outing would be the first time they'd been away overnight, and Danny had wanted to go so badly she'd almost agreed. But she still believed he would be too bored by the hours Jake could spend setting up his equipment, measuring the light and doing other unknown things before ever taking his first photo.

Hannah doubted they'd see more than the spur road up to Mount Shuksan and Mount Baker, however much Jake wanted a better look at the other mountains north of Snoqualmie Pass. It was a significant drive to Whatcom County—almost to the Canadian border—and he undoubtedly hoped to explore some of the trails. He pushed his body constantly, as if effort alone could make his injuries heal.

The rising sun had bathed the yard in pink light, and she saw Jake waiting by the Jeep, one eyebrow raised in challenge. "I figured you'd cancel after what happened Friday," he said.

Hannah put two bags and a soft-sided cooler into the cargo area. "You figured wrong. I still took you to see the avalanche lilies, didn't I?"

"Yeah, and didn't say a word to me."

"What else should I have said? You left the craft fair looking for a fight and we ended up kissing each other. End of story."

"Ah, that's more like it. Did you make coffee?"

Her eyes narrowed. "Considering the comments you've made about people in Washington being obsessed with coffee, I'm surprised you have the nerve to ask."

"Yeah, you're obsessed here, and yet the stuff at the pancake supper tasted as if it was made with dishwater and floor sweepings."

"That's firehouse brew—strong, cheap and easy."

Jake still looked hopeful, so she sighed and swung the knapsack off her shoulder. "I've got a thermos. I've also arranged for my mother to come over and check on your kitten."

"He isn't *my* kitten," he corrected hastily. "But that's great. I left a huge bowl of food and water and an extra litter box for Louie, but he'll probably get lonely without Badger visiting. You're aware that Badger came over on both Saturday and Sunday, right?"

"I figured that was part of the reason he wanted out a few times. You've named the cat Louie?"

"Just for convenience. It doesn't mean anything." Hannah struggled to keep from smiling.

Louie, I think this is the beginning of a beautiful friendship.

Did he remember the movie quote she'd thrown at him?

They headed down the highway with Jake driving, their coffee cups in the holders between the seats. The muted edge of hostility between them was still present, but at least they were managing to be reasonably civil.

And it wasn't really hostility, more frustrated sexual tension. Part of Hannah wanted to tell him to forget any more outings, but another part was too fascinated by watching him work. And, while she'd only seen a few of the photos Jake had taken, the mountains she loved were slowly emerging...no matter how impossible he might be.

Yet a smile tugged at her mouth as she thought about the kitten they'd left back at Huckleberry Lodge. Jake was so damned determined not to be tied down by relationships, but relationships came in all shapes and sizes, including a kitten with white paws.

"By the way, I got a wood train set for my nephew at the craft fair," Jake said after they'd reached the interstate and were headed north. "I know Will can't play with it now, but he might like it when he's older."

"That sounds nice. You can give it to your brother and sister-in-law when we see them."

"I had it shipped. I hadn't planned to visit."

Hannah's jaw dropped. "But we're going through Seattle. You don't want to stop to see your brother and the baby?"

JAKE WINCED. VISITING Matt hadn't occurred to him, but he could see Hannah's point. There weren't any fast bypasses around the city and they would drive within a few miles of Matt and Layne's house.

"Uh...yeah. Sure, we *should* stop," he said. "It's after seven now. Can you call for me and tell them we're coming?"

"Okay."

He explained how to find the number on his satellite phone, and a few seconds later Hannah had placed the call. From the tone of the conversation, it was clear that Layne, who'd answered, was somewhat shocked that her brother-in-law wanted to visit. Damn it, he wasn't a family person; he'd never claimed to be. Sure, there *may* have been times when he was growing up that he'd thought it would be nice to have stronger ties, but those moments hadn't lasted.

"If you're sure," Hannah said at length. "Mmm.... Yes...I know the area, I went to school in Seattle. It shouldn't be hard to find....I look forward to meeting you, too."

She disconnected.

"What was that all about?" he asked.

"We're meeting them at Matt's office. Layne says it's closer to the freeway than their house and she knows we're in a hurry."

"Then we're all set."

AN HOUR LATER Jake watched Hannah coo over his nephew and wondered if he was missing something in his genetic code. The infant wasn't related to Hannah, yet she'd excitedly asked to hold him, while he was afraid to go near the little guy. But it wasn't because William might spit up or cry. It was because he looked breakable. Life was fragile. Too many babies in the places he'd lived never grew up.

"Never thought this day would come, did you?" Matt asked while Layne and Hannah chatted as if they'd known each other for years. "Me, married with a kid?"

"Not after that party you threw the weekend we saw each other in Tahiti. I had a hangover for a week."

"Please don't mention that weekend to Layne. Jeez, isn't she beautiful?" he asked, looking at his wife with a goofy expression.

However attractive she might be, Layne didn't compare to Hannah, but Jake nodded dutifully. "Yeah. Uh, by the way, I'm having a gift shipped to your house for William. It's a hand-carved wood train with a circular track, so he won't be able to play with it for a while."

Matt grinned: "No problem, *I'll* play with it."

They were getting ready to leave when Hannah pulled a colorful package from her knapsack. "Oops, I almost forgot to give you this."

It turned out to be a finely crocheted baby blanket that his sister-in-law immediately wrapped around her son. "How beautiful," she exclaimed. "I love handwork."

"Me, too."

They exchanged phone numbers and email addresses, then Hannah kissed Will's forehead and left with obvious reluctance. Ten minutes later they were back on the freeway, and even Jake couldn't deny the whole thing hadn't delayed them for long.

He was expecting a comment to that effect when Hannah said, "I'm starving," and took a container of cookies from her backpack. "Want one?"

"Later." Jake glanced at her. "I must have seemed pretty awkward back there."

"No more than most bachelors."

The offhand comment was curiously reassuring, and Jake concentrated on negotiating the city traffic. Hannah had offered to drive, and he'd take her up on it after they left the freeway. Once in the mountains he wanted to focus all of his attention on potential places to stop and take photographs.

HANNAH LOOKED OUT the Jeep window at the city flashing past, aware of a vague ache around her heart. Will was such a sweet baby, and she'd always wanted more than one child. She loved Danny more than anything, but he was growing up so quickly, and who knew if she'd ever meet someone.

Jake, a voice in her head whispered.

Yeah, just the new father figure her son needed. Yet when she thought about the night with the skunk and Jake's admission about being sometimes scared, she had to wonder.

"Is there any more coffee?" Jake asked, breaking into her thoughts.

Hannah pulled out the thermos—a thirty-two-ounce stainless-steel thermos bottle her family had taken on outings for at least twenty years—and poured him a cup.

Jake sniffed the steaming brew with apparent appreciation. "Thanks."

"Do you have coffee when you go on one of your longer expeditions?"

"Sure. It doesn't taste like yours, though there's something special about drinking it in the wildest places in the world. There's nothing like being in a place few people have ever been before."

"Then a place isn't worth your time if a lot of people have been there?"

Jake frowned. "That isn't what I meant. Not exactly. But I want to take the most unique photos possible. How long will the drive to Mount Baker take?"

"Once we get to the town of Glacier, it's only about an hour," Hannah said, deciding that talking was better than thinking stupid things. "But it offers high-country views that you usually can't get without backpacking."

"Yeah, and that will have to do, since you refuse to take me to the more *in*accessible parts of the range," Jake said, an edge returning to his voice.

Hannah pressed her lips together. The moderate hiking they were doing was one thing; going into rough country with a heavy load was another. Jake had pushed for a backpack trip into the Enchantment Lakes Basin—particularly to Lake Viviane, considered by some to be the most beautiful alpine lake in the Cascades. But it was a strenuous climb and would take several days. She'd told him she would consider a trip there...when Owen Kershaw and a doctor cleared him for it. Jake hadn't been pleased.

"You can always hire someone else to take you around," she told him. "I'm not stopping you."

"I just wish you'd be more reasonable."

"I *am* being reasonable. Owen said you could pursue normal daily activity, but backpacking doesn't qualify."

"I'm improving much faster than anyone expected. It may not take a full year to get back to where I was."

Hannah didn't respond. They both knew the bruised nerves in his leg were healing the way nerves healed...slowly. She'd overheard Owen emphasizing it the last time he was at the lodge for a therapy session. And maybe the nerves didn't need to be fully recovered for Jake to return to his old life, but he'd be taking a chance.

At Burlington they left the freeway to take a state highway, and switched drivers. Hannah had brought Danny to Mount Baker the summer before, but he'd gotten scared on the switchbacks. It *was* nerve-racking—in some places the road almost felt suspended in air as it twisted upward.

Before long they'd passed the little town of Glacier.

"Do you want to visit Nooksack Falls now or after we go up the mountain?" she asked a few minutes later. "It's just a mile off the byway."

"After. According to the weather service, a small front is coming in, and that should make for dramatic pictures up at the viewpoint."

Hannah's fingers tightened on the steering wheel. She should have checked the weather herself instead of leaving it to Jake. *Her* priorities were quite different from *his,* including staying alive to raise her child. For a brief moment she considered refusing to go any farther, but they were less than twenty miles from Artist Point.

"Fair warning, I'm turning around if we get thunder and lightning out there," she warned. "And if it gets too bad, we're staying put until it's over."

Jake didn't look happy about it but didn't argue.

Shortly after passing the Silver Fir Campground, they emerged from dense forest and the road began snaking its way up the mountains. There were few people on the road—probably because of the weather forecast—and Hannah grimly concentrated on driving. It was only when they arrived at Artist Point and parked that she relaxed.

Though she wasn't thrilled about the gathering clouds, she helped Jake carry his equipment out to the spectacular vista of Mount Baker. Almost instantly, his expression intensified the way it always did when his photographer's instincts took over.

Hannah sighed and sat down with her book. It was going to be a long wait.

JAKE WASN'T AWARE of anything except the storm developing over the jagged peak of the mountain. It was eternally white, the most glaciated of all the volcanic peaks in the Cascades, which wasn't surprising considering the amount of snow it got in a single year.

And maybe some today, he thought as the clouds roiled. He took picture after picture, switching lenses and changing settings, compelled by the ice-carved landscape.

A spatter of rain distracted him only because he needed to protect his equipment. Automatically he held out his hand for one of the plastic hoods he used to shield his cameras…only to remember that Toby wasn't there any longer, anticipating his needs.

Damn.

He missed the guy, even missed his complaints. Missing anyone was a new sensation, and not one he particularly enjoyed. Jake pulled the protective hood from his bag, only to stop and look back at Hannah.

She'd fallen asleep, her jacket wrapped tightly around her. If it start raining much harder, she'd get wet and chilled.

Jake glanced back at the mountain with the weather front poised over it, perfect for photos… then rapidly broke down his equipment and stowed it away.

"Hannah." He shook her shoulder. "It's starting to rain. Let's get going."

She glanced at her watch. "You haven't been working that long."

"We can't stay—you'll get wet."

"Oh." She blinked, but didn't say anything else, for which Jake was deeply grateful. He didn't want to examine his reasons for stopping early; he *never* stopped working for something like rain. Some of his best shots had been taken during brief breaks in the weather.

By the time they'd hiked the mile back to the parking area where the Jeep sat alone, the rain was falling in fits and starts from a sky that had grown ominously dark. They stowed his gear and got inside as the clouds began dumping torrents, reducing visibility to only a few feet.

"We're not going anywhere," Hannah murmured. "We might as well have lunch."

She shimmied into the backseat and he followed, though it was a much tighter fit for him. He reached into the cargo area and pulled out the cooler bag. Two sandwiches and a hot cup of coffee from the thermos later, it was still raining, but they were warmer, since the survival gear they'd stowed in the Jeep included blankets. Jake hadn't thought the gear was necessary, thinking of the Cascades as little more than a kiddie playground, but after viewing the sharp slopes of Mount Baker and other peaks they'd seen driving up, he was realizing his mistake.

The windows were fogged, and he rubbed a clear space to look out. The rain was still so heavy, he could see little except rivers of water flowing over the ground.

"At least it isn't snowing," he muttered.

"Perish the thought. In some spots Mount Baker can get over a thousand inches of snow annually. We're at a lower elevation here, of course, though snow is probably possible any day of the year."

He instantly pictured more than eighty feet of snow rising around the Jeep. Even with his experience traveling in extreme terrains and weather, it wasn't pretty.

"So if you had the train set shipped to Seattle, what else did you buy from Vince?" Hannah asked. "You had two bags when we left the craft fair."

"I got a train set for Danny, too."

She blinked. "Oh. That's really nice of you. Vince Gilson does wonderful work."

"Yeah." Jake stirred restlessly. "He mentioned having a bum leg. Is that why he got into wood carving?"

HANNAH FINALLY REALIZED why Jake's mood had deteriorated so badly on Friday—talking to Vince had been a reminder about his own injury.

"Vince worked as a logger for more than twenty years," she said carefully. "He was hurt several times, but the last accident was the worst. He took up wood carving while he was laid up, and now has quite a reputation throughout the region. Galleries carry his work from Vancouver, Canada, to Portland, Oregon."

"I'm surprised he bothers making toys."

"I think Vince and Norma just love kids. They've got seven grandchildren. Norma helps him in the business, painting or staining the pieces and handling the internet orders."

Jake stretched and Hannah nearly groaned as she watched him. They'd come close to making love on Friday, and her body still remembered that she hadn't followed through.

"Can't they do anything for Vince?" Jake asked. "A better surgeon, maybe? I could call my orthopedist in Seattle for a consult. He's Layne's father. I'm sure he'd take the case. And I could help with some of the expense if money is a problem."

Hannah's heart melted. For all of Jake's faults, he *did* care about people…he just didn't want to acknowledge that part of himself. He'd even abandoned today's work because of her, and she'd seen enough of his photos to know he favored the dramatic weather that had been developing over the mountain.

She inched closer to him.

"You could talk to the Gilsons, but I know they've seen more than one specialist."

Her blanket had fallen to the Jeep floor and Jake lifted the edge of his and tucked it around them both. Heat suffused her, making her breasts throb and stomach clench.

Leaning over, he kissed her slowly and thoroughly. He started to draw back and her body screamed.

"Sorry," he muttered. "We're up here alone.... I'd never take advantage."

"Fine. I will." Hannah grabbed the lapels of his shirt and kissed him again.

Suddenly his hands were everywhere, tugging clothes aside, exploring and caressing. Her jeans were damp from the rain they'd walked through and it was difficult getting them off, but she finally kicked them free, and his fingers slid under her bikini briefs to cup her bottom.

"You feel so good," Jake breathed against her neck. "That night on the couch, I'd never touched anything so soft. Do you know how much sleep I've lost thinking about it? Not to mention the cold showers I've taken."

She nearly laughed. "What about last Friday?"

Jake tipped his head back and surveyed her. "You looked like a sun goddess. I wanted to see *all* of you. Every inch."

"I don't think exposing every inch is practical in the Jeep."

"Do you—"

A sharp tap on the window from outside of the Jeep startled them both.

"It's the Forest Service," called a voice. "Is everything all right in there?"

"Uh, *fine,*" Hannah called back, frantically pulling her T-shirt and bra into place. She kicked Jake when he didn't move, and he zipped his jeans. "Just a minute."

She somehow got her own jeans on, then rubbed a clear spot on the fogged window. A man in a Forest Service uniform stood nearby.

Hannah opened the door. There were a few drops of rain still falling, but the sheets of water inundating the parking area had stopped.

"Uh, hello. We didn't think it was safe to drive in the storm. We were eating a late picnic lunch and didn't realize conditions had improved."

"It's good you stayed put, but you should go down now that we have a break in the weather—the road could freeze over later. I'll lead the way, slow and easy."

She smiled brightly. "Wonderful. We'll turn the engine on and start the windows defogging."

"Yes, ma'am. Just flash your lights when you're ready." The ranger tipped his hat and returned to his vehicle. Though his expression had remained neutral, she had the feeling he knew exactly what they'd been doing.

Hannah cast a glance at Jake. He looked more

frustrated than she'd ever seen him. "Well, now you've had another cultural experience, though it's one most of us get out of the way as teenagers."

"What's that?" Jake asked grumpily.

"Necking in a car and getting busted by the cops with your pants unzipped."

To her astonishment, he burst out laughing.

CHAPTER FIFTEEN

HANNAH FOCUSED ON the forestry vehicle moving slowly ahead of them on the road and was grateful that Jake remained silent. The first ten miles were the most nerve-racking since the elevation dropped quickly, but her watchful tension didn't fully ease until the denser forest closed around them.

The forest ranger obviously agreed that the worst was over because he turned into the Silver Fir Campground and waved as they passed.

"Nice guy," Jake commented at last.

"Who probably thought we were crazy as loons to go up to the point with bad weather predicted," Hannah returned crisply. From now on she was checking the predictions herself *before* going anywhere with Jake.

"Don't start on that death-wish thing again," he warned. "I have a healthy appreciation for being alive. I just prefer taking a certain kind of photograph."

What's wrong with diversifying? Hannah thought wryly. "Okay, I take back the near-death-wish thing, but your 'certain kind of photograph' could still get you killed."

"Why do you care?"

"Because Danny idolizes you." *Among other reasons.*

"I didn't mean for that to happen. I won't tell him any more stories. Maybe that will help."

Hannah smiled sadly, thinking about the way Jake had stopped taking pictures of Mount Baker because she might get wet. Or how he'd helped out after Badger and Danny got sprayed by the skunk. For that matter, his friendship with his longtime photography assistant was endearing. There was a good person inside Jake, even if he didn't want to see it.

"It isn't just the stories," she said. "And Danny would think he'd done something wrong if you stopped telling them. But when you leave, he's going to read about you on the internet and never stop hoping you'll come back. He doesn't have a father like his friends, but now he has heroic Jake Hollister, intrepid photographer, to look up to."

"*Crap.* I'm no hero."

"There are all kinds of heroes, Jake, including guys willing to take the time to tell stories to a kid. And if something ever happened to you…"

"I'm not reckless, Hannah."

She no longer knew what to think. Her heart was too involved—so much that she'd found herself wondering if things could work out if they both made compromises. It wouldn't change her concern about

Danny losing someone he loved, but Jake *had* shown he could be a good father if he wanted to be.

Of course, it was ridiculous to have those thoughts. Jake was famous, both for his photographs and disreputable father. An internet search on his name turned up thousands of hits, and many art critics called him the Ansel Adams of the twenty-first century.

That was huge.

He'd end up in history books, be the subject of encyclopedia articles and was probably already in *Who's Who in America.* That kind of man didn't get serious about small-town schoolteachers.

Hannah flexed her fingers on the steering wheel, glad Jake had focused on his cameras, probably to avoid the awkward moment.

It was still wet, but the sun was peeping out through the clouds, creating a rainbow. In Washington the weather was often like that—it could be storming one minute, and the next minute sunlight could be glinting against rain-washed surroundings.

"See the rainbow?" she asked, pointing. It arced through a section of the sky, seeming to begin and end in turbulent, silver-crested clouds. "Jake, *look,*" she repeated.

"Uh, yeah," he said, barely glancing up. Apparently rainbows didn't inspire his photographer's eye the way the steep slopes and ice of Mount Baker had done. He'd been fascinated by Mount Shuksan as well, thinking it *was* Baker when first spotted.

They turned off to stop at Nooksack Falls, and though it wasn't a glacier-covered mountain peak, Jake spent the rest of the afternoon photographing the waterfall. Hannah read, occasionally watching him work, marveling that he could be surrounded by breathtaking beauty and still see no mystery or wonder in it.

Finally Jake packed his cameras away again.

"I'll drive," he said as they put his equipment back in the cargo area. "So you can get some rest…in case you're interested in continuing what we started earlier."

"I'm interested."

Making love with Jake could make things harder in the end, but at the moment she didn't care.

Jake's eyes gleamed, yet he insisted they drive all the way to Bellingham for lodging…then asked for two rooms at the registration desk, albeit *adjoining* rooms.

It was a nice hotel, the kind with bellhops, and one of them helped bring their belongings up to their rooms, though Jake moved his own photographic equipment. While he didn't seem to mind *her* handling his gear, he wouldn't let anybody else touch it.

"Thank you, sir. Is there anything else?" the bellhop asked eagerly after receiving a generous tip. Until then he'd been polite but not enthusiastic. Now it seemed he couldn't do enough for them. "Money talks" wasn't a cultural lesson Jake needed to learn about America, or maybe it was just true of most cultures.

"No, that's all."

When they were alone, Jake held up the plastic card key for her room. "It's your decision."

Hannah took the key and lobbed it over his head, into the room beyond. Even if it *was* a mistake to have sex with Jake, she'd made her decision.

He smiled and took a step backward. "Please, come in."

"Don't mind if I do. May I freshen up?"

"Not at all. My house is your house." He stopped and grinned. *"Literally."*

She went into the bathroom and nearly screamed at the sight of her hair, mussed and barely contained by its French braid. If the forest ranger *hadn't* guessed what they'd been doing behind those fogged windows, he was unbelievably naive. Undoing the braid, she combed her hair as much as possible with her fingers.

When she came out, the connecting doors between the two rooms were open and Jake was examining his wallet. "I'm going to run downstairs for a moment," he said, looking up.

Oh, great.

He needed condoms. It was a good thing they'd been interrupted earlier; she could imagine his reaction to a potential pregnancy. She wasn't sure how she'd feel about it herself. While she wanted another child, she didn't have a future with Jake, and it wasn't easy being a single mother of *one* kid, much less two. And would she be making the same mistake she'd made with Steven? Hadn't she learned anything in the past eight years?

Hannah showered quickly and changed into a nightshirt from her bag. It wasn't romantic or sensual, but better than clammy jeans. She turned back the bed and sank back on the pillows, hoping Jake would hurry…and that the hotel gift shop carried what he'd gone looking for.

JAKE WALKED AROUND the small shop in the lobby and finally located a discreet display of condoms. There were several different kinds, and he grabbed a box without paying attention to which one it was. Protection was protection; the important thing was using it. And normally protection was something he was *very* careful about, which made the interlude at Artist Point disturbing for more than one reason. He hadn't been carrying anything with him, and he wasn't convinced they would have stopped if they hadn't been interrupted.

Of course, Hannah might have had a cooler head and put the brakes on, but there were no guarantees.

Hannah was different from the women he'd known before…though he didn't want to think about those differences too much. Nevertheless, surely she understood that he wasn't someone to plan her future around. He frowned as he waited in line to pay for the condoms. Maybe he should talk to her and be sure they were seeing the situation in the same way, even if it cast a chill on things.

Back at the room he walked in and saw Hannah in the bed.

"My clothes were still damp," she said, gesturing to the oversize T-shirt she wore. Clearly she'd discarded her bra along with the rest of her clothes, and his mouth went dry.

"Uh, Hannah," he said, sitting on the edge of the mattress. "You remember that I'm...well, not *permanent*. Right? This is a break...a vacation from our real lives."

She rolled her eyes. "Just shut up and kiss me."

"Is that a movie quote?"

"I think so." Hannah frowned. "Probably. Hell, I don't know. Ask me when I care." Wiggling a little, she pulled off her T-shirt and threw it across the room.

Any thought of doing the prudent thing flew instantly out of Jake's head. His view of her on the hood of the Jeep had only been a taste of better things. He sat on the bed and fastened his gaze on the rounded slopes of her breasts, her quickening breaths causing them to rise and fall.

He put his finger on the hollow of her throat and slowly drew it down, tracing each responsive peak in turn.

Her hands reached for his arms and she arched backward into the pile of pillows. He teased her nipple with the tip of his tongue, then blew on it. A satisfying squeak sounded in Hannah's throat. Jake opened his mouth around her, drawing hard on the sensitive crest, loving the restless shifting of her legs.

He trailed his right hand down along her waist, finding the curve of her hip and sliding his fingers between her thighs.

HANNAH GASPED.

It had been so long since she'd been with a man that she instinctively clenched her legs before relaxing them. He brushed the apex, teasing and tempting before easing into her core. Almost instantly wave after wave of pleasure shuddered through her body.

When her heart finally slowed, she opened her eyes to see Jake watching her intently.

"Don't get too smug," she ordered. "And you're way overdressed…except for a condom. You did get condoms, didn't you?"

"Yeah, I got them, and it would be a shame if they went to waste."

Hannah levered her way to a more upright position, using extra shoulder action, which drew his attention back to her breasts.

"I agree. About all those clothes…?" she said deliberately.

"You want to help?"

"I'd rather watch."

Jake slid off the bed and pulled his shirttails free at the waist before beginning to unzip his jeans, at which point Hannah started humming.

He stopped. "What's that?"

"A striptease deserves music. That's 'Let Me Entertain You' from *Gypsy*. It's a movie about a famous stripper."

"Another movie, huh?"

"Growing up I used to regularly spend weekends at Huckleberry Lodge, especially after my great-uncle passed away. Great-Aunt Elkie loved movies. She had all the cable channels, and the guy from the video store would come out every week to show her the list of new releases. She ordered *a lot* of them."

Kicking his pants across the room, Jake stood with his boxers only.

"Why don't you help me? I dare you."

The sexy glint in his eyes was part laughter, part white-hot heat. Hannah climbed to her feet and had the satisfaction of seeing Jake's chest contract as she deliberately brushed her breasts against his arm. She slid her fingers under the waistband of his boxers.

Jake clearly had more experience than she did, but she refused to show any uncertainty.

"Do you enjoy this?" she asked, stroking down the lower part of his belly, finding his erection and exploring it, then tugged his shorts free until they dropped to the floor.

He didn't say anything, but his groan told Hannah all she needed to know.

"Not bad, Mr. Hollister," she murmured. She pushed him onto the middle of the bed and studied his body the way he'd examined hers. There were the scars, some jagged, some others straight and even. His body was also lean and muscular and incredibly well formed. Dropping to her knees next to him, she deliberately let her hair trail up his legs, a strangled sound coming from Jake's throat.

JAKE COULDN'T STOP another groan from escaping his chest. Hannah wasn't behaving the way he'd expected. She'd looked at his scars, but hadn't expressed sympathy or shown any particular curiosity. Instead she'd gone straight to seductive moves that were making his blood boil.

Opening the box of condoms, she pulled one out and dropped it on his stomach with a challenging smile.

He pulled her down on top of him, wrapping his arms around her slender waist and fastening his mouth on hers. Hannah tasted sweet, and he slowly rolled on his side to look at her as the condom slid against her belly.

Picking it up, he brushed his fingers against her neck, across her breasts and down to tease the soft curls at the apex of her legs. She squirmed.

"Slowpoke," she gasped. "I'm one up on you."

"Watching your pleasure is…pleasurable, as well."

"Sadist. Right now, you're just torturing me."

Suddenly unable to wait any longer, he jerked the package open.

"Let me." Hannah rolled it over his erection, and the minute she was done, he tugged her on top of him. She was hot and ready, and they moved together like waves surging and ebbing, yet the pressure inside only grew and grew until he couldn't restrain it any longer.

THE NEXT MORNING Hannah woke up before dawn and quietly tiptoed into the adjoining room with her bag. Having sex with Jake couldn't be repeated. It was exactly what he'd said: a vacation from their real lives.

Yet when she looked back at him lying sprawled naked on the mattress, her abdomen tightened all over again.

Look at the scars, she reminded herself. Death wish or not, there were plenty of them, a clear indication of the risks he willingly took.

Jake's leg, broken in the plane crash, was punctuated with red lines where the surgeon had pieced it back together. A six-inch jagged mark on his opposite thigh had the earmarks of a horrific gash that had probably healed without benefit of stitches. There were three long white slashes over his right ribs that looked suspiciously like claw marks. His knuckles and hands had dings and bashes, some older, some looking more recent.

There were other scars as well, but she didn't want to look closely. She'd felt them, though, as their bodies had moved together, her hands exploring his lean, hard length. It wasn't the marks themselves that she minded, it was what they represented.

Damn it.

It had been the best sex of her life, but she had to put some distance between them before she started thinking foolish things.

Just lust, she told herself firmly, going into the other bathroom and stepping into the shower. The worst part about lust was that there was no good way to get it out of her system. She could pretend it didn't exist, that they'd scratched that itch last night, but she knew it would sneak back in when she wasn't paying attention. And now she was going to compare every other man to Jake for the rest of forever, and they'd probably come up short. On the other hand, it was now more obvious than ever that she'd made the right decision breaking things off with Brendan.

Hannah shampooed her hair and rinsed it, wincing as she encountered a mass of tangles. Normally she braided it before going to bed, but hadn't gotten around to the task the previous night…though they'd made serious inroads on the box of condoms Jake had bought, in between ordering a late dinner from room service and finding it offered avenues for sensual play, as well.

Forget him, she ordered.

She stepped out of the shower and wrapped her hair in a towel, only to look up and see Jake watching her, his boxer shorts doing little to conceal his renewed arousal. Her breasts tightened in response, but she couldn't weaken her resolve.

FROM THE COOL expression on Hannah's face, Jake was fairly certain she wasn't interested in returning to bed with him. On the other hand, maybe her reserve had more to do with his coming in uninvited while she was showering. Modesty after the way they'd made love all night seemed a little odd, but he didn't understand the female psyche any better than he understood the U.S. And despite his claims to the contrary, he obviously *didn't* understand America or Americans.

Somehow that made him feel lonely, though nothing had changed except his perception. But part of him had always clung to the thought that he had a country where he belonged, even if he was never there.

"What are you thinking?" Hannah asked, sounding suspicious as she wound a larger towel around her body. While it provided coverage, it also teased and tempted, revealing the upper slopes of her breasts and an expanse of thigh.

"That you were right."

He almost laughed at the shock on her face that he'd admit such a thing.

"I'm a mother—I'm right about a lot of things. What particular thing are you referring to?"

"That I really *don't* know the customs of my own country. In some ways I feel more like a foreigner here than in Nepal and Tibet."

"You've probably spent more time in Nepal than here."

It was true. When he was a kid, the U.S. had been

a stopping place on the way to somewhere else, not a destination in its own right. And he was in the States even less often as an adult. There hadn't seemed to be any point in coming here, though he was starting to recognize that he might have missed a few good things about the place.

Hannah walked past him out of the bathroom.

"The Himalayas above Kathmandu are incredible," he said, following her. "An endlessly shifting environment of sunlight and mist. You should consider going there one day." He resisted calling it magical, though it *had* seemed magical when he was a boy, mist covering a mountain peak or stream as if an unknown force controlled how and where it moved.

"I'll put it on my to-do list. But schoolteachers' salaries usually don't lend themselves to trips like that. Especially ones with a kid to send through college. I'll be happy if I can take Danny to Europe or Japan someday."

She sat on the edge of the king-size bed and pulled the towel from her head. Jake smiled ironically. His preconceptions about schoolteachers had *never* included a sexy, scantily clad woman with damp ropes of hair tumbling almost to her waist. *Lady Godiva,* he thought. He just had to get that towel away from her and the image would be complete. Well...except for the horse in the legend.

"Ouch." Hannah had been combing her hair with her fingers and had tried to yank through a knot.

"Do you have a comb? I'll help. After all, I'm partly responsible for those tangles."

She regarded him for a long minute. "On the bathroom counter."

He fetched the comb and sat behind her, easing the teeth first through the ends of her hair, gradually working out the snarls as he moved higher. Working on a woman's hair was another new thing for him, and strangely satisfying.

"Aren't you anxious to get back into the mountains?" she asked eventually.

"We'll get there, but I don't think they're going anywhere." Jake paused and thought of the horrific eruption of Mount St. Helens. "Not today, at least."

"What about our plan to drive the North Cascades Highway?"

"Maybe another trip."

"Summer won't last forever. The road is closed part of the year, and I'll be teaching after Labor Day."

He didn't like thinking about it, though if he hadn't been working around Hannah's committee meetings and parental needs, he'd be getting a hell of a lot more accomplished. Jake thought about the previous day when he'd packed up his gear because rain was coming. In the past he'd gotten soaked, half-frozen, nearly struck by lightning, even attacked by animals in his search for the perfect photograph. He *never* quit while there was an opportunity for a good photo, but yesterday he'd stopped because Hannah Nolan might get wet.

Yet his brain shied away from thinking too much about it. He liked Hannah and respected her, but he couldn't let her become too important to him.

Remember Toby, his self-protective instincts reminded him.

Toby had quit because Vera didn't want him traveling so often. Still, Toby hadn't looked unhappy about it, either. And as much as his former assistant had complained, he'd enjoyed the travel almost as much as Jake himself.

"There's something I don't understand," Hannah murmured. "You love the high villages of Nepal in the Himalayas, but I understand the Sherpas are very spiritual, offering prayers in a multitude of different ways. You don't believe in anything like that. How can you love the place and the people and not have any appreciation for their beliefs?"

Jake's hands stilled in Hannah's hair.

"It's not a question of appreciation," he said carefully. "I simply accept it as their way of life. And sadly, a good deal has been lost or changed since Sagarmatha was first climbed by Sir Edmund Hillary."

"Sagarmatha?"

"It's what Mount Everest is called in Nepal. In Tibet it's Chomolungma…'goddess of the world.'"

"I like those names."

"Me, too. Tourism has changed the Sherpa villages. They were once so isolated. It's a strenuous two-week walk over mountain trails to climb to the Khumbu highlands of Nepal from Kathmandu, but now there are landing strips for small planes, and it takes under an hour. Thousands of people arrive yearly, some who just want to see the country, and others who want to challenge Sagarmatha or other peaks."

"Are you saying the Sherpas have lost their spirituality?"

"No, they still pray. They burn juniper with their morning prayers and in small shrines. They make prayer wheels and carve stone tablets and rock walls along trails. It's part of the face of Nepal. Prayers are written on flags and banners and hung from trees or poles or stretched ropes. I think the people believe they'll be carried to heaven by the elements."

"It sounds beautiful."

It did have a curious beauty, yet Jake no longer knew how he felt about it. Was it simply a charming tradition of people who lived in a harsh land and needed a primitive crutch to survive? Or was it a genuine sensing of something greater and more powerful around them?

Abruptly he recalled Josie's anger when he'd written a few words and hung it with the other prayer flags, thinking of the climbers who'd lost their lives. She'd ripped it down, angry her son would participate in an "archaic ritual." It was the only time she'd shown any emotion about the disastrous attempt to climb Sagarmatha and he'd wanted to scream at her. At least he'd *done* something by writing the words; he hadn't just drunk coffee and silently stared at the mountain as if resenting the defeat.

Jake realized he'd suppressed the memory for years, and an ache grew in his gut.

Somehow the disastrous expedition when he was eight was getting mixed up in his head with the crash in the Arctic. Death had followed both, and he'd never talked to anyone about it…just attempted to take part in a custom that seemed to comfort the Sherpas. And curiously, he didn't think Gordon would mind a prayer being written for him in a distant land. He'd seemed to have a universal acceptance of the world and how he was connected to it.

"Do you think they have pancakes on the room service menu?" he asked, determined to change the subject. "Or French toast?"

"Probably. But not huckleberry syrup."

"Too bad. They'd make a fortune."

They ordered a huge breakfast, along with a picnic lunch to take with them. He decided to keep their rooms for a return that night, though he suspected Hannah would keep the connecting doors firmly closed between them.

It should have been reassuring that she didn't expect more. Instead it was damned annoying.

CHAPTER SIXTEEN

BARBI DROVE OUT to Silver Cottage early Thursday evening for a tutoring session and saw Jake down by the lake, taking pictures across the cove. He was out there a bunch. She didn't expect him to see her. He got weird when he had his camera, as if the rest of the world was invisible.

She climbed the steps of the guesthouse and noticed Danny sitting on the lakeshore near Jake, intently watching the photographer.

Hannah opened the door before Barbi could knock.

"Hi. Since Jake is out by the lake, let's work in the kitchen," Hannah suggested.

That suited Barbi. She hadn't thought she minded people knowing she was studying for her GED, but it wasn't true. Hannah was okay. She understood about Vic, even if she didn't know everything. And Luigi had been pushing her to do it practically from the first day she started working for him. But she didn't want anyone else to know, especially Brendan, though her reasons had changed.

"Do you want coffee?" Hannah asked. "Or something to eat? I've got Chinese-chicken salad leftover from dinner, and Danny will just take it to Jake in the morning if you don't have some."

"Naw, I'm fine. I saw Danny outside. Doesn't he get bored watching Jake take pictures?"

"He wants to go on some of the photography trips with Jake, so he's trying to prove he can be quiet and not be restless."

"Think it's gonna work?"

"Not a chance."

Barbi fidgeted with her books, then glanced at her friend. "So how's it going with Brendan?" she asked casually.

Hannah's face went blank as she sat down. "Actually, we broke up. And to be honest, I haven't missed him. I know that sounds terrible, but I think we just *thought* we should be a good couple. It isn't that we were bad together—we just weren't *anything*."

Relief flooded Barbi. "Then, um, would you mind if I...uh...asked him out?"

"Be my guest. But I have to say I'm a little surprised. You fight all the time. Well, except at the pancake supper—it was nice that you ate with him."

"We fight, but I sorta like him under all that stuffiness. Only I'd never, *ever* do something if you weren't okay with it."

"Heavens, I know that," Hannah assured her. "Don't worry, I'm not the least bit interested in Brendan, except as a friend. Now, let's talk about what you worked on while I was gone."

Barbi took out the sheet of equations and wrinkled her nose. "I hate this stuff."

"I'm not crazy about math, either, but it's part of the test, and you're very good at it."

The praise was encouraging and Barbi watched as Hannah went over the papers, checking her work.

It was a relief to know Brendan was available. Eating pizza in the park hadn't been a date, any more than having pancakes together, but she'd felt funny about it. Hannah was her friend, and between her different jobs and the problems with her father, Barbi didn't have that many friends.

The question was how to make her move. She'd only had a few regular boyfriends—guys usually did a fast retreat when they eventually bumped into Vic, not wanting the hassle of dating someone with a dad like that. Who could blame 'em? Hell, *she* was leaving Mahalaton Lake to get away from Vic. It would take a while since she still needed her GED and to get a job that showed she had marketable skills, but she was going.

So why not have some fun with Brendan in the meantime?

It wasn't as if she expected it to last. He was a freaking lawyer and she hadn't even finished high school. And he had a rich, snobby family back in Boston who'd *never* approve of her. His ancestors would probably jump out of their graves if she showed her face east of the Mississippi, especially the ones who'd rubbed elbows with John Adams before he became president of the United States.

After an hour with Hannah, Barbi left with a new set of math problems to work out. She debated for a little while, then drove toward Brendan's condo, deciding there was no point in being subtle. She might as well give it a shot and see what happened.

BRENDAN FLIPPED THROUGH the hundreds of on-demand offerings from the television cable company, unable to find a single thing that appealed to him. There wasn't much else to do, either. Mahalaton Lake was devoid of nightlife except on weekends when there was a community event, but normally that didn't bother him much.

Tonight he was just bored and restless for some reason.

There were restaurants, of course, and a bar just outside town. But a roadside bar didn't hold any appeal—he had an uncle with a drinking problem and had always been cautious of alcohol because of it.

The internet was no more tempting. There'd been another email from his father giving the schedule of Massachusetts's bar exams. Probably what made his father so successful was that he didn't accept answers he didn't like. He pushed and pushed, and as a result was one of the most sought-after litigators in the state. As for Brendan's mother, she'd written that the two youngest Chester sisters were still single. *Hint, hint*. The Chester girls were interchangeable to Brendan, but his mother liked their social desirability.

Tossing the remote control to one side, Brendan glanced around the living room. Kind of empty and dull. Even when he'd been sick, he'd noticed how Barbi had brightened the place up with her blond hair and impudent smile. What an idiot he'd been not to see beyond the clothes and in-your-face attitude earlier. He'd met her months before meeting Hannah.

The bell rang and he considered not answering, but finally got up and opened the door.

"Barbi," he said in shock.

"Hey, Brendan." She smiled sassily. "I understand you and Hannah aren't an item any longer."

"That's right."

"Good. Because I'm coming in."

Confused, he stepped back while she marched through the door, kicking it shut behind her.

"Would you, uh, like a glass of juice or cola?" he managed to ask. "I don't have any wine or beer."

"I don't drink…and I'd much rather have a glass of *you*." She tugged her tight tank top over her head and threw it across the room.

The sight sucked the air out of his lungs. He'd thought her tight clothing left few unanswered questions about her figure, and he was partly right… and partly wrong. She wasn't wearing a bra and her breasts rose high and full above her slim waist, just waiting to be touched.

"Aren't you going to take your turn?" she demanded before he could react.

"What do you mean?"

"This is like tennis. I take off a piece, then you do. Then I do. Then you do. Whoever runs out of something to take off *last* gets to be on top."

Now *there* was a game he liked…and wanted to lose.

He loosened his tie and threw it behind him. Barbi tugged at the waistband on her jeans, then stopped and grinned. She unfastened her beaded necklace instead and dropped it on the coffee table.

Brendan quickly evaluated how much he was wearing…and how much Barbi had left, and knew he'd finish last unless he got creative. But at least he wasn't still wearing his suit jacket and vest. He shrugged out of his shirt, somehow getting his hands free of the cuffs without removing his cufflinks. A faint ripping sound accompanied the effort and the links went flying, but he didn't care…as long as Barbi ended up on top.

One of her bangles landed on the table next.

Good, she had at least three more on her wrist. That would help. Brendan unfastened his pants and let them fall, managing to get both his shoes off at the same time he kicked free of the pants. His socks didn't cooperate—they remained on his feet.

She grinned.

"Mmm," she murmured, looking at the tight fabric

of his underwear with approval. "From what I can see, that's some impressive equipment."

"Yours is better," he said, unable to keep his gaze from her perfect breasts.

Her ankle bracelet followed, then his right sock, her left sandal and his left sock.

"We're tied," he announced, glancing at the wisp of lingerie around her hips. His own briefs felt so tight he wanted to howl.

"Nope," she said with a speculative examination of his lower body. "I've still got three bangles." She dropped a second bangle on the table.

"Yeah, I have the damnedest luck," he observed, his heart pounding with anticipation.

"You're next." She inspected him boldly.

His briefs dropped to the floor a moment later, and he closed the gap between them. "You win, but that means I get to help take off everything you have left."

"I like good losers," she whispered, tracing her tongue down the side of his neck and shimmying a little against him.

The movement nearly brought him to his knees.

Hooking his thumbs through the narrow fabric on her hips, Brendan dragged it down, kissing her neck, between her breasts...and the smooth, taut skin of her belly. He eased the underwear farther down, taking his time, until it lay on the floor.

"Okay. Into the bedroom, pal," she ordered. "You're gonna want something soft beneath your butt."

He grinned and grabbed her hand.

JUST AFTER DAWN Brendan woke and looked at Barbi lying asleep in the bed next to him. Never in his wildest dreams had he imagined he'd be with her, particularly after the way they'd argued over the past fourteen months.

Foreplay.

He'd never been with anyone like her. She awakened things he'd never experienced—adventurous, gut-level responses that made him feel fully alive for the first time. It wasn't just the sex—it was the way she attacked life, with no holds barred.

Of course, the sex *was* spectacular, and Brendan's grin grew as he remembered making love in the kitchen, the shower…even the closet where they'd landed accidentally, not realizing the door was open. Around midnight they'd gone searching for a fresh supply of protection and had risked getting arrested when they stopped to use some of it at a pullout on the highway coming back from Lower Mahalaton.

"What are you grinning at?" Barbi asked sleepily.

She was curled on her side and he smiled. "I was just thinking my car had to be better than your small Chevy for making out. 'Fess up—you're glad we took the Lexus."

"It wasn't bad."

"Not bad, she says. I would have broken my back

in your little car." Barbi lightly dragged her finger-nails up his thigh, sending instant heat to his groin.

"Not that I would have minded," he said hoarsely.

"That's better."

Brendan frowned at a set of faded bruises on the inside of Barbi's wrist where she always wore her bangles. He lifted her hand and lightly brushed the yellowing marks. The way the bruises were aligned looked suspiciously like someone had grabbed her, digging in hard with their fingers.

"What are these from?"

"Oh, nothing." She shrugged.

"They don't look like nothing. Did one of your pizza-delivery customers do that?" he demanded. "You don't have to put up with stuff like this, Barbi. Call the police and get them arrested for assault."

"It wasn't a customer. I just banged something. I do it all the time."

"Barbi—"

"Brendan." She mimicked his tone. "It's fine. I clean offices and work in the bakery and stuff, so I always have bruises. Right now I'd rather take another shower than discuss something this tedious."

Brendan's body instantly went on alert. He'd chosen his condo because it had a huge walk-in shower with jets on two sides and a glass firebrick wall that let in natural light at the end. The sun was coming up, and Barbi would look great in the morning glow. Of course, she looked great anywhere.

She bounced out of the bed, vibrant and flushed

with desire, her silky blond hair tumbling over her breasts making her look like an impudent mermaid.

"Slowpoke," she said, stretching slowly to great effect.

BARBI LICKED HER lips, deliberately catlike, and disappeared into the bathroom.

She'd hated fudging the truth about the bruises, but Brendan didn't need to know about her father. Not yet. Besides, a long, hot shower *did* sound nice; her muscles were deliciously tired from the workout she'd given them. It turned out that missionary position wasn't the only way Brendan liked sex. As a matter of fact, he liked it just about any way. And he was awfully good at it, too.

She grinned as she heard footsteps behind her. Flipping on the water, she turned to look at Brendan.

He stepped forward, his arousal already protected by a latex sheath. He soaped his hands, exploring and teasing her breasts, tugging her nipples and whispering sexy suggestions that didn't sound the least like a staid barrister from Boston.

She was startled when he lifted her abruptly and thrust fiercely into her, muttering, urging, demanding, until the world became focused entirely on the juncture of their bodies, whirling faster and faster until she shattered.

Much later she lay draped across Brendan's chest on the bed, sated and lethargic before she glanced at his clock.

She bolted upright. *"Ohmigod, is that the time?"*

Brendan glanced at the bedside clock. "Yeah. I may call in and tell my secretary to cancel my appointments. All two of them. Friday is usually a slow day, thank God."

"I have to go to work."

"But Luigi's doesn't start delivering until four this afternoon. Aren't women supposed to like afterglow? Where's my afterglow?"

"Sorry, but I clean at Memorial Hall on Thursdays and Fridays." She scrambled away, hunting for her clothes. However much she'd love to spend the day in bed with Brendan, she couldn't blow off her jobs. He wasn't permanent, and it wouldn't be right to leave her various employers in the lurch.

"See ya," she said, giving him a kiss with plenty of tongue action.

"Tonight," he replied firmly. "Meet me here after you're done at work. I'll get a can of whipped cream."

"Whipped cream?"

"Yeah. I can't wait to taste it on you. Better than any ice cream sundae."

To Barbi's astonishment, her face actually heated. Hell, she wasn't a virgin to be embarrassed by something like that, though maybe it was because *Brendan* had said it. She wouldn't have expected a guy with his background to have such sexy fantasies. Still, it was nice that he'd gotten rid of all that morning-after awkwardness with an assumption they'd be together again that night. It made things much easier.

"Uh, okay," she said, and his delighted laughter followed her out the door.

HANNAH MET WITH the rescue squad fund-raising committee on Friday morning and showed them the two photographs Jake was donating to their Christmas in August raffle. He'd emailed the digital files to a processing company he'd worked with before, asking for a rush job on the printing and framing. One of the photos had been taken in early-morning light, the other at sunset. And while they were from virtually identical locations, the lighting made each unique.

"They're beautiful," Gwen exclaimed. "And the custom framing...it must have cost a fortune."

Hannah shook her head. "According to Jake, the company donated their time and supplies when they learned it was for a fund-raiser."

"Excellent, and I see they're signed," said Vince Gilson.

"The framer fixed it so Jake could sign and date the outside mattes, then fasten everything down tight. Jake has also provided a certificate of authenticity stating these are limited first-edition prints." Hannah turned one of the photos around so everyone could see the envelope affixed to the back.

Gwen rubbed her hands together. "This is great. We've been selling the raffle tickets locally, but it'll really pick up now that people can see the photos. I also emailed the information to a number of businesses in Seattle and Portland. When I checked our PayPal account this morning, over a thousand tickets had been sold."

Everybody looked suitably impressed.

"To be honest, I was worried Mr. Hollister would change his mind about donating the prints and we'd have to refund the money," Gwen confided. "Now I can relax."

"Jake believes in supporting rescue workers," Hannah said. She didn't add what he'd told her about the Inupiat villagers saving his life. It wasn't a secret—articles about the plane crash had spoken of the Inupiat rescue efforts—but he didn't like talking about what had happened in Alaska. And if she said anything to the committee, somebody might mention it to him.

Ironically, in their phone conversation before Jake arrived, Andy had mentioned his client was determined to return and finish the photographic study of polar animals as soon as he was fit enough.

Hannah's breath caught at the prospect, yet she didn't have any right to complain or ask him to stop recklessly risking his life. *It's just because he reminds you of Collin,* she tried to tell herself. She'd never forgotten her first love, and losing him in such a terrible way had always stayed with her. It was just her bad luck to get involved with another adrenaline junkie.

Except Jake *wasn't* an adrenaline junkie, and that argument was no longer believable.

"Now that the raffle business is concluded, I want to be sure everyone knows the times they're supposed to be at the booths for the street fair," she said.

The festival started a week from Monday and she was frazzled about getting everything done. Well... she was mostly frazzled by Jake and trying to figure out how big a mistake sleeping with him had been.

Or maybe it hadn't been a mistake.

She was annoyed that he had the gall to act as if he knew more about love than she did, but she *had* gotten a little set in her ways...not that she needed to get blasted out of those ways by a man guaranteed to break her heart. And Danny's heart. Except that was going to happen no matter what—her son already adored Jake.

Jake's travel stories *were* exciting, and they debated and argued and kept each other on their toes. And sometimes she saw a loneliness in him that caught her throat.

Even his growing fondness for Louie showed there was more to him than his skill with a camera. He'd never admit it, but he'd become goofily attached to the stray kitten, playing with him, letting him sleep on the bed or ride around on his shoulders. She'd even spotted a number of pictures he'd taken of Louie, though he'd hastily made an excuse about experimenting with interior locations and not wanting to let his skill at photographing animals get rusty.

It was frustrating. Jake had so much to offer, yet he was stubbornly determined to spend his life on glaciers and mountains and in jungles, detached from people.

Pictures were fine and he was a great artist, but why couldn't he let himself be more than just a camera?

LATER THAT EVENING Brendan waited for Barbi, practically jumping out of his skin every time a car drove by outside. He didn't want to think she might have changed her mind, but it was always a possibility.

When the clock ticked over to ten-thirty he was convinced she *had* decided their night together was more than enough. Luigi's stopped delivering at ten on Fridays and Saturdays, and it wasn't a big town. It was less than ten minutes from one side of Mahalaton Lake to the other.

Then there was a knock and he lunged off the couch.

"Hiya, Brendan," Barbi said as he opened the door. She was holding a pizza box.

"Hi."

He pulled her into a kiss that seared right through his soul. Yet when he lifted his head, he could see she looked pale, which wasn't any surprise considering their lack of sleep the night before...or the fact she'd been working since early that morning.

"Did ya get the whipped cream?" she asked with a grin.

"Sure did. Have you eaten?"

"Luigi always feeds me, but I brought some pizza for you so we'd both have garlicky breath."

Brendan almost refused, but there was a flash of pride in Barbi's eyes. "That's great."

She put the pizza box on the coffee table and they sat on the couch. The pizza was his usual sausage, onions and olives, but he decided not to wonder if there was a hidden message in that. He steadily ate a couple of pieces, anxious to take up where they'd left off that morning, then glanced over at Barbi.

She'd fallen asleep.

Though disappointed, Brendan was also glad. She worked hard, and they could make love after she'd gotten some rest.

Groaning a little, he got up and put the rest of the pizza in the refrigerator, then returned and lifted Barbi's legs onto the couch. She was really quite small and delicate—it was her attitude that was big…the defiant attitude that he'd despised and now found so appealing.

Maybe he'd *always* found it appealing, but it had scared the hell out of him to feel that way. A man didn't change who he was in a week or a month. Or even a year. But he *was* changing. While he couldn't totally abandon his upbringing, he was seeing a new way of doing things.

He put her feet on his lap and slipped off her shoes.

One day at a time, he thought.

Yet at some point he had to make a decision about his life, and that included a real commitment to staying in Mahalaton Lake. The people here weren't stupid. Deep down they'd probably guessed he wasn't really putting down roots. So maybe taking care of their legal needs should include making them feel he was one of them, and not just passing through.

CHAPTER SEVENTEEN

ON SUNDAY NIGHT Danny turned on his side as Hannah tucked the blankets around him.

"Are you excited about vacation Bible school?" she asked.

"Uh-huh. Are we really gonna camp out?"

"You sure are, just like the olden days." The counselors had come up with a new idea this year—the VBS had deliberately been scheduled for the week before the Christmas in August celebration started, with the theme centered around ancient biblical journeys. They were going to have the kids sleep over the first and last nights at the church, pretending to be the ancient travelers to Bethlehem…the wise men, the shepherds and the other people going to be counted in the Roman census.

"Where's Badger, Mommy?"

"Probably putting Louie to bed," she said. She suspected when Jake went back to his old life, they'd end up giving the cat a home. "I'll go check on him."

Danny yawned. "Okay."

Hannah waited a few minutes until she was sure he was soundly asleep, then walked over to the lodge. Jake met her at the door. "Your dog thinks he's a nursemaid."

She stepped inside and saw Badger doing his best to give Louie a bath, while Louie, greatly improved in appearance and looking fatter over the ribs, just wanted to play with his tail.

"Badger, come."

The retriever gave her a slightly harried look, probably similar to the one she'd worn when Danny was a baby and *nothing* was going the way the baby books said they were supposed to.

"Where do you think we should go this week?" Jake asked, freeing Louie from Badger's overenthusiastic grooming and draping him over his shoulder. A loud purr instantly rumbled through the air.

Hannah reached up to rub the top of Louie's head. "Oh, I thought we could go down to Mount Adams and maybe to the other side of Mount St. Helens. A two-day trip to allow for extra time with your camera."

"Sounds good for Wednesday and Thursday. But what about hiking part of the way up Mount Mahala tomorrow?"

She hesitated. "We've talked about that. The best views are pretty high."

"I'm tired of taking it slow. I'd like to go tomorrow."

"Fine." Hannah walked over and grabbed Badger's collar, tugging firmly. "Come on, boy, Danny wants you."

The retriever's ears tilted forward at the name and he followed her obediently, though he looked at Louie on Jake's shoulder, a worried wrinkle between his eyes.

"It's okay, Badger," Jake surprised her by saying. "I'll take care of Louie. You don't need to worry about him."

It was probably the first time he'd ever tried talking to the dog as if he could understand, and Hannah's heart ached even more.

JAKE KNEW HANNAH wasn't entirely comfortable about hiking Mount Mahala with him, but it wasn't as if he was suggesting they go up Sagarmatha. While pretty, Mount Mahala was one of the more minor peaks in the Cascades, barely high enough in elevation to maintain its three small glaciers.

Besides, Hannah had said there was a trail where mountain-climbing gear wasn't required, and he wanted to push his leg harder than he'd been able to on the less-strenuous trails they'd taken to date.

Badger came along the next morning, trotting easily on the forest paths and on the steeper rocky tracks.

As they climbed higher, the avalanche lilies appeared, their showy blossoms nodding gently in the light breeze, growing so thickly they could almost be mistaken for ground cover.

The names of the flowers rolled off Hannah's tongue, blending together in his head—columbine, lupine, shooting stars, penstemon…tiger lilies. The tiger lilies looked like something he might see in formal gardens. Hannah explained it was a wild lily that was so popular with gardeners, a lot of people thought they were domesticated bulbs gone wild.

When they approached the first snowfields, Hannah stopped to put on a jacket and Jake followed suit, though he wasn't cold yet. The biggest problem was his leg; it was aching badly from the effort of keeping it straight, and he dreaded having to call a halt. Luckily they soon reached a small widening of the trail and Hannah cleared her throat.

"I thought this might be a good place for you to work."

Jake's jaw was clenched from the strain of climbing with a heavy pack of equipment, and he was drenched with sweat, but he turned his head and everything else was forgotten. To the north, one of the larger peaks stood sentinel over the surrounding range, a giant that looked sleepy and peaceful, belying the geologic power that lay beneath.

As for Mount Mahala, old-growth forest surrounded the base and lower slopes, and below was Mahala Lake. The town wasn't visible from their vantage point and the lake was the distinctive milky green of glacial meltwater.

Hannah was gazing intently up at Mount Mahala. "'The whole mountain appeared as one glorious manifestation of divine power, enthusiastic and benevolent,'" she quoted softly, "'glowing like a countenance with ineffable repose and beauty, before which we could only gaze in devout and lowly admiration.'"

"John Muir," Jake said absently. "From *Steep Trails*. One of the climbers I knew as a boy loved that quote. He planned to leave a copy at the top of Sagarmatha, but he didn't make it."

"Maybe he'll try again someday."

Jake shook his head. "His body is still up there. When someone dies too high up, it isn't always possible to recover them. The oxygen is too scarce, and more lives could be lost." He looked at Hannah. "Doug loved the prayer flags in Nepal. I tried putting one up for him after the accident, but Josie didn't like it."

"Your mother has strong views."

"Yeah. I…uh, I've put them up since." It was the first time he'd admitted it to anyone, but now it seemed all right with Hannah. "I've never seen any harm to the practice. If nothing else, it's a form of remembrance."

She touched his arm. "I hope it makes you feel better."

"It does," Jake confessed. "And it's funny, I've mentioned some of the Tibetan and Nepalese spiritual practices to Ruth and she wasn't the least bit offended, even though they have a different religion."

"I don't recall you talking about that with your grandparents when they visited."

"Well, I thought about what you said…about making up my own mind about the MacDonalds, so I've called them a couple of times. They don't seem to be the way Josie described them—all dogmatic and Bible-thumping. Maybe they've changed."

"People *do* change," Hannah said, looking thoughtful. "But I'd better let you work."

She went over to a low rock and sat down, Badger leaning against her leg as Jake selected a camera. Before his accident he'd believed solely in the here and now, *the provable*. It wasn't so clear any longer.

JAKE WORKED FOR at least six hours before he noticed Hannah walking up and down and swinging her arms. He vaguely recalled gulping a cup of coffee and swallowing a sandwich in the middle of those hours, but little else.

"Cold?" he called.

"I'm not warm. We're above the snow line."

Damn.

Hannah was far too nice. Toby would have been complaining from the minute they'd started up the mountain.

"Sorry about that. Let's go."

Hannah came over and helped pack the cameras. She was becoming proficient with his equipment, handling it carefully and ensuring everything was secure in the packs.

The hike down was slow. Jake's leg and knee had seized up badly and he noticed Badger stayed close to his side, rather than ranging ahead, the way he usually did. Hannah didn't say anything for a long time, though she periodically cast worried glances at him.

"Did you bring any pain medication?" she finally asked.

He almost snapped at her, then managed to control the impulse. "No, I just need the hot tub. It's better than anything else."

"We're miles from a hot tub, Jake."

"I'll get there. And taking a pill might make me woozy enough to slip."

"I know."

It was another three miles to the Wrangler, and by the time they got there, Jake's muscles were shaking.

Hannah drove down the mountain, and the jolting over dirt and gravel roads was enough to make Jake's jaw tighten again. Clearly, he hadn't recovered as much as he'd hoped, and the knowledge sat in his stomach, in a cold, indigestible lump.

"Don't we have to pick up Danny from your parents'?" he asked when she drove straight through town to Huckleberry Lodge.

"No. Vacation Bible school started today. The leaders are having the older kids sleep over as part of the lesson."

"Oh. So Danny is away tonight," Jake murmured speculatively, though he was hardly in any condition to take advantage of Hannah's unexpected freedom.

"Don't get any ideas," she warned as she parked near the front door of Huckleberry Lodge.

"Does that mean you're refusing to share the hot tub with me? I can't think of a better way to relax and get warm, can you?"

HANNAH WAVERED. IT was a cool day, and though they'd had the heat on during the drive back, she was still chilled. And her muscles would stiffen up even more, no longer being accustomed to such strenuous hiking, so she could imagine how lousy Jake felt. He had set the pace with a grim determination. Impatience was his biggest barrier to recovering.

"Uh, sure. I'd love to."

"Good, I'll meet you on the deck."

Jake headed into the lodge, limping heavily, with Badger sticking close to his side. Over the past couple of weeks the hesitation in his gait had almost vanished, but Hannah wasn't surprised it was back. At least if the overexertion was a problem, Owen would have something to say about it when he came tomorrow for Jake's therapy.

Hannah changed into a swimsuit and grabbed a robe, then hurried over to the lodge. A fire had been lit in the master bedroom, and Badger and Louie were lying in front of it in obvious bliss. The golden retriever still treated his new feline friend like Little Orphan Annie, but Louie was starting to show his independence, so the relationship would quickly equalize.

Outside, Jake was already in the churning water. Hannah dropped her robe on a bench and slipped into the warmth with a sigh. A bathtub was okay, but it couldn't compete with a hot tub.

"I'm surprised you haven't installed one of these over at Silver Cottage," Jake murmured after a long time, the lines of strain on his face beginning to ease.

"Until you leased the lodge, we were always able to come over and use this one between our short-term renters."

"You still can use this one. I invited you, remember?"

"You just did that to annoy Brendan."

"I was bored and he's an easy target. How did he take it when you broke up with him?"

"He was a perfect gentleman."

Initially, Hannah had felt guilty about Brendan, but now she suspected he'd forgotten all about her.

While Barbi and Brendan might be an incongruous pair, there was a rightness to it, as well. Brendan needed someone who'd lighten him up, and Barbi needed someone solid and dependable, willing to make a commitment and stick to it.

So do I, Hannah thought dismally.

Brendan obviously wasn't the right man for her, but she still hoped to find someone with his solid values...and Jake's sex appeal. Hannah squirmed at the thought. She strongly suspected that Jake was naked beneath the churning water, and just the thought was enough to send prickles shooting through her tummy.

The sun was low in the sky, and she closed her eyes, letting the bubbling water swirl around her.

When the timer for the jets ran down she stayed quiet, listening to the sounds of evening. A few minutes later the cry of a loon rippled through the air.

Jake sleepily opened his eyes. "That was a loon, right?"

"Uh-huh. Some people think it sounds like a weird sort of laughter, so that's where the expression 'crazy as a loon' comes from."

"I probably would have guessed it had something to do with the moon. You know, loon...lunar?"

"Mmm. You should see the birds with their young. They're wonderful parents. Amazingly affectionate, swimming with their babies or carrying them on their backs. I'm so glad they've come back to the lake."

The cry came again and they were both silent, listening to the haunting, flutelike notes.

"I've gotten pictures of a large bird with a baby on its back," Jake murmured. "Black-and-white spotted, with a black head and a couple of bands below. I'm sure they're loons from the photos I've seen in books."

Hannah smiled with delight. "That's great. They're really shy, which is partly why their nesting habitat has shrunk so much."

"I didn't go near them, just used my telephoto lenses," Jake assured her. "Shall I put the jets back on?"

"I'll do it." Hannah stood before he could get up, turned the timer on, then slid into the water again.

"Chicken."

She raised an eyebrow at him. "About what?"

"Seeing me in my birthday suit."

"Ha. That's nothing I haven't seen before."

"True. I just don't see the point of wearing shorts. And to be honest, I didn't think about it before you came out in your swimsuit. I might tease, but I didn't mean to offend you."

"You didn't." The reason she'd wanted to turn on the jets herself was out of concern for his leg, but he probably wouldn't want to hear it.

"I got an email from Toby last night," Jake said unexpectedly. "He and his fiancée got married in Hawaii last weekend."

"And you disapprove."

"No."

Hannah lifted an eyebrow and Jake sighed. "I've finally accepted it. But I'm still going to miss him. I never expected to have an assistant, then the magazine foisted him on me for a trip to Indonesia. I'd cracked a couple of ribs and they thought someone should go along and do the heavy lifting."

"That was nice of them."

"Not exactly—they always want more control than I'm willing to give them. It pissed me off. There I was, saddled with a guy who cursed and complained endlessly…yet didn't think twice about throwing himself into a raging river to pull me out."

"So you became friends."

"Yeah. And that wasn't the only time he saved

my life. Toby is a great guy. I'll never be able to replace him. I'm not even going to try. From now on I'm working solo."

Hannah swallowed. It was hardly a secret that Jake had nearly died more than once, but she didn't enjoy being reminded of it, either. *Or* of his determination to continue being a lone wolf. On the other hand…she thought about some of the things Jake had said over the past few weeks, little hints that there was more going on than his resentment over feeling trapped by his injuries.

"Why solo?" she asked carefully.

"It's easier. Toby could have been killed in that plane, the same as the pilot."

"I thought the pilot died of heart failure," Hannah said, startled that Jake had brought it up.

"Gordon *was* having a heart attack," Jake said, almost as if to himself. "The beds of his fingernails were blue, he was having trouble breathing, his chest hurt and he lost consciousness just before the crash. I was told it was his heart that killed him, but his injuries were severe, as well. It was probably just a race as to which caused his death."

"It's terrible, but there was nothing you could do."

"Not exactly. He was in the plane because of me, the same with Toby. If I hadn't hired him, he might have been closer to a doctor."

Hannah looked out at the lake. It was beautiful and serene, and the mountain above it glowed in the setting sun…the mountain where Collin had died.

Jake was expressing the same illogical guilt that she'd felt after Collin's accident, though there was nothing she could have done to prevent his death. Collin had gone too far, just as he always did, and that time it had killed him.

Jake wasn't as disconnected as he wanted to believe. He was compassionate and decent enough to care that a man had died, and was troubled that his friend could have been lost, as well.

Oh, hell, what about when he'd stopped taking pictures of Mount Baker because she was there and would be caught in the storm with him? Or had worried that she was upset about Brendan being sick, so he paid to have Barbi get him groceries? Or admitted to Danny that he got scared, just like anyone else?

That nearly brought tears to Hannah's eyes each time she thought about it. Men didn't confess that sort of thing easily. And yet Jake had admitted it to a child who hero-worshipped him, simply because he'd realized it was better for Danny to know that fear was normal.

It was the sort of thing a father would do.

"Jake, we've talked about my boyfriend who died on Mount Mahala," Hannah said slowly, and he nodded. "A group of us kids went up together for a climb. It was supposed to be an easy day, but Collin could never let well enough alone. He always needed to push things a little bit further and take a few more risks than anyone else. We didn't have the right equipment for anything more than casual climbing and I begged him not to take this one rock face, but he was determined. And then when he died...I felt so guilty."

"Even though it wasn't your fault?"

"Yeah. It was survivor guilt, Jake. It's not logical, but it's real. Maybe it was even worse because he wasn't killed instantly, and all we could do was wait for help to come. The what-ifs haunted me for a long time."

"And you think that's what I'm feeling."

"I'm no expert, but you're alive while someone else isn't. It's bound to cause mixed emotions."

"That's an understatement."

Hannah shifted closer to him, their legs brushing in the bubbling water. "Jake, working as a pilot was what Gordon chose to do. His death is very sad, but it wasn't your fault for hiring him. And Toby could have refused to go on any of your expeditions, right? No one forced him to go."

"Of course not."

"People have to make their own choices. Collin chose to do something reckless that got him killed. Gordon became a bush pilot, even though bush pilots are often far from medical facilities. Toby freely took the job as your assistant. Would you rather have been alone all those years instead of having the friendship you shared with him?"

"The risk of any relationship," Jake murmured, almost to himself. "I heard a climber say that in Nepal after he lost a friend in an avalanche."

"Caring about someone is always a risk in one way or another," Hannah said softly. It wasn't a revelation, but since being with Jake felt like playing with fire, the idea had been on her mind a great deal. "I know I'm a fine one to talk, but would you rather be alone or take the risk of caring about someone? You seem to take every other risk in the world."

JAKE DIDN'T SAY anything as he stared at the bubbling surface of the hot tub, remembering both the disastrous expedition on Sagarmatha and his feelings about the plane crash. Josie had put the climbing team together, determined to stand on the world's highest peak and take photographs that would astonish everyone.

Photographs that would cement her reputation as the foremost female photographer in the world.

Damn.

Jake would never know whether the fatalities were Josie's fault, but he knew that he'd been eight years old, dealing with death for the first time. A flicker of the old anger he'd barely acknowledged came back to him. Josie may have had her own demons to fight, but she'd stayed separate from the son who'd needed her. Doug's widow had been the one who'd sat next to him and held his hand.

Then Josie had gone *back* to Sagarmatha without telling him. He'd been furious when he'd learned about it, thinking the photographs wouldn't have been worth her life.

Lord. What sort of hypocrite did that make him, readily sticking his own neck out for a great photo but disapproving of someone he loved doing it, as well?

"Do you want to see the Arctic pictures?" Jake asked, surprising himself. "There are a few of Gordon in the collection."

"I'd like that."

"I'll get the computer." He got out, still in some pain, but the warm water had helped. Wrapping a towel around his waist, he fetched his laptop from the library. Back in the bedroom he found Hannah sitting on the love seat by the fire, wearing one of his T-shirts. Though too big, it looked far better on her than it ever had on him.

Jake sat next to her. The computer booted quickly, and he opened the Arctic file. For the first time in his career, he didn't try to just display the pictures that met his standards; he simply passed the laptop over.

He didn't know what to think or believe any longer.

Hannah was making him feel as if setting down roots would be perfectly all right as long as she was with him. In fact, those roots were looking damned appealing, offering possibilities he'd never considered.

He'd never been anywhere long enough to get invested in a place or a person—his mother's restless spirit had moved them constantly when he was a boy, and he'd lived the same way ever since. Hell, he wasn't even close to Josie, and the nearest thing he had to a home was his studio in Costa Rica.

Was that how he wanted to spend his entire life— moving, without any real sense of belonging?

It was a troubling question. He loved the travel and excitement of new places, though there *were* times he felt lonely. And it would be harder now that Toby wouldn't be with him. Toby had become a good friend, someone he trusted, and that wasn't something that could simply be replaced by hiring someone new.

HANNAH LOOKED AT the pictures on the screen, swept into a world of ice and stark landscapes. Many photos she'd seen of polar bears and other Arctic animals didn't capture their wildness, but Jake's did. Some were so stunning they literally took her breath away.

Oddly, since Jake rarely took pictures of people or human habitation, the most unusual photos were of the Inupiat villages he'd visited. Though she knew little of Inupiat life, it appeared modern conveniences were mixed with more traditional tools. One shot showed both a snowmobile and a dogsled.

"That's Gordon," Jake said when she clicked on the next file. "He had this funny, wry way of looking at things. And he carved intricate chess pieces, using polar animals in place of the traditional figures."

The man on the screen was smiling and holding a

coffee cup. His age was hard to determine, but there was something in his tranquil eyes that suggested he had seen a great deal.

As she continued clicking through the pictures, she saw more of Gordon. She loved the ones of him playing with the children, and yet the pictures of him conferring with the village elders suggested long familiarity and respect for their customs. There was a natural feeling to the photos that made her almost believe she'd stumbled on to something going on in the next room.

"These are amazing," she said. "Lots of photos like this seem posed. These don't, but they have great composition."

"The magazine asked for a few pictures of Inupiat tools," Jake explained, looking almost embarrassed. "I wasn't intending to take pictures of Gordon and the others—it just happened."

"But these pictures *should* be part of the article. These people's lifestyle is part of the world up there."

"I'll think about it. I have to go back anyway, to finish the assignment."

Before she could think about what that meant, Louie suddenly jumped onto Jake's poorly protected lap. He shot to his feet with a yelp, while Hannah laughed so hard she had to grab the computer to keep it from landing on the floor.

"Damned cat," Jake growled.

"Poor baby. I'm talking about the cat, you understand." She leaned over and patted an offended Louie, who'd leaped onto the arm of the love seat.

"Hey, he could have done serious damage."

"Probably mostly to your pride. But I'll take a look."

She put the laptop to one side and tugged the damp towel from Jake's hips. He glared, unabashed, as she examined his thighs and groin.

"Looks as though it still works," Hannah said, touching his arousal with her finger. "But you do have a tiny scratch right here." She kissed the red mark on his thigh.

"Are you just tormenting me, or are you planning to do something about it?" he demanded grumpily.

"I'm not sure." Hannah stood up and stretched, aware of his gaze fastened on her. "I could call the Mahalaton Rescue Squad."

"That isn't funny."

"Only if you don't know where those condoms are."

"I know exactly where to find them."

Jake relaxed, grinning as he pulled the T-shirt over her head and peeled the bathing suit from her body, taking his time as he uncovered her breasts, teasing her nipples before dipping his tongue in her belly button.

"That tickles," Hannah protested.

"You laughed when the cat skewered me."

"Yeah, but I kissed and made it better." She looped her arm around his neck.

"Just give me a chance, lady."

Hannah's last rational thought was that she'd love to give him a chance; she just didn't think he wanted the chance she most wanted to offer.

CHAPTER EIGHTEEN

BRENDAN FELT RIDICULOUSLY happy as he got out of the Lexus with Barbi and they walked toward his condo. He wasn't sure where his relationship with her was going, but he'd never had more fun in his life. She had an amazing ability to find pleasure in the simple things.

Yet it wasn't just about sex.

They were spending every free minute together and tonight they'd gone miniature golfing down in Lower Mahalaton. Naturally she'd played as if it was a national pro tournament...all the while deliberately wiggling her butt and distracting him from *his* shots.

"I want a rematch," he said. "But you're wearing a sweat suit next time, not those tight capris."

"You think that'll work?"

He hugged her and laughed. "Probably not. I guess you get to be on top," he whispered in her ear. "Who could have guessed that losing would make me the winner? Any other bets you'd like me to lose?"

"Maybe. Are you *sure* you're from Boston?"

Barbi still teased him about his New England upbringing, but she was getting him to loosen up in all sorts of ways. It was like having fresh spring air blowing through a stale attic. Everything was opening up inside him, making room for new things. He loved it. It was as if he'd been a genie trapped in his bottle, suddenly given freedom.

"So this is where you been hiding, girl," a slurred voice said from behind them. "Somebody told me you got a fancy new boyfriend."

Barbi's back went rigid and she turned around. "Please d-don't do this. Go away, Vic."

"I'm lonely. I need a bottle." The man grabbed her arm and jerked. "I'm your daddy, and you owe me."

Brendan instantly remembered the bruises he'd seen on Barbi's arm. "She owes you nothing. Leave her alone," he ordered, angrier than he'd ever been before.

"It's none of yer business."

"I'm making it my business." He stepped toward Paulson. The guy threw a punch, but Brendan sidestepped easily and employed a move from his high school boxing team days.

Vic Paulson went down with a thud.

BARBI COULD HARDLY breathe as she watched her father lying on the ground, clutching his stomach.

She could see genuine fear in Vic's eyes, and memories rushed in of all the times he'd terrified her as a child, and then later as an adult. She suddenly understood that leaving town wasn't the answer. She had to deal with Vic, or else she'd be running her entire life whenever something scared her.

Mahalaton Lake was her home and she wouldn't let anyone take it away from her. If she left, it needed to be her own choice.

When Vic finally stopped gasping, Barbi leaned over and looked him in the eyes. "You're not sponging off me any longer, Vic. Not one more dime. Don't come around ever again. I don't want to hear about how lonely you are, or how hard it was to lose Mom. It was hard for me, too. I was just a kid and needed my father, but you quit. If you ever touch me again, I'll press charges and make sure you go to jail. And I'll use this on you."

Barbi pulled out the pepper spray she carried in her pocket, but had always been too frozen with fear to use.

"Right in the eyes," she promised, pointing it at him for effect. "You'll wish you were dead."

As Vic scooted backward in the grass, Barbi realized he was a coward at heart—as most bullies were. He hadn't been able to face the loss of his wife and raising a child alone, so he'd dug a hole and climbed in it with a vodka bottle.

"You wouldn't do that to your own father," he whined.

"Yes, I would. *In a second.* And you'd be smart to leave town, because I don't care anymore if people know how lousy you are. I'm getting a restraining order, and you'll be arrested if you come anywhere near me."

She'd loved him once, but that had been a long time ago.

Barbi turned to Brendan, hoping he wouldn't be so disgusted he didn't want anything more to do with her. But if he was, that was his problem. She refused to apologize for who she was, ever again. "Let's go in. Our ice cream is melting."

"Yeah."

Brendan kissed her forehead before picking up the grocery bag he'd dropped during the confrontation with Vic.

Inside he insisted on checking her wrist, looking angry again when he saw the red marks on her skin. "*Damn it,* how long have you been dealing with him like this?"

"Since I was nine and my mom died. It's too bad you had to get involved."

"No, it isn't. You were only nine? That's terrible. Why didn't somebody do something about it?"

Barbi put the ice cream in the freezer. "Well, I kind of protected him, you know—cleaned up when he got drunk, and didn't tell people when he knocked me around."

"Don't you *dare* blame yourself," Brendan said adamantly, and she felt more of her tension and uncertainty fall away.

"To be honest, I've been so scared of Vic, I hardly ever fought back. I guess I could have stopped him a long time ago, but I didn't know how. But when I saw Vic lying there, I realized he was a bigger coward than I could ever be."

She couldn't tell much from Brendan's expression, but he almost looked...*proud*.

"I think you were wonderful."

"You should also know I never finished high school. I dropped out to get a job, but I'm studying for my GED now. Hannah has been helping me."

BRENDAN COULD TELL Barbi expected him to reject her on the spot, but he'd sooner cut off his right arm.

If he'd been looking for meaning in his life when he moved to Mahalaton Lake, he didn't have to look further. He loved Barbi. He'd told her things he had never told anyone...things about his family and Maria and the reasons he hadn't joined Townsend & Associates back in Boston. And she understood him in a way no one ever had.

With Barbi, the world was full of possibilities.

"I know you can do anything you want." He gently kissed the marks on her wrist. "I realize this isn't the most romantic setting, but I've lost too much because I focused on the wrong things and kept biding my time. I love you, Barbi. If you'll have me, I can't imagine a better life than being a lawyer and a husband, right here in Mahalaton Lake."

Barbi looked shocked. "You're crazy. Your family expects you to marry a proper society girl, someone good enough to be a lawyer's wife."

"You *are* good enough—more than good enough. I can't imagine anything more boring than a proper society girl. And if you won't marry me for such a crazy reason, I'll quit the law—I'm not losing the best thing that's ever happened to me."

"I thought Maria Walther was your best thing."

"I loved Maria," he acknowledged, "but she didn't make me a better person the way you do. Being successful lawyers together was more important than what we were as a couple. That's not 'best,' it's not knowing any better. How about it? Is there any chance you could love me, too?"

BARBI BIT HER LIP. Never in her life would she have thought that a man with a college education and re-fined manners would want to marry her, but now Brendan Townsend was saying she was the best thing that had ever happened to him.

Should she say yes?

Loving him wasn't the problem. She loved him so much she could burst with it, but it wasn't as if they wouldn't have problems. On the other hand, she'd gotten the courage to tell her father to leave her alone, and that was huge. Maybe Brendan had helped by getting him on the ground, but she'd still waved that pepper-spray bottle in Vic's face, making sure he knew she'd use it if he bothered her again. If she could do that, she could do anything.

"Your parents wouldn't come to the wedding," she said. "Not if they meet me first."

He shrugged. "That's their loss."

Barbi smiled slowly, suddenly feeling very sure about the future. "How about another bet?" she suggested. "If you win, I marry you."

"Uh-uh," Brendan said, walking toward her with a gleam in his eyes. "I love you too much to take a chance on losing."

"In that case, I guess I'll have to marry you anyway...'cuz I love you, too."

He pulled her close for a kiss, everything she'd always wanted and never thought she could have.

HANNAH DIDN'T FEEL in the Christmas in August spirit, but nevertheless, on Saturday she helped decorate the fire station and the rescue squad headquarters. At least the rest of the town seemed to be having a grand time preparing for the festival, and all the motels were fully booked, so the tourists were looking forward to it, as well.

The city maintenance department had put up the street decorations on Friday, and people were wandering around humming Christmas carols under their breaths. Normally Hannah loved it, but she had too much on her mind to feel festive.

Her parents always got into the spirit so much they put up lights around the house and a tree. Her mother had invited Danny to spend a few nights with them during the festival, saying it felt more like Christmas with a child in the house, but Hannah knew it was also to make her expeditions with Jake easier to coordinate.

"But, Mommy, can't you and Jake stay at Grandma and Grandpa's, too?" he asked that night as Hannah packed some of his things before bedtime. He was at his grandparents' house so often he had plenty of clothes there, but there were a few items she thought he might need.

"Jake is working on his photographs and I'm helping," Hannah explained. "Now hop into bed. You can read for a while before going to sleep."

He sighed and climbed under the blankets with his book while Badger jumped onto the mattress beside him.

Hannah went into the living room and wished she didn't feel so unsettled. She'd woken early Tuesday morning and had thought about leaving before Jake awoke to avoid another potential morning-after discussion, only to see him lying sprawled on his back, Louie tucked into his armpit, looking so endearing that she'd almost cried.

The risk of any relationship.

She pressed her arm over her stomach, remembering the hollow tone in Jake's voice when he'd said those words. Caring about someone was always a risk because there were so many ways to lose them.

The phone rang and Hannah's eyes widened as she saw the display. Why was *Brendan* calling her?

"Hello?"

"Hey, Hannah, it's me."

Relief flooded her. "Barbi? Hi. How's it going?"

"Pretty good. Um, could I come out tomorrow afternoon?"

Hannah quickly sorted her mental schedule and to-do list. "Sure, that would be fine. What time?"

"Is one o'clock all right? I'll bring pizza."

"You don't need to do that."

"I want to."

"Well…sure."

It was only after they'd said goodbye that Hannah frowned. Barbi had sounded pretty excited for someone setting up a tutoring session. Of course, she was calling from Brendan's condo, so she was probably a little tense, not wanting him to know about her studies…and exhilarated because she was with him and able *to* call from his condo.

PROMPTLY AT ONE the next day, there was a knock on the door, and Hannah went to answer. But instead of just Barbi, Brendan stood there, too. And Jake was coming out of Huckleberry Lodge, obviously headed for Silver Cottage.

"Um, hi, everyone."

"Hey, Hannah." Brendan kissed her cheek. He was holding three giant pizza boxes and looking more relaxed and happy than she'd ever seen him. "Hope it's all right, we asked Jake to join us for lunch."

"Oh. Okay."

She stepped back and Barbi, Brendan and Jake

trooped inside. Catching Jake's gaze, she raised her eyebrows, but he just shrugged.

"Hi, Danny," Brendan called. "Half of this top pizza is just cheese, the way you like it."

"Yum."

Confused, Hannah suggested they sit on the deck, but it wasn't until they were eating that she noticed something flashing on Barbi's left hand. She leaned closer and saw a diamond-and-sapphire ring.

Barbi laughed. "Yup, we're engaged. Can you believe that?"

"We're getting married in September." Brendan looked so proud his buttons were in danger of popping.

"That's wonderful." Hannah hugged her friend as Jake and Brendan shook hands, their former animosity apparently forgotten.

"It isn't gonna be a big wedding," Barbi said. "But you'll be my maid of honor, won't you?"

"Of course."

They discussed the wedding for the rest of the meal, but when she was finally alone and Danny was playing in the upstairs family room, Hannah felt like crying. She was thrilled for Barbi, yet her heart ached. Before Jake's arrival in Mahalaton Lake, everything had seemed so clear to her. If she fell in love again it would be to a solid, dependable man like Brendan—but hearts didn't always make logical choices.

"Danny, let's go for a walk," she called up to the family room.

"Coming, Mommy."

He clattered down the steps with Badger at his heels, and they walked down the trail toward one of the huckleberry patches, with Danny throwing a stick ahead of them for Badger to chase.

"Brendan says I can call him Uncle Brendan," Danny said after a while. "'Cause you and Barbi are real good friends."

"I thought you didn't like him."

"I didn't *used* to like him, but he's pretty nice now," Danny told her earnestly. The only thing that had changed was Brendan was no longer a potential stepfather, but Hannah didn't point that out.

At the huckleberry patch, Hannah looked at the ground where Jake had lain taking pictures, and her stomach knotted up even more. She wanted to be sensible, both for herself and Danny, yet saying she didn't want to fall in love with someone like Jake hadn't kept her from doing it.

Maybe it was too late to protect her own heart, but she still had Danny to think about. He would be devastated if his hero died, but it would be even worse to lose someone closer.

On the other hand, Jake had shown the potential to be a good father, and that was important, too.

"Mommy, do you have a bag?" Danny asked. "I wanna help pick berries."

She pulled a small plastic bag from her pocket.

It was the time of year she always carried them for huckleberries.

He diligently began picking the fruit, and Hannah sighed. One of the reasons she'd tried to keep Jake and her son apart was her fear that Danny would turn out like his biological father if he had a similar role model. But Jake *wasn't* like Steven.

Hannah pictured her ex-husband. Beneath his charm, Steven was deeply unhappy, though she hadn't recognized that when they were dating. Perhaps he simply lacked something within himself, and that was what made him restless and discontented. But Danny was a sweet, generous, outgoing kid with love enough to spare. There wasn't any real reason to think he'd go off, wandering the world, making other people miserable along with himself.

As for Danny having daredevil tendencies, Jake had discouraged *that* in a hurry. She'd been alarmed when Danny had talked about whacking a bear on the nose, but Jake had handled it far better than she'd expected.

Of course, she was probably being ridiculous to think about the future. Jake had made it clear from the beginning that he wouldn't be here long-term.

JAKE RETURNED TO Huckleberry Lodge, wondering if he'd had anything to do with kindling Brendan and Barbi's relationship. It was possible—he'd thrown them together on at least two occasions.

It was also possible it was the first time he'd ever affected someone's life enough to make a difference.

The thought was sobering.

Living in Mahalaton Lake was making him see that his world was even more different from other people's than he'd ever thought. Hemingway had written that most men led lives of quiet desperation, but that wasn't Jake's experience. His every memory was of distant places and adventure. Josie had ensured he'd seen the wonders of the world and known freedom like no other child, and he'd charged into adulthood in the same spirit.

Yet he didn't have traditions or a family whose faces lit up at the sight of him. Instead he had a sister-in-law who was shocked that he wanted to visit her and her newborn son. He had editors waiting for his photographs, yet they probably wouldn't recognize him on the street. And he had critics who evaluated his work with no idea of what kind of person he might be.

Hannah was the one involved with her community. She was concerned about the quality of education children were receiving. She cared about the land and animals. And she worked hard to make sure Mahalaton Lake had the emergency services it needed.

Jake stepped out on the deck and looked at the lake. He'd taken hundreds of thousands of pictures, but if he'd died in the crash, other people's lives would have gone on, little changed because of it.

Still, there *were* people who cared about him.

The MacDonalds had made the effort to visit, while Matt had chartered a flight and rushed him to a hospital in Seattle after the crash. Josie and Sully had each been concerned in their own ways. And three of his sisters—Oona, April and Tamlyn—had dropped everything to visit him in Washington, along with his eldest brother, Aaron.

It was less complicated to live without ties to other people, but he'd never realized how alone he'd felt before coming to Mahalaton Lake and meeting Hannah and Danny.

Maybe he should give Aaron a call and find out if he and Matt still wanted to visit Mahalaton Lake with their families. It might be nice to see them all again.

CHAPTER NINETEEN

"MORNING, OWEN," HANNAH said as she hurried into the sunroom on Tuesday. She'd just finished cleaning the lodge and wanted to get back to Silver Cottage to make lunch and a fresh pot of coffee. "I got a copy of the festival schedule for you. It just started yesterday, so you haven't missed too much. The big events are next weekend."

"Terrific. We bought the *Clarion* a couple of times so we'd have it, but somehow both editions ended up lining the cat's litter box."

Hannah handed him a sheet of paper, glancing at Jake. Louie was lying across the back of the couch, basking in the sunlight from the window, while Jake scratched his neck.

Louie, I think this is the beginning of a beautiful friendship.

She'd shown *Casablanca* to him the other night and Jake had groaned, suddenly realizing why the name had popped into his brain. Curiously, he hadn't said anything recently about finding Louie a home.

"I'll see you Thursday, Owen," she said, her smile fading.

In her own kitchen Hannah noticed she had a missed call, so she picked up the phone and dialed her parents' house.

"Hey, Mom. What's up?"

"Not much. I'm baking a gluten-free cake for the Cub Scouts meeting tonight. I've got the fried chicken and potato salad you made, but Charlie's mother called to say he's been diagnosed as gluten intolerant. She wants everyone to know because Charlie is rebelling."

"Uh-oh, there's flour on the chicken."

"We're covered. Your dad checked, and Luigi's has a gluten-free pizza."

"If there's pizza, all the boys will want some."

"We're getting a couple. They can have salad, pizza, chicken and gluten-free cake."

"Better get some wings, too. I'll pay you back for everything."

"You will not," Carrie said indignantly. "It's bad enough you brought the fried chicken and potato salad. You've got enough to do without feeding your father's Cub Scouts troop."

"I like to do my part."

"You've *done* your part. But I better get going. The kids are sleeping in the fort tonight with your dad, so I need to air out his sleeping bag."

"Tell him to have fun."

Hannah started the coffeemaker and quickly made some ham and turkey sandwiches. Sandwiches were the easiest food for when Jake was working—usually he barely noticed he was eating anyway.

TWILIGHT WAS FALLING as Jake drove the Wrangler toward Mahalaton Lake that evening. They'd gone to Mount Rainier, but curiously, Jake had mostly looked for places to get more distant photos of Mount Mahala.

Pleasantly tired, Hannah took a sip of coffee from her cup. She loved the long summer days in Washington, though Jake had reminded her that *Alaska's* summer days were almost twenty-four hours long. It *would* be interesting to experience something like that, but while she'd enjoy seeing other places, she'd want to go home before too long.

"Damn it to hell," Jake cursed as two deer suddenly ran in front of the Jeep and froze in the headlights. He braked and veered around them while the lid flew off Hannah's cup and coffee sloshed over her jacket and jeans.

"Crap." She grabbed some napkins and dabbed the brown stains. "I thought I'd gotten the top down tight."

Jake didn't say anything and she glanced over. His lips were pressed tightly together.

"Is something wrong?" she asked.

"No."

Yeah, she believed that.

She waited another few minutes, then pulled out the thermos and refilled her cup. "Want some?"

He shook his head and Hannah sighed in exasperation. Men accused women of being moody, but she had news—they were the biggest offenders. And Jake, for all of his unconventional upbringing, wasn't any different.

"Don't worry, the coffee spilled on me, not on the Jeep."

"I don't give a damn about the Jeep."

Okay, she hadn't thought he was obsessed with his vehicle, though some people were, but she was trying to break the tension.

She kept trying to get him to talk the rest of the drive back to Huckleberry Lodge, and her own temper had frayed by the time they pulled in next to the garage. Monosyllabic replies did *not* make a conversation.

"What's wrong with you?" Hannah demanded, getting out and slamming the door.

"Nothing, but I've made a decision. I won't be responsible for something happening to you, so you aren't going out on shoots with me any longer." Jake turned on his heels and stomped toward the lodge.

"Of all the insane... You aren't making sense!" she shouted after him.

The door of the lodge slammed, only to bounce open again, and Hannah stalked inside.

"Jake, what is your problem?"

"Don't you get it? We almost hit those deer. Two huge bucks. There could have been an accident. *You could have been killed.* Danny could be an orphan right now."

The breath caught in Hannah's throat because Jake's concern seemed very real.

"We live in the mountains," she tried to say reasonably. "Deer are always jumping out. It's one of those things we accept about Mahalaton Lake. We're just extra careful, especially at times of the day when they're more active."

"No. Risking my own life is one thing, but I won't take a chance on endangering someone else I care about."

He cared about her?

Hannah crossed her arms over her chest and tried to look stern, even though her pulse was jumping. Saying he cared wasn't a declaration of love, but at least it was something.

"We've *had* this discussion, Jake. People make their own decisions. You didn't chain me to the SUV and drag me out on the road. I agreed to work with you because I love the Cascades and wanted you to understand that beauty isn't just something found in remote, exotic locations."

"That doesn't change what could have happened."

"Please, don't be so dramatic. I'm going to jump in the hot tub to relax. You can join me if you stop acting like an idiot." She walked past him, pulling off her jacket.

JAKE STOOD IN the living room, his fists clenched against a rush of emotions. Nothing in his life had prepared him to care about someone the way he cared about Hannah and her son. She'd been his first thought when the deer had jumped onto the road. Perhaps they hadn't been in real danger, but it was close enough for him to realize that it would kill him to lose her.

After a moment he hurried into the master bedroom and looked out in time to see Hannah's silhouette on the deck, her bare body painted in light and shadow. She lifted her arms, twisting her hair up off her shoulders before descending into the bubbling water.

She was deliberately tempting him.

He removed his own clothes and grabbed a condom before stepping out and closing the doors behind him.

"We weren't done talking, Hannah."

"*I* was done."

"*Hannah.*"

"*Jake.*" She stared at him, almost daring him to say more. "I'm the one who's supposed to fuss about dangerous stuff, not you. Remember?"

She grasped the edge of the hot tub and lifted one of her legs above the surface, turning her foot back and forth as if inspecting it. Blood rushed into his groin, sweeping everything else away. He got into the hot tub and saw a satisfied smile on her face.

"Much better," she purred, half swimming toward him. "You're lucky. I was always good at water sports."

His hands slipped over her breasts, full and slick in the churning bubbles. He was lucky all right.

Damned lucky.

THE SUN WAS rising, flooding the bedroom with pink light, when Jake opened his eyes. Hannah lay against him, her head on his shoulder and hair wrapped around them both.

He *had* overreacted the night before. Perhaps it was partly from lingering survivor's guilt, but it had mostly been the blinding realization of just how important Hannah had become to him.

He loved her and he loved her son, and leaving them wouldn't erase those feelings; it would just make it worse because he wouldn't be part of their lives.

Perhaps that was what Josie had been doing all these years—trying to escape any pain or sorrow or regret. But he couldn't escape what was inside him. No one could. And Hannah *was* inside him…she was inside his heart.

Jake gazed out at the mountain standing guard over the lake, its white-crowned peak glistening in the dawn light. Loving Hannah and choosing a life with her would mean changes. And compromises. Whether she'd be willing to make those compromises with him was anyone's guess. After all, she had Danny to think about, and she was as protective as a mother polar bear when it came to her son.

When they'd met, he'd never expected to find someone with her depths. She loved the land and family and tradition, with a sense of home and place he'd never experienced. She was also prickly and had a quick temper, but that made two of them. They'd fight and make up and fight some more; it was inevitable.

He smiled. They'd made love half the night and he wouldn't mind picking up where they'd left off, but he needed a fresh supply of condoms. Hannah wanted another baby and he was okay with that, but until she agreed to marry him, he wasn't going without protection.

IT WAS AFTER eight when Hannah woke up and slipped out of bed. Jake was asleep, his morning stubble dark on his face, and Louie lay curled on a fluffy pillow. For a stray, the kitten had developed a remarkable fondness for his creature comforts. Jake was careful about keeping the exterior doors shut, but Louie had shown little interest in the great outdoors—he'd landed in clover and he knew it. He wanted the best tuna, the softest pillow and long snoozes in a sunny window.

She had a stack of huckleberry pancakes made when Jake wandered into the kitchen, wearing a disreputable pair of sweatpants and scratching the scars over his bare ribs.

"Good morning."

He smiled sleepily. "Good morning."

"Sit down. Breakfast is ready."

"I thought I smelled something good."

Hannah piled the pancakes on plates and brough[t] them over with butter and maple syrup.

"Oh, wow," Jake said, taking his first bite. "I don'[t] know which way I like these best. We'll have to pic[k] a lot of huckleberries."

"I always do."

They'd finished eating and Jake was on his thir[d] cup of coffee when he shook himself and starte[d] looking more alert. "Sorry about last night," he mu[r]mured.

"Which part?"

Jake grinned. "*Not* the part that requires anoth[er] trip to the drugstore. Mostly I've been thinking abou[t] us."

"Oh?"

"Yeah, I think we should get married."

Hannah stared. She didn't know what she'd e[x]pected, but certainly not a proposal. "That can't b[e] what you really want. You've had your life turne[d] upside down by the plane crash and everything els[e] that's happened."

"You're right…except for the part about n[ot] knowing what I want. If Gordon's death and m[y] injuries are ever going to be more than just a frea[k] accident, I *need* to look at where I'm headed an[d] what's important."

Hannah traced the rim of her cup. "Careful… you're beginning to sound like someone who believes in karma."

"Who knows? You've made me see that there *has* to be more to life if I can love you and Danny this much. Otherwise everything is just a series of chemical reactions."

A bubble of hope rose inside of her. She'd been scared of falling in love with someone who'd leave or get killed, and equally worried about Danny experiencing that kind of loss. But that could happen with anyone they loved. And in different ways. Barbi's father had abandoned life, even though his body still continued, pickled by vodka and memories of his lost wife.

Life was uncertain, whether you worked as a wildlife photographer or taught elementary school. It was just a little *more* uncertain with Jake.

So what she had to decide was whether it was worth the risk.

"I don't know if it's that simple," she said, stalling. "You've always avoided relationships, even with your siblings."

"True, but I've realized some important things in the past few weeks. And I think the biggest reason I haven't gotten close to my family is because I didn't want them to be hurt if something happened to me. Then something *did* happen, and it turns out they cared, whether I wanted them to or not—even my grandparents, who'd never met me. It just took a while to work it out for myself."

"How will Josie feel about you being in touch with her parents?"

"I'm not sure," Jake said, yet his eyes were curiously untroubled. "My mother has some problems. I'll try to make her understand, but that's all I can do."

He lifted her left hand and traced the length of her ring finger.

"Hannah, I finally get it. I don't have to live the way my mother does, because I'm not her. And I will *never* be casual about risking my life again—I have too much to live for. I love you. I want to be here for both you and Danny and any other children we have, and I want the home I've never had. I know that if we both make compromises, we can find a solution with my career and traveling and everything else that will work for us both."

Hannah let out a breath.

She *did* love Jake.

He'd shaken up her comfortable world and she'd never be the same, but *could* it work between them? Barbi and Brendan seemed to think they could make their unlikely romance successful, and judging by the happiness in their faces, they were off to a good start.

Things were more complicated for her and Jake—especially because of Danny—but not impossible. The fact he'd proposed in the first place showed he'd changed. The Jake Hollister who'd informed her that marriage and family were career enders would never have considered any compromise to his life acceptable.

"I don't want to give up teaching," Hannah said slowly.

Jake smiled, obviously recognizing she was thinking seriously about his proposal. "I wouldn't expect it, though I'd want you to use the SUV to drive into town, at least in bad weather."

"That's reasonable. I wouldn't have to teach summer school, though...even when they have the funding for it."

"Okay. I have to finish my photography assignment in Alaska," he said. "But I'm willing to limit my time away each year to two or three months, in the spring or fall whenever possible," he said. "However, I'd like you and our children to travel with me for a few weeks during the summer, whether I'm working or not. I like the idea of sharing the world with them. And with you."

The thought of Jake returning to the place that had nearly killed him was frightening, but Hannah also understood. At the very least, he had to face what had happened up there. "Hmm, children...that's a switch for you, maybe even bigger than getting married."

"I realize that. But I keep thinking about my own childhood. It was lonely growing up that way. I want

Danny to have the kind of family I might have had
if my parents had been different kind of people."

"You still have a family. A big one."

"I know, and I'm finally learning to appreciate
them. But no matter how close I might get to my
brothers and sisters, you've made me want more."

Hannah nodded, trying to be sensible, but it was
difficult when her pulse was racing so hard. "So how
many kids are we talking about?"

Jake leaned forward and kissed the tip of her nose.
"At least one or two more, don't you think?"

A shiver of anticipation went through her. "That's
workable."

"I'm not your ex-husband, Hannah," he whispered. "Please trust me. I don't make promises I
won't keep, and I would do my best to never let you
and Danny down. I love you both."

She looked into his face and knew her heart already trusted him. "I love you, too."

Jake grabbed her close and began kissing her, tasting coffee and syrup and huckleberries. There would
be time for plans and babies and everything they
could build together.

Most of all, there'd be love.

* * * * *

LARGER-PRINT BOOKS!

HARLEQUIN *Presents*

PASSION GUARANTEED SEDUCTION

GET 2 FREE LARGER-PRINT NOVELS PLUS 2 FREE GIFTS!

YES! Please send me 2 FREE LARGER-PRINT Harlequin Presents® novels and my 2 FREE gifts (gifts are worth about $10). After receiving them, if I don't wish to receive any more books, I can return the shipping statement marked "cancel." If I don't cancel, I will receive 6 brand-new novels every month and be billed just $5.05 per book in the U.S. or $5.49 per book in Canada. That's a saving of at least 16% off the cover price! It's quite a bargain! Shipping and handling is just 50¢ per book in the U.S. and 75¢ per book in Canada.* I understand that accepting the 2 free books and gifts places me under no obligation to buy anything. I can always return a shipment and cancel at any time. Even if I never buy another book, the two free books and gifts are mine to keep forever.

176/376 HDN F43N

Name _____ (PLEASE PRINT) _____

Address _____ Apt. # _____

City _____ State/Prov. _____ Zip/Postal Code _____

Signature (if under 18, a parent or guardian must sign)

Mail to the **Harlequin® Reader Service:**
IN U.S.A.: P.O. Box 1867, Buffalo, NY 14240-1867
IN CANADA: P.O. Box 609, Fort Erie, Ontario L2A 5X3

**Are you a subscriber to Harlequin Presents books
and want to receive the larger-print edition?
Call 1-800-873-8635 today or visit us at www.ReaderService.com.**

* Terms and prices subject to change without notice. Prices do not include applicable taxes. Sales tax applicable in N.Y. Canadian residents will be charged applicable taxes. Offer not valid in Quebec. This offer is limited to one order per household. Not valid for current subscribers to Harlequin Presents Larger-Print books. All orders subject to credit approval. Credit or debit balances in a customer's account(s) may be offset by any other outstanding balance owed by or to the customer. Please allow 4 to 6 weeks for delivery. Offer available while quantities last.

Your Privacy—The Harlequin® Reader Service is committed to protecting your privacy. Our Privacy Policy is available online at www.ReaderService.com or upon request from the Harlequin Reader Service.

We make a portion of our mailing list available to reputable third parties that offer products we believe may interest you. If you prefer that we not exchange your name with third parties, or if you wish to clarify or modify your communication preferences, please visit us at www.ReaderService.com/consumerschoice or write to us at Harlequin Reader Service Preference Service, P.O. Box 9062, Buffalo, NY 14269. Include your complete name and address.

HPLP13R

LARGER-PRINT BOOKS!
GET 2 FREE LARGER-PRINT NOVELS PLUS
2 FREE GIFTS!

HARLEQUIN®

Romance

From the Heart, For the Heart

YES! Please send me 2 FREE LARGER-PRINT Harlequin® Romance novels and my 2 FREE gifts (gifts are worth about $10). After receiving them, if I don't wish to receive any more books, I can return the shipping statement marked "cancel." If I don't cancel, I will receive 4 brand-new novels every month and be billed just $4.84 per book in the U.S. or $5.24 per book in Canada. That's a savings of at least 19% off the cover price! It's quite a bargain! Shipping and handling is just 50¢ per book in the U.S. and 75¢ per book in Canada.* I understand that accepting the 2 free books and gifts places me under no obligation to buy anything. I can always return a shipment and cancel at any time. Even if I never buy another book, the two free books and gifts are mine to keep forever.

119/319 HDN F43Y

Name	(PLEASE PRINT)	
Address		Apt. #
City	State/Prov.	Zip/Postal Code

Signature (if under 18, a parent or guardian must sign)

Mail to the **Harlequin® Reader Service:**
IN U.S.A.: P.O. Box 1867, Buffalo, NY 14240-1867
IN CANADA: P.O. Box 609, Fort Erie, Ontario L2A 5X3
Want to try two free books from another line?
Call 1-800-873-8635 or visit www.ReaderService.com.

* Terms and prices subject to change without notice. Prices do not include applicable taxes. Sales tax applicable in N.Y. Canadian residents will be charged applicable taxes. Offer not valid in Quebec. This offer is limited to one order per household. Not valid for current subscribers to Harlequin Romance Larger-Print books. All orders subject to credit approval. Credit or debit balances in a customer's account(s) may be offset by any other outstanding balance owed by or to the customer. Please allow 4 to 6 weeks for delivery. Offer available while quantities last.

Your Privacy—The Harlequin® Reader Service is committed to protecting your privacy. Our Privacy Policy is available online at www.ReaderService.com or upon request from the Harlequin Reader Service.

We make a portion of our mailing list available to reputable third parties that offer products we believe may interest you. If you prefer that we not exchange your name with third parties, or if you wish to clarify or modify your communication preferences, please visit us at www.ReaderService.com/consumerschoice or write to us at Harlequin Reader Service Preference Service, P.O. Box 9062, Buffalo, NY 14269. Include your complete name and address.

HRLP13R